Child of Eynhallow

Anne Kinsey

Castell Books

ISBN-13: 978-0615539300

Castell Books

2342 Shattuck Avenue, Suite 141

Berkeley, CA 94704

CHILD OF EYNHALLOW

PART I

CHAPTER 1

On a summer evening in the year of grace 1143 when the day's work was finished, twelve-year-old Isabel and her cousin Meg ran from the village to play under the waterfall at the edge of the woods. They ran along the muddy ditch which separated the garden plots from the open fields, their bare feet sinking into the soft, receiving earth. With a running dive, they splashed into the water. The pool was delightfully cool and clear, the air charged with the twilight magic of the setting blood-red sun. The waterfall's steady rhythm pulsated with life, as comforting as a heartbeat. The deep spray of water caught the sunlight and turned into a cascade of glittering diamonds.

"Look what I learned," Meg said. She lifted her knees to let the water fall between her legs. "It's great fun. You try."

Isabel moved to sit near Meg where the soft rock formed a seat at the edge of the waterfall, where the stream was gentler.

"Like this," Meg said.

Isabel lifted her knees as Meg was doing. The water flowed over her belly and between her legs.

"What about it?" Isabel asked.

"Just wait," Meg said. "It will happen."

Isabel waited. Nothing happened.

"Well?" asked Meg. "Did you feel it?"

Wanting to please Meg, Isabel lied. "Yes," she said.

"Doesn't it feel amazing?" Meg's cheeks were flushed bright pink.

"Oh, yes," Isabel lied again. "Amazing."

Next afternoon, because Isabel was curious and felt loyal to Meg, she returned alone to the waterfall to see if she could find out what Meg had been talking about. She settled into the soft reclining rock in the shallow water. Lifting her knees, she leaned back and enjoyed the gently pulsating rush of water. The soothing water soon lulled her and her thoughts drifted lazily. Then, what started as a slight tingling sensation between her legs changed to a vibrancy that spread up her spine. The sensation built to a feverish explosion, making her twitch and shudder with a pleasure she felt all through her limbs, leaving her breathless and astonished.

Meg was right. The feeling was amazing.

Next time Isabel and Meg were at the waterfall, after both had a chance to sit on the reclining rock, Isabel said, "Did you tell your sisters about this?"

"No," Meg said. "I'm afraid they'd laugh."

Meg had five sisters, two older and three younger. Meg's sisters didn't approve of Isabel and they warned Meg not to befriend her. Indeed, there was something about Isabel which made all the villagers suspicious of her. The excuse Meg and her sisters and others gave for shunning Isabel was that her mother was a foreigner. In a village as small as Brotton, not only did everyone know everyone else, but if family trees were traced back far enough, most villagers were related by blood. Isabel's mother, Nan — who had died seven years earlier — was an exception. Nan had been found abandoned on the monastery steps shortly after a wave of the plague swept through that part of Yorkshire. Everyone assumed Nan's parents had been killed by the plague. The problem was, nobody knew who her parents were, and if the villagers didn't know a person's parents, that person was forever cast as a stranger.

Isabel was not beautiful according to the villagers' standard of beauty which required that a girl have pale hair, blue eyes, and a delicate frame. Isabel's eyes were brown flecked with gold, her hair a deep rich chestnut. There was a sensuousness about Isabel in the fullness of her lips and the upward slant of her heavily lidded and thickly-lashed eyes which made the villagers uncomfortable. A young girl, in the opinion of the villagers, was supposed to be demure and sweet. Isabel was neither. She had a way of standing with her feet slightly apart and her arms akimbo, looking around without fear.

In fact, Isabel felt lonely and envious of others around her, all of whom seemed to have close friends and loving families. Isabel held herself the way she did because she felt she needed to protect herself and vie for things which came naturally to others. For example, because Isabel and Meg were exactly the same age, born on the same day, it seemed to Isabel that she and Meg should be friends. But Meg was usually surrounded by her clannish and judgmental sisters and Isabel had to compete for her attention

The wooden church sat on a slight eminence overlooking Brotton, its white-washed bell tower visible from everywhere in the village. Like the spokes of a wheel, all the streets led away from the church.

The village consisted of about fifty half-timbered cottages with sunburned mud walls and moss-covered thatched roofs. The best cottages were of post and beam structure, but even these leaned and sagged as they got older. Each cottage had sheds serving as stables and barns, and chicken yards fenced by hedges or wooden stakes tied together with hemp. The cackling chicken never stayed in their pens, though, and had to be constantly rounded up from the neighboring yards. Surrounding the village were crofts and garden plots. About the village hung the scent of chickens and dung, which Isabel noticed only when she returned from the pastures or stream.

On Sunday, Isabel walked to the church with her father and half-brothers, the children of her father's first marriage. She wore her everyday skirt and mantle, undyed, woven by Lester, who lived at the edge of the village and owned Brotton's only loom. Because it was Sunday, she laced her golden-brown ribbon through her braid and wore her best frock, freshly bleached and ironed. Her boots, laced up her ankle, disappeared beneath the hem of her skirt.

There was much noise as the villagers wandered into the church. Stray roosters and geese entered with nobody bothering to put them out. Meg approached with her sisters and parents, but as usual when her sisters were around, Meg was cool and distant. Isabel sat on one of the benches toward the rear of the church, watching as Meg and her sisters spread a blanket over the straw-covered floor and settled on the blanket like birds settling on a lawn.

The new parson entered and stood behind the pulpit. The old parson had been wonderful — merry and understanding and kind. This parson seemed to Isabel to have been sent by the devil instead of God.

"I am called to carry out God's work," he said. His thin, bony frame and slightly hunched back gave him a comical, crooked look. His face reminded Isabel of a rodent, pale with beady, shifty eyes. His lashes and brows were light, his cheeks gaunt. When he preached, his entire face came alive as if he were possessed by the very demons he preached against.

"Together we must fight Satan and his demons who have the power to destroy us all, demons who unsettle the senses, stir low passions, disorder life, bring diseases, cause alarms in sleep, and arouse the passions of carnal love!"

As he spoke his tempo increased and his voice trembled. "The moment you open your soul to the devil, he takes possession of you. You know when you're in his grip because you forget yourself completely. Touch your body sinfully, and you invite the devil."

Isabel watched Meg's back stiffen with fear. She knew Meg was thinking about their game under the waterfall. They had touched their bodies sinfully, and — as their physical responses had demonstrated — had felt the devil within them. She knew why Meg was afraid. The torments devised for sinners were shocking and dreadful beyond imagination: biting snakes, scorching flames, starving people chained just out of reach of bread. Once, when they were much younger, Meg had burst into tears as a visiting monk described the horrors of hell.

"Please Meg," Isabel begged silently. "Don't listen to him. It won't happen to you. Please, Meg, don't be frightened."

"I warn everyone here of one thing," the parson shouted, "if you have committed any sin so horrible that you dare not confess for shame, I urge you, in God's name, to rid your soul of the onerous burden. Confess your sin, and I will absolve you by the authority vested in me!"

It seemed to Isabel that he was talking to Meg, looking directly at her, deliberately speaking the words which would go straight to her heart and frighten the life from her. ·

Isabel stopped listening when he launched into a familiar fable about three revelers who met death because they failed to guard themselves against Satan. She listened instead to the nervous shuffling of feet and the cackling of fowl, silently imploring Meg not to be afraid.

When the sermon was over, a line formed near the confessional booth. Isabel was not surprised to see Meg join the line. She knew she too should join them. Not confessing would make her sin worse, but she hated confessing to the parson. How she wished the old parson was here, or even the friar who wandered through Brotton on his round of villages. The friar was a dimply, ruddy-faced man who gave light penances. Unlike the self-righteous parson, the friar's eyes sparkled with life and everyone knew that he was friendlier with the barmaids in each town than the local priests. It was rumored that the friar didn't have the power to hear confessions at all, but the people who preferred his easy penances didn't care.

Isabel was one of the first to leave the church. Soon all the villagers would troop down the hill to change from their best clothes and go about their daily tasks. In Brotton, with the occasional exception of a holiday, there was no such thing as a day of rest.

Isabel wandered to a stump near the churchyard to use as a chair. Meg would confess everything, no doubt about that, then there would be trouble. Like a trapped animal, Isabel could do nothing except wait. First Meg's sisters, then all the villagers would learn of their game. Already Isabel could see the disapproving frowns and shaking heads. Her father would become angry in his off-hand and detached way, and her brothers would gloat to see her in trouble again.

From where Isabel sat high on the church hill, she could see past the sprinkle of cottages to the yellow barley fields and lane which broadened just past the windmill at the foot of the castle hill. Isabel's father and his oxen team would soon be in the fields wearing their long smocks, bare-legged except for their high boots, leaning on the left bale of the plow so that they seemed to lurch as they walked. Beyond the fields, a flock of sheep grazed in the far pastures. Tending the sheep was Isabel's favorite task. She wished she were on the sloping emerald green hillside instead of sitting on a stump outside the church awaiting the outcome of Meg's confession. She fought the impulse to run and hide. Better to wait to see what would happen.

In the distance, past the yellow fields, the black haunted forest stretched to the north and west of the village. It was said that demons lived there, and elves, too, but the demons were the worst. The church bells rang every hour to frighten them away from the village. Crossing oneself or whispering the Lord's name also scared them away. It was said that to the west the forest grew blacker until there was no sunlight at all. There was supposed to be an ancient Druid fairy ring where the most evil of spirits swarmed.

Isabel watched the church door. A cold sense of impending disaster came over her. If only Meg would come out. She felt she could not endure the suspense another minute. Each time the door swung open and someone who had been ahead of Meg in the line emerged, the weight in Isabel's chest grew heavier.

At last Meg appeared in the doorway, squinting against the bright sunlight. Her skin was white as dried plaster. She looked at Isabel, then scurried away like a frightened mouse. Isabel felt irritated by her timidity.

When the church door opened again, the parson appeared and walked purposefully toward Isabel.

"Do you have something to confess?" His beady eyes glittering angrily.

Isabel felt herself shrink, her irritation with Meg changing to sympathy. No wonder Meg had turned meek and frightened.

Reluctantly, Isabel followed the parson into the church, which was now empty. She knelt in the darkened booth, the black coarsely woven curtains creating a narrow rectangle, enclosing her like a coffin. She dropped her head in her hands. The rough woolen curtain scratched her cheek.

"Bless me father, for I have sinned." She paused, unsure how to confess this particular sin. "I played a game under the waterfall."

"What kind of game," he asked, as if he didn't already know.

"I let the water fall between my legs."

"You touched your body sinfully. You have invited Satan into your soul. I am frightened for you." He paused dramatically. "The priest will be here tomorrow. He'll exorcize the evil spirits. You are to be here at daybreak."

Isabel shrank further into herself, knowing what the exorcism would involve. There would be foul-smelling candles in the darkened church and frightening chants. This would be much worse than she imagined. The villagers would not merely be disapproving, they would be angry, for anyone who beckoned the demons endangered the entire village.

"I can think of no penance severe enough," were the parson's final words

That evening Isabel creaked open the cottage door as her father and half-brothers settled about the oaken kitchen table. Even with the light of the log fire that blazed under the wattle-work chimney hood, the low-ceilinged room was chilly and dank. Dried meat hung from the rafters, tied out of reach of the cats. Tall andirons hanging from hooks supported two kettles over the flames. The hearth was surrounded by cooking utensils and earthenware pots and jugs, now in disarray from the supper preparations. On the table was a pile of cold mutton, chunks of black barley bread, and a large jug of ale. The dogs sniffed about, waiting for scraps.

Nobody acknowledged her entrance, not even the hounds, as if they were all in conspiracy to let her know that she was shamed. Her father was tense and pale, his usually bland face twisted into an expression that was both angry and bewildered. Usually he was carelessly jovial and absent-minded in his treatment of her. His anger was frightening because she could never guess his thoughts.

Her father turned to Marc, the eldest of Isabel's half-brothers who still lived at home. "Tell her," her father said.

Marc turned to Isabel and, puffing up his chest, said importantly, "You're to be at the church after the Lauds bells."

"I know," she snapped.

"You've never been anything but a problem," her father said flatly, "but this is the worst yet. Tempting the devil like the evil-minded child you are. You're just like your mother."

The absurdity of this accusation baffled Isabel. People were always saying she was like her mother, but Nan had been meek, passive and quiet-voiced.

"Jack the wheelwright says any girl who beckons the devil should be whipped," offered another of Isabel's half-brothers.

"And," added another, "he said that Nan was a foreigner and probably a pagan devil-worshipper, and Isabel probably is, too."

Isabel glared at him, her anger rising. "She was not, and I'm not either." Her mother had prayed as devoutly as anyone. Isabel remembered her kneeling in the candlelit church, her forehead pressed to her knuckles, murmuring the required responses. Where did they get these ideas and these accusations?

"What a little hussy you are," Marc said. "How dare you answer back that way?"

She was about to crash her fists against the tabletop, but stopped herself. If she had such a fit, they would say she was fully possessed, and then she'd really be in trouble.

Her father tore off a chuck of bread and took a bite. Her brothers watched her with gloating half smiles.

She turned and stamped to the ladder that led to the loft. As she climbed, she knew they would divide up her share of the food, but she didn't care. Her limbs trembling, she flung herself onto her straw sleeping pallet and glared at the heavy ceiling beams.

The entire family slept in the loft, which was partitioned into individual cubicles with rough woolen hangings. High above her pallet, a tiny window was cut into the wall, but the overhanging eaves and crude shutters blocked most of the moonlight.

Soon she heard the clanking of dishes and utensils as the table was cleared. Next came the sound of the trestle table being folded. She expected to be called because washing the knives and bowls was her task, but to her vast relief, they left her alone. She pulled the heavy sheepskin blanket over her head to keep out the chilly air and to shut out the sounds of her father and half-brothers moving about.

She didn't want to face the exorcism in the morning. If only she could disappear. If only she could close her eyes, open them, and find herself in some faraway place.

She had learned early what it was to be a girl in a family of boys. The youngest child and only girl might have brought out the protective instincts of her brothers, but no such thing happened in Isabel's case. Her fierce independence combined with her brothers' inclination to imitate their father resulted in her role as the family loner. At a young age she had learned to fight, and she was not afraid to stand up to any of her brothers who tried to bully her. She was often covered with bruises, but she held her head high and proud.

There was something queer about her father's family, everyone said so. They held themselves apart, but not in a clannish way like Meg's family. It was said that the Coles had always been strange, aloof, and dour. They had wanted little to do with Isabel's mother, and now they wanted little to do with her.

Meg's father, in stark contrast to Isabel's father, was a jovial man who laughed easily, often tossing his daughters into the air and catching them as they squealed with delight. Isabel had often compared him to her own father, who was whey-faced, with a blank vacuous stare and very little to say to anyone. Occasionally, watching Meg's father with his daughters would bring her a sharp pang of what she missed. Later she would gaze at her own father and try to imagine him hugging her. The moment of longing would pass because the repulsive idea of her father hugging her put all such thoughts from her mind.

Isabel had only the vaguest recollections of her mother. In her memory were wisps of a pale, sweet-voiced woman bent over the neat rows of her vegetable garden. Isabel had been too young to understand that Nan was pallid and quiet partly because she was incurably tired. Her father had five children by his first marriage. When Isabel was an infant, Nan had a household of eight to care for.

Isabel must have dozed sometime during the night, but when the first gray dregs of dawn lit the cracks in the shutters she felt she hadn't slept at all. Shortly after the bells of the distant monastery announced the sunrise, she heard the sounds of her father and brothers. She knew their morning noises so well that she knew what each of them was doing. The eldest of her brothers was dragging his pallet down the loft stairs to shake it outside. Her father trimmed his beard himself, not caring that it was always uneven.

She braided her hair, letting it fall down her back where it hung nearly to her knees. She pulled on the first tunic she laid hands on, the one on top of her stack of clothes folded neatly in a wooden crate at the foot of her bed. It was not one of her best, patched in several places and tattered at the hem, but she didn't care. She paused to fold her coverlet as tightly as possible into the chest to suffocate the fleas and bedbugs and prevent new ones from finding their way inside.

The sun was just over the horizon when she climbed the hill to the village church. The door creaked noisily as she pushed it open. The church was darkened, all shutters pulled shut and the candles lit. Meg was already inside, kneeling before the priest who was studying the book that lay open on the table in front of him. There were those who suspected the priest couldn't read but merely recited from memory, pretending to know what was written on the page. Because nobody in the village could read, there was no way to know.

The parson stood nearby with the bailiff. The baron's bailiff was included in all important rituals. He had a sweet babyish face, and an easy going manner, always trying to keep trouble to a minimum. Isabel could almost hear him saying: "Is all of this necessary?" and the parson responding by launching into a sermon about the works of the demons.

They all turned toward Isabel as she entered. The soft leather of her shoes tapped against the earthen straw-covered floor as she crossed the church and knelt beside Meg.

The priest chanted the mysterious language of the church, lifting his arms over the candles. The flickering flames threw his shadow across the wall where it touched the ceiling boards. The bailiff and parson bent their heads as if in silent meditation. All the while, Meg muffled her frightened sobs in her hands.

Isabel saw the whole scene as if from a great distance. The priest's performance seemed unreal and a bit ridiculous. The only thing that was real was Meg's fright. Isabel found herself growing annoyed with Meg's sobs.

Then, from the distance came the faint clicking of hooves. As the sound grew nearer, the priest dropped his arms and listened. The bailiff and the parson looked at each other. Horsemen seldom rode through the village. The hoof-beats pounded up the road to the church. Soon the horsemen were close enough for those in the church to hear the jingling of harness chains. Geese honked loudly, no doubt fluttering and scrambling to get out of the road.

"Where the devil is Christopher?" came a shout from outside.

The priest and parson turned to the bailiff.

"It is Edmund," the bailiff explained awkwardly, "the baron's son."

The bailiff crossed the chapel and creaked open the door. Sunlight flooded in.

"I'm here," the bailiff said.

"What the devil are you doing in there? Have you suddenly taken to praying?"

A broad-shouldered young man stood silhouetted in the doorway, framed by the bright sunlight. He strode into the church, followed by his attendants. Isabel had never seen anyone so splendidly dressed. He seemed to glitter as he walked. He wore a mantle of dark woodland green, a white shirt with gold embroidered cuffs, and a black velvet cap. His hair, the color of sunshine on a wheat field, glowed in the dim candlelight. He stopped and looked about the church with the haughty glance of ownership.

"Open that window," he commanded. "I can't see a thing."

Quickly his attendants threw the shutters open. As the wide beams of sunlight streamed in, he turned to look at Meg and Isabel.

"What is going on?" he demanded. Meg dropped her face into her hands and continued sobbing.

"We are exorcizing evil spirits from these girls," the priest explained.

"What have they done?"

"They have tempted the devil into their souls."

"Really?" he asked. "How?"

"I'd rather not say, sir."

This caused Edmund's brows to arch. "Come now, I want to know," he said in a friendlier, coaxing tone. Looking back again at Isabel, he asked, "How old are they?"

"Old enough to tempt Satan, sir."

"They're children. What they have done?"

The priest leaned forward and whispered into his ear. He listened intently.

"The waterfall?" he exclaimed, his face suddenly animated and bright. "How clever."

"I'm so ashamed," Meg sobbed into her hands.

"What about you?" he asked Isabel, his amused smile transforming his face into something wonderfully alive, as if his face was lit from within. "Are you ashamed?"

Isabel was so deeply startled by his evident amusement that she could only stare at him mutely.

He walked toward her and Meg, crossing the space between them with a few long strides. Meg looked up at him as if at a horrible apparition. Instinctively, Isabel rose to her feet. She was tall. Already she stood as high as many village men, but the baron's son dwarfed her. He stood close enough for her to smell the warm musky scent of horses.

"I suppose this interesting activity was your idea?" he asked.

As a matter of fact, Meg had discovered the game, but who would believe it? Summoning all her energy, she squared her shoulders and lifted her chin, glaring silently at him.

"You brazen girl," snapped the parson. "You answer his lordship when he speaks to you."

"Never mind," the baron's son said to the parson. To Isabel, he asked, "What's your name?"

"Isabel."

"Of course," he said, as if her name could possibly be familiar to him. "I must ask the witch to tell me all about you."

For a moment Isabel was too confused to realize who he meant. What could he know of the village witch? But even worse, what could the village witch possibly tell him about her?

"I think the demons have been exorcized enough," he said, turning back to the priest and the bailiff. "Let these girls return to their families."

The priest nodded to Meg and Isabel. "You may go."

Meg leapt to her feet and fled from the church. Slowly Isabel turned to leave, aware of the baron's son watching her. She didn't want to take to her legs in Meg's undignified fashion. Instead she held her head high, and pretending she was a royal princess, walked from the church with as much pride as she could muster, closing the door softly behind her.

CHAPTER 2

On the outskirts of Brotton lived a strange old woman named Alis who everyone said was a witch. She was perhaps fifty years old, older than everyone else in the village. Her cottage stood in the shade of a thick clump of trees and shrubs, completely hidden by the heavy foliage in the summer, separated from the village by a stretch of marshy bogs. Surrounding her rich vegetable gardens were rows of beautifully tended lilies and roses. Abundant honeysuckle and ivy framed her doorway. Her cottage, housing only an elderly woman, should have seemed empty, but instead it burst with life.

There were many strange peculiarities about her. She lived alone, which was unheard of for a woman, even a widow. She should have had a son or nephew to care for her, but nobody claimed her as a relation. She had obviously been beautiful once. Her cheeks were soft and rounded, her hair snowy white. The skin around her piercingly blue eyes was loose and folded gently with age.

Everyone knew that she was a stranger from York. As a young woman she had married a villager named Barnabe and moved to Brotton, and after her husband's death, she had remained in his cottage. She had lived in the village for as long as anyone could remember, but like Isabel's mother, she was of foreign birth and thus had never been fully accepted into village life. Each week she came to church and each year she paid her rents and tithes, but she kept to herself.

Alis understood the mysteries of herbs and furnished medicines from her gardens. A few children claimed to have seen her emerge from the black part of the forest where the evil Druid spirits lurked, but that was too preposterous to believe. It was said that she could foretell fortunes, and even members of the baron's family had gone to her for advice.

How had she learned the art of healing, the villagers wanted to know. She gave the same answer every time she was asked: "I learned after I came to Brotton, from an old wise-woman who peddled her cures through Yorkshire."

Few villagers were old enough to remember the wise-woman, and those who were old enough admitted that it might be true, or it might not; it was difficult to remember back that far. It was whispered that her magic was black, and she had really learned sorcery in pagan lands.

"She does not practice black magic," the bailiff had explained in his diplomatic way, "her magic is natural. There's a difference."

"Magic is magic," the parson said, "and it's against the laws of the church." He gave his usual reason: "Herbs cannot work without prayers, but prayers work without herbs."

The villagers were most upset by the times Alis became so absorbed in her task of inducing her medicines to work that she forgot to utter the accompanying prayers. This proved, they said, that she was pagan. But they needed her remedies, so other than a few whispers and jeers, her presence was tolerated.

The next Sunday at church, Isabel caught Alis watching her with what felt like a special kind of intimacy, her smile gentle and kind.

Isabel looked away. I'm imagining things, she told herself. She wanted to look back at Alis, particularly after the things the baron's son had said, but she didn't dare. She was still in enough trouble after the waterfall incident. The last thing she needed was for people to think she was friends with the witch.

One evening not long after, in the shadowy, fading light of early evening, Isabel was in the whortleberry thickets near the start of the black forest, a half-filled basket on her arm. She poked around the thickets, searching for berries, when Alis appeared at her elbow. Startled, she dropped her basket.

She and Alis looked at one another. A kind smile came to Alis's face. "You've been in some trouble, haven't you? The exorcism must have been unbearable. Such nonsense."

Isabel's shock deepened: How dare Alis speak this way? The baron's son, of course, could get away with making light of the exorcism, but Alis speaking such words in such a tone, if heard by those who hated her, would confirm the rumors that she was secretly a pagan who despised the teachings of the church.

"Don't you believe in demons?" Isabel asked, standing with her feet slightly apart in that way which made the villagers whisper that she was brazen.

"Of course I do," Alis said.

This wasn't what Isabel had expected. She herself wasn't sure she believed in them.

"Have you ever seen one?" Isabel asked.

"Demons can't be seen," Alis said, smiling again. "They're the parts of ourselves that we can't control. Mostly they have to do with our bodies where we're not supposed to touch."

Isabel took a step back. "Why were you watching me in the church?" she asked.

"I have always watched you."

"Why?"

"You're like your grandmother," she said. "You look like her, you even speak like her. She would be proud of you."

"I'm nothing like her," Isabel said. She was tired enough of people saying she was like her mother, but this was worse. She remembered her paternal grandmother well. She had been thin, flighty, and as wiry as a humming bird.

"I'm speaking of your mother's mother," Alis said.

Isabel blinked at this. "She never lived in this village," she said, not bothering to add that nobody knew who she was.

"That is true," Alis said.

"Do you know who she is?"

Alis looked away, as if studying something in the distance. "Of course I know who she is."

"How do you know?"

"She was my sister."

For a moment Alis's words had no meaning for Isabel. They sounded like pure nonsense. Then the meaning crashed like a clap of thunder. She caught her balance and told herself that it couldn't be true. Her mother had no living family, or so everyone said.

"It isn't true," Isabel stammered at last.

"But it is." A smile played at Alis's cheeks.

"Then why did my mother never tell me? Why did *you* never tell me?"

"We drink milk until we are ready for meat," she said. "I am telling you now, even though you still may not be ready, because I see how you're misunderstood. It might help to know that your grandmother would have been proud of you."

"*Proud* of me? Why?"

"You are very much like her. You are brave and strong and spirited, like her. It hurts to watch you trying so hard to befriend girls like Meg who are completely unworthy of you."

Suddenly Alis became very still, like a deer catching the scent of danger on the breeze. Before Isabel could say another word, Alis was gone. Moments later, Isabel heard the laughter of a group of approaching village girls.

Quickly Isabel picked up her basket and returned to gathering berries, trying to regain her composure. As she poked around the whortleberry bushes, she found the path that Alis must have taken. With a jolt, she realized that the path led in the direction of the black forest. So the rumors were true. Alis did go alone into the haunted forest.

When the girls approached with their baskets, Isabel nodded in absent-minded greeting. Then she realized the girls were crossing themselves and that Meg was among them.

"How can you come here alone, so near the black forest?" one said.

"Quickly cross yourself," said another. "There are demons nearby."

Isabel obliged. During the week since the exorcism, she had waited for Meg to break the silence between them, but Meg had kept her distance. Now, as before, she avoided looking at Isabel.

Isabel thought perhaps she should speak first. "Hello, Meg."

"Here you are," Meg said, "still beckoning the demons. Haven't you learned?"

Isabel and Meg stood looking at each other. There was fear in Meg's eyes.

"Stay away from her from now on," one of Meg's sisters said to Isabel. "You're to leave her alone."

Isabel watched Meg to see how she would respond. Meg slowly and deliberately turned away. Isabel stared at the familiar curve of Meg's back and the wispy curls of her braid. Isabel's cheeks burned with the humiliation and injustice of it all.

She tried to think of something to say, something cruel and conclusive, but she couldn't. The girls turned and walked away, laughing and talking again among themselves. Isabel turned toward the village, listening to their voices fading behind her.

That night in the darkness of the sleeping loft Isabel thought about the silver amulet, a charm shaped into a beautiful floral pattern that she kept hidden between the layers of her straw pallet. She'd had it for as long as she could remember, although she didn't know where she had found it. Once her father had taken it away. Grasping it by the rope she had tied around it, he threw it into the swampy bogs down the hill from their cottage, saying, "It's an ancient pagan charm." It took three long afternoons of wading through the puddles until, miraculously, she found it, which she wouldn't have done if not for the rope it was tied to. After that she kept it hidden.

Now she dug into her pallet until she found it. The cold metal, so heavy in her hand, thoroughly frightened her. She wanted to run and throw the amulet back into the bogs. She sensed that possessing this amulet widened the gap between her and the villagers. She didn't want to feel so separated and alone. She wanted her father to smile at her as he often smiled at her half-brothers, with a bit of life coming into his empty eyes. She wanted Meg and her sisters to include her in their circle.

Even though she wanted these things, and even though she felt a wild urge to throw the amulet into the bogs, she tucked it into a pouch.

The following day, she wandered slowly past Alis's cottage. She knew that Alis, bent over the fragrant rows of her herbal garden, was aware of her, but there were villagers in sight, so she said nothing. As Isabel gazed longingly into her yard, she spun an enticing fantasy: Alis was indeed her kin and the villagers put aside the notion that Alis was a witch. Isabel would then live with her in her lovely cottage instead of her father's crowded, musty loft.

Alis continued to pull weeds as if Isabel were not lingering about. Slowly Isabel turned and, dragging her fingers across the hemp fence, wandered away.

In the weeks that followed, Isabel sometimes walked slowly past Alis's house and other times lingered about the thicket near the path that led from the forest. She came as often as she dared, whenever she could spare a few moments from her daily chores.

Finally Alis appeared near the thicket again. This time Alis didn't even try to hide the fact that she had come from the direction of the black forest. She smiled and waited for Isabel to speak, as if she knew that Isabel had something particular to say.

Isabel held out the amulet so Alis could see it.

"That was your grandmother's. I gave it to you."

"You did? When?"

"You were very young, no more than three or four years old. I told you to take good care of it. I said it was magic and would protect you."

"Where did she get it?"

"She brought it from Eynhallow."

Eynhallow. The name had a faraway, mysterious sound. Isabel wanted to know where this place was, but instead she asked, "Do you know the baron's son?"

"Of course I know Edmund."

"How?"

"When he was a young boy he came in search of me, saying he was looking for a witch, assuring me he wasn't afraid."

"Can you read the future?"

"Hmm," Alis said, smiling. "I can tell some things. I know that you, for instance, will not stay many years in this village."

"How do you know that? Because of your black magic?"

"I don't practice black magic."

"They say you do."

"They say many things, and most of the time they're wrong."

"Then how do you know?"

"Because I can see what kind of girl you are. You're restless, curious, and strong-willed. You are simply not like the others in this village. You'll not remain content here for long." Something like admiration came into Alis's voice. She seemed to think highly of Isabel for the very reasons the villagers disliked her.

Isabel could think of nothing at all to say. At last, with great effort, she said the only words that came to her: "I wanted to visit you."

"Come when you are ready," Alis said, "and I'll tell you your secrets."

CHAPTER 3

During the months that followed, Isabel often thought about visiting Alis, but she never did. Sometimes she thought she didn't go because she was afraid. Other times, she knew the real reason. She wasn't ready. *We drink milk until we are ready for meat.*

Years passed. Isabel was sixteen and Jake two years older the summer of their friendship. Isabel wasn't quite pretty — her features were too broad and overpowering — but her face was striking. She had an earthy sensuousness that repelled and fascinated the villagers. There wasn't a village boy who didn't look at her with the hot light in his eyes that she had learned to recognize. Jealous girls might point out Isabel flaws, but the village boys declared her the beauty of Brotton.

Despite Jake's awkwardness, she preferred him to the others. He had an impish, fun quality that she liked. He had reddish hair which stood straight up in places, giving him a rumpled look. After he had visited the port of Grimsby and spoken to several sailors, he spoke of it constantly. He was filled with dreams of adventure, and she enjoyed listening to him talk.

"They sail to distant lands," he told Isabel, "to strange places in the Orient. One day I will sail on such a ship."

Jake had fallen into the habit of joining her as she tended the sheep along the bright green bank of the stream at the bottom of the hill. He lounged easily beside her upon his deerskin cape which he had thrown across the grass. His legs, which were too long for his breeches, crossed carelessly, his knees showing through the garment's many holes.

It was a bright September day, and nearly time for apple picking. From where they sat, they could see the baron's castle. Beyond the castle, on a faraway hilltop, a long walk away but visible when the air was clear, was the closest monastery. All around were the scents of late summer, the sweet tangy fragrance of ripe apples, the smell of the clover, the fragrant cowslip. It was a perfect day.

"And how will you get onto such a ship?" She didn't know of a single villager who had ever left.

"Merchant ships always need crew members. One of the sailors told me that. All I have to do is offer to work."

"How do you know it's so wonderful in the east?"

"That's what the sailor said. There's a place marked on the map he showed me where heaven and earth meet."

The notion of such a place, which must surely be magical and lovely, quieted Isabel for a moment. "Can you sail there?" she asked.

"Yes, but it's far away, at the end of the earth. A paradise with every kind of flower, and trees that grow as high as the clouds."

"Is that where you'll live?"

"Nope." He leaned back, turning his face to the sunlight. "I don't think anybody lives there. It's just a place to visit. I'll live in the Orient."

"The Orient is pagan," she teased. It was the only thing she knew about the east.

"I don't care. They wear gold and satin and sleep on silk beds stuffed with feathers. All the men are rich, and have harems filled with wives."

"I suppose you want such a harem."

"Indeed I do."

"Have you confessed this desire to the parson?"

"Bah, what does he know about it? I'll have hundreds of wives, and I want them all to look like you."

He leaned toward her, but she drew away and looked toward the baron's castle, perched on a distant hilltop, high above the surrounding countryside. She had chosen this spot because Jake liked to look at the castle. It always prompted his talk about the great things in the world that were waiting for him, like feathers waiting to be plucked for his cap.

The year before, when Edmund's father had died and Edmund's brother had become the baron, Isabel had watched the ceremonial procession pass through Brotton. She saw Edmund from a distance and thought he seemed nothing like the laughing man who had interrupted the exorcism and ordered the parson to open the church windows.

"You're thinking about him, aren't you?"

"Who?" she asked, knowing very well who he meant.

"The baron's brother. You met him once."

Although their encounter didn't quite have the dignity of a meeting, she liked the way it sounded. "I thought him very haughty."

"If he comes around looking for you, stay away from him."

"Why would he come looking for me?"

He looked at her a long moment before answering. "He might."

She smiled. "I believe you're jealous."

"I don't want a knight looking for my girl. I've heard stories about what they do. They come around with presents and gold, and then leave you with a big belly. If I have to fight him, I will. You're my girl and he's to stay away."

The bravado in his voice was false. Isabel knew as well as he did that he'd never be able to fight an armed knight. Knights had real swords and armor. Fighting men from the fields, like Jake, carried pikes and axes and had no shields.

"Am I your girl?"

"You know you are."

She looked back toward the castle. On rare days when the fog lifted completely, the castle was visible from everywhere in the barony, constantly appearing and reappearing over the hills and treetops. She liked it best when the fogs were heavy and the red sandstone towers glowed through the mist as if touched by magic. After seeing Edmund up close, she imagined that the entire place glittered like him.

She looked back at Jake. He smiled and pulled her close.

She shook him off. "I refuse to fall in love with you. One day you will be on a ship sailing to the east, and I'll be left here."

"I'll come back for you."

"To fetch me for your harem?"

He pulled her to him, folding his arms around her, caressing her back. "If you'll be my wife," he said.

"One of them, you mean."

He kissed her, and she relaxed. He slipped his hands into her shirt to rub her bare skin, lifting his fingers to touch her breasts. The first time he had touched her that way she had jerked back, startled. He had merely smiled patiently and waited, as if he knew that any girl who had played the games she had under the waterfall as a child of twelve would soon find the forbidden irresistible. Sure enough, unable to set aside her fear but tempted by curiosity, she had let his hands wander over her.

Something made Isabel turn and look toward the path that led to the village. Sensing someone watching her, looked toward the fields and found herself looking directly at a plowman who stood watching them. His eyes were wide with watching everything. He stood on the balls of his feet as if poised for flight. She pulled her shirt back into place, but it was too late. He had seen everything.

The plowman hurried away.

Jake also saw him and bolted upright. "Did you see who he was?"

"I think it was John Durbey," she said.

A gloominess came over Jake. John Durbey was his uncle. John Durbey would soon report what he had seen, and everyone would talk about them. Again Isabel would be a lusty, evil-minded girl.

"I hate everything about Brotton," Jake said.

"Me, too."

"I want to be on a ship sailing far away," he said.

Isabel sighed. There would be trouble, and she wasn't looking forward to it. Silently, gloomily, they rose and returned to the village, separating when they came within sight of the first cottages.

That night Jake ran away. Isabel knew he had gone to the port of Grimsby to join a ship's crew, but the villagers saw things differently.

"He ran away so he wouldn't have to marry her," was the general opinion in the village

CHAPTER 4

Edmund Decourcey's monastery cell always smelled musty, even though a servant aired it twice daily. The fine linen on his mattress and fresh carpet of rushes on the floor were dank and smelled of mildew. The cell was no more than four paces across. Edmund could not stand up straight without his head brushing the ceiling. There was no window, and the thick walls shut out all sound.

"You'll only be there two years," his brother's advisors had said when he complained, "you know that."

"Why can't I continue with tutors in the castle?"

"You're going to be a priest," his brother's chaplain had answered. "Unless you want to be a lowly parish priest, tutors are not enough. You need a formal education."

The problem was, Edmund didn't want to be a priest at all. He tried to remember back to a time when he had wanted to enter the church, when its mystique and wealth had beckoned to him, but he could not.

He would have preferred the monastery nearer the castle, but the decision to send him instead to the stricter Fountain's Abbey had been made by his brother's advisors, who arranged for his admission and paid the necessary tuition.

Most sons not destined to inherit could ride out into the world in search of adventures and fortune, but a royal decree had ordered

Edmund into the church. It would thus be impossible to join the king's army, and unless he lied about his identity, he was barred from the retinue of any English lord. His father had attempted to free Edmund from his fate by leaving him a substantial amount of money, enough for him to join any noble retinue which would have him. But within days of his death, a royal decree came voiding the will, leaving every bit of his gold to his older brother Albert, except what Edmund would need to enter the priesthood and obtain a respectable post.

Edmund closed his eyes, thinking about the endless days and weeks stretched out before him. He guessed about an hour had passed since Matins, the midnight Mass. If only he could sleep, the nights would go faster and the days would be less tedious.

The door to his cell opened so quietly that for a moment Edmund thought he had imagined it. The corridor outside was as dark as the cell, so he couldn't know for sure that the door had opened, but there came the unmistakable whisper of a movement, the lightest swish of clothing.

"Who's there?" Edmund demanded.

"Shh," came a soft whisper. "It's me."

"Who?" Edmund demanded more loudly. It had to be one of the tutors, for none of the novices or other students would have the courage to enter his cell. Edmund guessed that his visitor must be Brother Craig — but, on second thought, surely that was impossible. Brother Craig was overbearing and rude to everyone, particularly Edmund.

"Shh."

The intruder's soft, reassuring whisper did nothing to stop Edmund's heart from pounding. Whoever it was moved across the cell, the floor rushes snapping softly beneath his feet.

What do you want, Edmund wanted to ask as the man lowered himself to the mattress, but his words caught in his throat. Edmund wasn't accustomed to this helpless feeling of sheer terror. Unable to speak past the tightening in his throat, he withdrew into himself, like a cat about to pounce.

"Are you afraid?" came the hesitant, tentative whisper.

"No," was Edmund's instinctive response.

"I knew you wouldn't be," the intruder sounded pleased and satisfied. "I would have come sooner had I dared."

Cool air touched Edmund's legs as the visitor lifted the blanket. Edmund drew away, his back against the wall near the corner of the cell, his knees drawn up protectively in front of him.

"Shh," the visitor said again, as if that was all he needed to say, and Edmund would obey.

A silky hand touched Edmund's thigh.

"No!" Edmond said. He rocked back and, and with all his force, sprung his legs in a kick intended to push the intruder away. The crushing impact of his weight sent the man sprawling against the far wall.

"For God's sake!" said the intruder.

"Brother *Alfred*?" Edmond said.

"Well, who did you think? Jesus, you didn't have to try to kill me. I would have left if you told me to."

Edmund realized he was trembling, his limbs weak from fright. He breathed deeply, forcing his composure to return. From the sounds Brother Alfred made, Edmund knew he was smoothing himself, also regaining his composure.

"I thought you were Brother Craig."

"Well, I'm not. I thought you knew who I was."

"You have no business coming in here."

"I'm sorry. I was clumsy and stupid, but you didn't have to try to kill me."

A curse on this place, Edmund thought. He was tired of the penances and the rules which were meant to be broken. He understood why Brother Albert had come: the penance for touching another man was lighter than the penance for touching oneself.

In that very moment, Edmond reached a decision.

"I'm leaving in the morning," he said. If he stayed another day, he would surely explode. As soon as it was light, he would write the necessary letters. To his brother, he would write that he was ill and needed fresh air for his health. To the king's advisors he would plead the need for a temporary respite. Then he would join Tristin.

"Don't blame me," Brother Alfred said. "You've wanted to leave for months, but you've needed an excuse. Now you've got one."

Edmund heard the soft patter of Brother Alfred's footsteps as he walked from the cell to the corridor. He settled back onto his mattress. Brother Alfred was right, of course. He had wanted to leave for months.

A distant female voice, soft and comforting, came from far back in his memory. It had been a long time since he had thought about Alis. Now, her long ago prediction came back to him like a prophetic warning. "You will find yourself alone in that place," she had said. "You will be the most miserable resident in the entire the monastery."

Edmund had not thought much about her prediction at the time. Nobody was happy in a monastery; monasteries weren't intended for that purpose. But he had discovered that, unlike the other residents, he could find no way to make life bearable. Brother Geoff contented himself with his frequent visits to the town, where he was treated like royalty by the barmaids because of the clinking gold in his pocket and his famed generosity. Edmund sometimes joined him, but the hours in town did nothing to make life at the monastery more bearable.

Some of Edmund's fellow students considered monastery life one of complete freedom and independence. Other students and novices genuinely wanted nothing more than a life of meditation and study and were thus content in the monastery. They managed to find a camaraderie from which Edmund felt excluded. Alis's prediction had indeed come true: he was very much alone, and utterly miserable.

Before meeting Alis, he understood there were two kinds of witches: young and beautiful girls who lured men to destruction, and wicked old hags who unabashedly did the devil's work. After hearing stories of a witch who spent time in the dark and haunted part of the forest, he decided to go in search of her.

Sneaking away from his governess, he had made his way down the back of the castle hill, through the dense and tangled brush. At last the land leveled off and he emerged into an open glade. In the glade was a large circle of blanched white stones. There was an old woman sitting on the clay stoop of a sagging wattle hut which looked like it had been hurriedly erected. Calmly she set aside her whittling and stood up.

She was not a young temptress or an old hag. She was kind and gentle-voiced, with pale skin, white hair, and bright blue eyes. She had an air of quietness about her, a manner which was both compelling and gentle. There was something magical about her, as if a light radiated from within her.

"Hello, Edmund," she had said.

"How did you know my name?" he had demanded.

She smiled. Instead of answering, she said, "Of course I know who you are. You're very brave to have come here in search of me."

"I'm not afraid of witches."

"I can see that. But the truth is, I'm not a witch."

"What are those stones?" he said, lifting his finger and pointing.

"A magic ring," she said. "Long ago, pagans danced among them, worshipping the earth goddess."

"There's no such thing as the earth goddess."

"Are you sure?"

He felt he should have been frightened, but he wasn't. He said, "If you have the magic Sight like everyone says, tell me my fortune."

"It doesn't take the Sight to know that baron is your father, but the baroness is not your mother. Your birth is considered illegitimate, so you must go into the church."

He was only ten, but old enough to grasp the significance of the word "considered." He had thought his illegitimacy was a fact.

"What do you mean *considered*?"

"Your father *did* marry your mother."

"He did?"

"Of course, but according to her local customs. She was from far to the west, you know, the farthest reaches of Wales. The bishop says the ceremony wasn't legal because it wasn't a Christian ceremony."

"Then," he said, "if the ceremony wasn't legal, I'm illegitimate."

"According to the bishop."

"But—"

From the distance came someone calling, "Edmund! Edmund."

"I have to go."

"I hope you will visit me again."

He did visit again, many times. Then one morning just after dawn when he was eighteen a page brought him a cryptic message which read like a command: "Know where Brotton's bailiff is at sunrise."

"Who sent this message?" Edmund had asked

"A village woman brought it to the gatekeeper," said the page. "She said it must be given to you immediately."

Edmund hadn't thought that any of the villagers, even the parish priest, could read. The message was scratched on a scrap of parchment with a piece of burned wood. The handwriting was large and messy, as if written by a young child. Intrigued, he dressed and searched the castle for Christopher, the bailiff. The men-at-arms were just then clambering to their places on the walls and towers, replacing the night watch. The grooms were busily sweeping the stables in the courtyard, and already the smith was at work in the forge, the pounding of his anvil ringing through the yard. Edmund asked each of them where Christopher was, but none knew.

Edmund then took a horse from the stables and rode through Brotton. At last a villager directed him to the church, where he stumbled upon the ridiculous exorcism ritual.

He understood right away that the witch had sent him the note so that he would interrupt the exorcism and spare the girls the ordeal. One of the girls, who was frail and blonde, had been terrified. The other, a beautiful girl with large velvety brown eyes and burnished bronze hair, had not been afraid at all.

"The simple folk will never accept the word of our Lord," the priest had later explained, "if we don't frighten them a bit. You understand, I'm sure."

"No," Edmund had snapped. "I don't."

After eighteen months in the monastery, he had not changed his mind.

Edmund ignored the Lauds bells, remaining in his cell to pack his things. He was reading through his letters, mostly correspondence with Tristin, deciding what he would burn and what he would take with him, when the door swung open. Brother Craig stood on the threshold.

"You slept through Lauds," he said, his voice hard and flat, accusing.

"No, sir, I did not," Edmund said, drawing himself up to full height. "I chose not to go."

"The penance is for missing Mass is —"

"I don't care what the penance is," Edmund interrupted. "I am leaving this morning."

Several beats of time passed. "Just like that?" his stern face softening with curiosity.

"I've been ill. I need air."

"I will write your brother the baron to the contrary."

"Then he will receive both our letters at the same time. Let him believe who he will." Edmund had no fear of his brother. Disobeying a royal order was another matter, but Edmund would worry about that later.

Brother Craig turned and stalked down the corridor. Calmly Edmund continued packing. About a half hour later, he heard someone behind him, and spun around to face Brother Alfred. Brother Alfred's eyes that seemed always to crinkle with laughter provided a welcome contrast to the dour and hostile Brother Craig. Then Edmund remembered the incident in the night and folded his arms across his chest.

For a moment they studied one another's eyes, as if afraid of each other.

"Where are you going?" Brother Alfred asked

"To meet up with a friend. The last I heard he was riding with the Duke of Northumberland's retinue."

"I will ride with you as far as the inn near Pately Bridge. They have thick ale which always raises your spirits. I don't mind if you leave hating Brother Craig, but we were friends."

Edmund felt himself softening. "All right," he said.

CHAPTER 5

On a brisk afternoon in late autumn a few months after Jake ran away, three monks came to Brotton from the nearby monastery in search of youths capable of learning. The village boys up to the age of sixteen were gathered in the front of the church, with the other villagers ranging behind. The monks looked them over haughtily, as if wondering if any might possess enough wit to join the lofty rank of educated churchmen.

The church had recently announced a policy of giving its offices to the most intelligent and capable clerks, regardless of their birth. Although no Brotton youth had ever been educated, a boy had been selected from a nearby village several years before. It was supposed to be possible for a poor plowman's son possessing ambition and a quick mind to enter that mysterious place of learning and come out a richly clad prince of the church.

The chapel, lit by candles set in latticed casements of colored glass, looked its best for the monks' visit. The wooden walls glowed warmly, the air was lovely and still.

Isabel sat between her father and one of her brothers near the back of the church. Two of her brothers who were young enough to enter the contest sat in front with the other boys.

The eldest of the monks, who also seemed to be the leader, stepped forward and cleared his throat, his voice shattering the stillness. "We are here to select the brightest youth for a convent education. We will pose two riddles. Any boy to answer both questions shall return with us." The boys leaned forward eagerly.

The door opened and a newcomer shuffled in. Isabel turned to see who had entered. It was Alis. She set down her basket and pulled off her woolen gloves. She looked over the crowd and seeing Isabel, she smiled.

"Please stand," the monk said, "if you can solve the riddle: Who killed one quarter part of all people in the world?"

Silence followed. Not a boy rose to answer the riddle. Isabel waited for one of them to answer. The riddle was an easy one. Isabel turned to look at Alis. The old woman nodded sharply as if she knew Isabel had the answer. "Go ahead," Alis seemed to nod, "stand up and give the answer."

A bubble of courage rose in Isabel. She stood up, and in a clear voice said: "Cain, when he killed Abel."

Everyone in the church turned toward her. Her father stared, shocked and uncomprehending. Thinking they had not understood, she opened her mouth to explain, but the parson snapped: "Sit down, you impertinent girl."

"Who are you?" asked the monk, as if the parson had not spoken.

"Isabel Cole." Isabel suppressed a smile, enjoying the deliciousness of the moment.

"How old are you, Isabel Cole?"

"Almost seventeen years old, sir."

"Perhaps, Isabel, you can answer the next riddle. A house full, a yard full, but you cannot catch a bowl full. What is it?"

She smiled. "Smoke."

The silence that followed was broken by the awkward shuffling of feet and a nervous cough near the front of the church. Her father, astonished, was simply staring at her. Her brother wore a strange little smile that she couldn't read. Again, thinking they had not understood, she explained: "Smoke can fill the yard and a house, but not a bowl."

The monks turned away and put their heads together. They whispered for several minutes, and turned back to Isabel.

"We are awarding you tuition for three years study with the nuns."

For a moment nobody spoke. Then the parson stepped forward. "Please sir," he said. "You don't understand, she's not suitable at all."

"I disagree," said the bailiff. "It is an honor to the entire village. She must be permitted to go."

Isabel, still standing, could look over the crowd. Some villagers were nodding. Meg and her sisters were staring, but nobody moved to object.

So Isabel would receive an education in a world of luxury, for the nearby convent was known to be one of the richest in all Yorkshire. She would learn to read and write like the daughter of a nobleman. She remembered Alis's prediction: *You will not remain long in this village.* Isabel looked at Alis.

Alis was smiling at her.

Next morning, when Isabel walked proudly from the village, she wore her best skirt, the one with a single patch that hardly showed, and her favorite tunic with sleeves laced from wrist to elbow. The silver amulet was sewn into her hem. She had scrubbed her boots until all the mud stains were gone, and in the hazy morning light they shone almost like new. Her hair was carefully combed and braided, her face and hands clean.

She marched down into a valley and up the next hill, feeling a rush of excitement as the convent towers grew nearer and larger. She was leaving behind a familiar world, and entering one that would bear it no resemblance. Ahead were the convent towers, which were not red sandstone like the castle, but a creamy stately gray. Even the crisp air and whispering trees that arched overhead seemed exciting and new.

The recent rains had turned the road to mud, so by the time Isabel arrived, a layer of muddy slime covered her hem and boots. The watchman at the gate glared at her as if at her presumption in approaching the convent, but when she gave her name he swung open the wrought iron gate. The gates opened majestically as if she were a long-awaited, honored guest.

He rang a bell. Then he pointed and said, "That way."

She walked toward a courtyard trellised with carefully tended roses of red, pink, and white. The cloister walk was paved with smooth stones and shaded with ivy-covered canopies.

A nun came forward and greeted her. "I am Sister Agathe," she said. "You must be Isabel Cole. Follow me."

Isabel followed her down the cloistered walk, past one elegant stone building after another, past a quiet duck pond, along a seemingly endless row of stone pillars.

"This is the dormitory," she told Isabel as they walked up a set of wide steps to a large carved door. "The other girls are in the schoolroom."

The floor of the wide chamber was spread with a thick carpeting of fragrant rushes mixed with flower petals and bay leaves. In a corner of the room, a marble statue of the Virgin Mary was mounted amid an array of ivory and pewter crucifixes. There was a row of enormous beds, and at the foot of each were two beautifully carved chests.

"You'll share this bed with Elizabeth," said Sister Agathe, "and this chest is yours."

The wooden chest at the foot of her bed was so large all Isabel's belongings would fill a single corner.

Then, to her surprise, Sister Agathe took her bundle of clothes. "You won't need these," she said, holding the bundle away from her, as if it were infected. "Clothes for you are in the chest. I suggest you wash before the girls return." She pointed to a ceramic basin.

Without another word, Sister Agathe turned and left Isabel alone. Filled with wonder, Isabel touched the bed, and realized that the fine linen sheets were stuffed with feathers. Gingerly she sat on it, feeling like an angel falling into a cloud. She smiled at the delightful absurdity of sleeping on feathers. With a surge of triumph, she wished Jake could see her. "I will sleep on a feather bed," she wanted to tell him, "surrounded by silks and satins. Can the Orient be more luxurious than this?" He had escaped from the village searching for better, and she had, too.

Then she noticed that a bit of dust from her skirt had smudged the snow-white linen. She tried to brush the sheet clean, but the stain deepened. Water from the basin turned it to a muddy splotch.

Not knowing what else to do, she quickly washed herself. In her trunk she found a stack of clean white muslin shifts made from finely spun cloth. After she was neatly dressed, her braid tucked into a cap, she tried again to remove the stain from the sheet, but again failed. She supposed her tunic would also be taken away, so she removed the amulet from the hem and hid it in a corner of her chest. That done, she wandered to the small window clad with wrought iron tracery.

The thick ledge formed a window seat. She sat on the cushion and pressed her cheek to the cool iron casement. She could see past the neat gardens and orchards, over the convent walls to the rolling hills beyond. She saw the bell tower of the nearest village, a village much like Brotton. How tiny it seemed, as if the entire village could fit in her palm.

Soon she heard the tapping of dozens of feet and the whisper of skirts across the floor rushes. She jumped up and faced the door as the girls trooped in. Nobody said a word. The silence was eerie. The girls were all dressed alike in crisp white linen shifts and soft leather slippers. They flocked to a cupboard and passed around large metal hoops and balls of thread.

"You must be the new girl," came a barely audible whisper.

"I'm Isabel," she said aloud to the girl who had spoken, her voice filling the room like a physical presence.

"Shh! There's a rule of silence. Whisper. If anyone comes, say nothing."

A yellow-haired girl bent over Isabel's bed, running her finger over the mud stain on her sheet. She turned toward Isabel, her face twisted into a scowl.

"Did you do this?" she whispered harshly

Isabel swallowed. "I'm sorry."

The girl, who Isabel guessed was Elizabeth her bedfellow, crossed the room and haughtily inspected Isabel, her gaze lingering on the traces of dust remaining on Isabel's elbow. Elizabeth's face was thin and angular, her eyes narrow. Anger bubbled inside Isabel as she stared at the imperial lift of Elizabeth's head. Would she be treated no differently here than in the village?

One of the girls handed Isabel a metal hoop with a square of linen and another passed her a ball of thread. Isabel had no idea what to do with them. The girls sat on stools scattered about the room and began embroidering, twisting their needles expertly in and out of the fabric.

"What are you waiting for?" someone whispered.

"I," Isabel swallowed, "I don't know how."

They all turned to look at her.

"You're filthy, and you can't embroider," said Elizabeth. "Where are you from?"

"Brotton," Isabel answered mechanically, "a nearby village."

"How did you get in here?" Elizabeth demanded.

Isabel drew herself up proudly and said, "I correctly answered the monk's riddles and—"

Elizabeth leapt to her feet, her embroidery frame clanging to the floor. "You're a common villager?" she said aloud. "I'm to share my bed with a common villager?"

"Enough of that," came a cool voice from the doorway. "Sit down and quiet yourself immediately, Elizabeth."

Humbly Elizabeth's bent and scooped up her hoop.

The speaker in the doorway was a strikingly pretty girl wearing a full nun's habit. She was no more than eighteen or nineteen years old.

"Mary," she said to one of the girls, "you will teach Isabel to embroider."

"Yes, Sister Clare."

Isabel stared at Sister Clare. How lovely she was! Her gently curving brows were jet black, her white skin tinged with peach, her eyes deep green. She held herself proudly, her shoulders squared, her chin high, speaking in a voice accustomed to giving commands. Even her white linen habit seemed luminous. Later Isabel learned the reason: it was made of the finest silk from the Orient.

Sister Clare turned to look directly at Isabel. Isabel expected a steely haughtiness. Instead, Sister Clare first studied her curiously, then flashed a friendly smile. She was dressed primly, but her eyes held a sharp intelligence, her expression a wild defiance.

Mary leaned forward to show Isabel how to hold the needle and make a simple stitch. Isabel concentrated on making the stitch. When she look up again, Sister Clare was gone.

The girls worked silently. As hard as Isabel tried, her stitches were uneven and her thread broke continually. The needle was tenacious in its refusal to let her control it. Once it pricked her finger and drops of her blood stained the linen. Never had she felt so awkward and clumsy. After the reprimand Elizabeth had received from Sister Clare nobody said a word, but Isabel had the feeling they were laughing at her clumsiness.

When the supper bell rang, the girls silently returned their embroidery hoops to the cupboard and filed into the cloister walk. Isabel followed along.

Sister Clare appeared, fell into step beside Isabel, and whispered, "Don't worry. Nobody learns to embroider in a single day."

Isabel smiled gratefully. Sister Clare walked ahead, catching up with the group of nuns who walked ahead of the students. Isabel thought Clare's face was sweeter than the Virgin Mother painted on the cloister-walk mural.

They ate standing up in a room called the refectory. Supper was bread made from fine white flour and a bit of chicken. At first Isabel enjoyed the sweet taste of the white bread, and thought the texture light and delicate, but its thin lifelessness left her with the feeling that she hadn't eaten at all. She wished for a piece of thick barley bread. Would she ever grow accustomed to this place?

After supper, just as the sun set, they all flocked to the chapel for Mass. The grandeur of the chapel surpassed anything Isabel had ever imagined: there were polished floors, enormous vaulted interiors, marble statues and jeweled crucifixes. She felt small and awed. The baron's own castle could not be more splendid than this. Perhaps even the king's palace fell short of this magnificence.

Back in the dormitory, the girls changed into night-shifts and got into bed. A calm serenity descended over the place as night fell. In the darkness, Isabel heard the girls whispering among themselves. Whenever footsteps sounded in the hall, the whispering stopped. When she listened to Elizabeth's uneven breathing, she had the feeling Elizabeth was waiting for her to break the silence between them, but Isabel had no such intention. She, too, had her pride.

When the Matins bells rang, Isabel's eyes popped open. For a bewildering moment she couldn't remember where she was. The sweet fragrance of the herbal floor rushes, the luxurious feel of fine linen, and utter strangeness of everything made her feel that she had awakened in another world.

The girls were out of bed, dressing quickly for midnight Mass. Isabel did the same.

She walked with the others through the velvety blackness of the cloister walk, feeling that she were still enveloped in the mists of sleep. In the moonlight, the neat rows of flowers and perfectly trimmed shrubs seemed unreal. The smell of herbs reminded her of

Alis. *You will not remain long* in this village, Alis had said, and she'd been right. But hadn't she helped make it happen by silently encouraging Isabel to answer the monk's questions?

Mass was said and Isabel was back in her bed, drifting into sleep, feeling that the interlude had been a dream. The next time the bells rang it was morning. A gray misty sunlight streamed in, bathing the walls in luminous silver.

As the girls dressed, Elizabeth took a mirror from her chest, propped it against her writing desk, and combed out her hair. Her yellow hair shone enticingly when combed.

Sister Clare entered the dormitory. Elizabeth tried to slide the comb and mirror under a garment draped across her bed, but the mirror slipped and fell to the floor rushes with a soft thud.

Sister Clare, her eyes twinkling mischievously but her face carefully impassive, said, "You know, Elizabeth, every minute that you spend combing your hair adds centuries to your time in purgatory."

Elizabeth missed the playfulness in Clare's green eyes. She sat for a long time staring into her lap, her eyes wide, her hands clutched together.

"I guess it's not worth it," Elizabeth said.

Sister Clare looked at Isabel, her eyes still sparkling with amusement. In response, Isabel came close to smiling. For a delicious moment, they were conspirators, sharing a joke at Elizabeth's expense.

Isabel's first few day passed in a confusing round of trips to the chapel to hear Mass, hours wrestling with the embroidery needle, meals in the refectory, and lessons in the schoolroom, none of which she understood. The oppressive rule of silence gave the place an air of deadly stillness.

That evening, as the girls were dressing for bed, one of the girls whispered to Isabel, "I think Sister Clare likes you."

"Maybe," said Isabel. "Who is she?"

"Her father is the Earl of Weston, so she is the highest ranking resident of the convent. People say she could have married the eldest son of a duke, and one day would have been a duchess. Instead she chose a cloistered life."

Another girl sitting nearby said, "Her family gives large amounts of gold to the convent and the adjoining monastery, so the abbess bows to all Clare's wishes. She's already taken her vows so she has the status of a full nun."

Next morning, as the girls walked along the trellis-covered walk toward the supper room, Sister Clare fell into step beside Isabel.

"How are you adjusting to life here?" Sister Clare asked.

It was a hard question to answer because Isabel was afraid she wasn't adjusting well at all. "I'm not sure," she said.

"It gets easier," Sister Clare said. "Just pretend you're a sheep."

Isabel was too astonished to answer.

"Do you miss your village?" Sister Clare asked

"Not at all." What was there to miss?

"There is no young man?" Sister Clare's voice was suddenly teasing. "There must be."

"Not anymore. He ran away, in search of adventures." Then, made bold by Sister Clare's questions, she asked: "Is it true that you could have married the son of a duke?"

"Nobody else has ever dared ask me that."

Isabel was instantly ashamed. "I'm sorry, Sister Clare."

"First, we can dispense with 'sister' when nobody can hear. I hate the sound of it. And I don't mind you asking. Anyway, it's true, but he was a fat, disgusting bore. After I tried to run away, my father locked me up here."

Now Isabel was even more astonished.

"I told you my secret," Clare said. "So you tell me yours. Tell me about your man who ran away."

Isabel stole a sidelong glance at Clare and saw the friendly face of a girl about her own age, eager for gossip. Could Clare, too, be lonely? Could it be possible that she was merely searching for a friend?

"Jake was nothing special. The truth is I used to think about someone else when he kissed me."

"See, I knew there was someone. Any girl who looks like you must have had dozens of admirers. Who did you think about?"

"Someone I saw once when I was only twelve. He had a good laugh at my expense. He wouldn't even know me if he saw me now."

40

When they passed a band of hooded monks from the other side of the wall, they fell silent. They had only one more chance to speak. Clare said, "However dreary village life may be," said Clare, "you will long for it after a little while here."

When Isabel rejoined the other girls, she noticed a change in their manner. At first she thought, from their tense, curious frowns, that they were angry. When they stared wistfully and asked what Sister Clare had said to her, she realized that they were jealous. Even Elizabeth gazed at her enviously.

Isabel soon realized that Clare was right about the dullness of the routine. She often had the feeling that she moved like a sleepwalker from one Mass to the next, and one lesson to the next.

The rule of silence was frequently broken, but the rule against laughter, which was far more serious, never was. "Christ never laughed," the abbess told the girls as they sat in the school room. "Three times he cried, but never once in the entire Scriptures is there an instance of the Lord laughing. Laughter is a meaningless convulsion that contorts the face, produces a hideous sound, and mocks the Lord. Worst of all, laughter invites the demons into the soul."

Breaking the rule against laughter brought the harshest of penances.

Once each month Isabel was given free time which she was expected to use to visit the village and her family. She spent her free afternoons within the convent walls, wandering among the gardens or groves.

Her favorite time was each week when the girls were permitted to sit behind a veil at the back of the boys' schoolroom and listen to the scholars debate the great philosophical questions. The rule of silence didn't apply to the boys' studies. They could ask whatever questions they wished and participate in the discussions as far as they were able. Isabel found some of the questions ridiculous: How many angels can fit on the head of a pin? Others were more interesting: If God is all-good and all-powerful, why is there evil in the world?

The girls spent several hours each day in the school room. They were only expected to learn enough Latin to understand the responses of the Mass, but Isabel studied hard. In the beginning her reading was slow and clumsy. She skipped the many words she didn't know, managing to get a general idea what the text was about. Gradually her reading became fluid and effortless.

Copying texts was the task that most students despised, but Isabel liked it, because the time flew by as she became absorbed in her reading. The girls sat in a large drafty vaulted chamber upon high wooden stools. Lettering was done with a quill, the decorative borders of flowers, fruit, and birds colored with light washes. Several hours of labor each week were required of everyone; there was no other way to preserve the ancient books, and although many were filled with pagan, heretical ideas, it was the duty of the students to preserve them.

One day, while copying a text of Aristotle's, Isabel discovered a quote which delighted her: "Man is a rational and mortal animal capable of laughter." From the context, Isabel understood Aristotle had meant that laughter set man apart from the animals and was thus valued. Aristotle said this, and he was the reigning authority upon which church doctrine was based.

"Aristotle was not always correct," the abbess said when Isabel called attention to the passage. "Particularly in this instance. Never again are you to question your lessons here."

"Yes, Madam," Isabel said, but she felt triumphant at her discovery.

"Good for you," Clare whispered later. "I had a feeling you would liven up this place."

From the west gate of the convent, Isabel could see the baron's castle. Sometimes she wandered to the gate to look at the gates, which beckoned to her like the gates of a distant paradise. She had always regarded the inhabitants of the castle the way churchmen regard angels, as beings of another sphere. But now that she was in so fine a place as this, the castle held a fascinating allure, as if she could approach it and find something for herself.

CHAPTER 6

✢✢✢

On a day in early spring, about a year after Isabel came to the convent, Elizabeth nudged her as they knelt in the stillness of their pew. Isabel knew from the eager way she leaned forward that she had exciting news.

"One of the kitchen maids was caught worshipping the devil," Elizabeth said. "She will be tried by water after Mass."

Isabel had no idea what that meant, and was afraid to ask. When the service ended, the residents of both the monastery and nunnery assembled on the banks of the large fish pond within the inner monastery walls. The sky was a cold steely gray, the chilly air piercing, the bare trees stretched against the sky like prickly webs.

A grim-faced monk tied the kitchen maid to a pole with swift, sure tugs at the leather cords. She stood as if petrified, her eyes wide and frightened, her skin very white. Her hair, a dark tangled mat, spread over the back of her ragged shirt. As she was lowered into the pond, Isabel's stomach lurched, but the residents watched calmly as the bubbles rose to the surface.

When it took less than four minutes for the bubbles to stop, the abbot raised his arms and said, "We have proof that she was guilty. Let us celebrate the death of a devil-worshipper."

As her lifeless body was lifted from the water, a cheer went up among the usually staid and quiet students and novices. It was joyous cheer, one that Isabel never expected to hear within the convent walls. The nuns and monks bowed their heads, permitting the shouts and spontaneous outpouring of emotion.

"Death to the devil-worshipper!"

"Her soul has been cleansed!"

The girl's body was lowered back into the water and held there as the students and novices continued cheering. Horrified, Isabel remained silent. When the girl's body was pulled out again later, white and water-bloated, a bitter-sick feeling rose in her chest. She kept her head bowed, afraid her face would betray her disgust.

Back in the cloister walk, Clare whispered: "It sickens me."

Isabel nodded, grateful that she was not alone in her horror.

For the days and nights that followed the drowning of the kitchen-maid, Isabel was haunted by the memory of the girl's bloated, water-soaked face. After that, the debating of the scholars seemed silly and trite, the gray walls even more stifling. She came to hate the convent as she had hated life in Brotton. She liked to imagine there was a distance, a cushion of space, between herself and everything around her.

The monotonous routine of the convent was occasionally broken by visitors. Although not a great abbey on a main road, the convent received its share of overnight travelers. Most guests stayed the night in the guest house, just outside the gates, where any traveler, whatever his rank, was entitled to a one-night stay. More distinguished visitors were given luxurious apartments inside the monastery gates.

One morning soon after the drowning of the kitchen maid, a noble entourage arrived. The wide gates swung open and servants from the monastery hurried to greet the visitors and take their horses. The abbot himself came to convey them to prayers, a sure sign that a nobleman was among them. As the girls passed along the walk to the refectory, Isabel, like the others, tried to catch a glimpse of the entourage.

That day was Isabel's free afternoon, but the idea of idling in the carefully tended gardens held no appeal. Flowers were supposed to sprinkle themselves over a meadow in lush patches, not grow in perfectly neat columns. Clare had told her that the thickets leading to the river were a wonderful place to be alone for those precious few hours of freedom.

During the past few weeks, the buds had opened and the woods had come to life. Spring usually came gradually, starting with a light watery green like the first wash of a painting spread over the bare woods. But this year the bright, vibrant colors seemed to have appeared instantly.

The sunlight filtered through the new green, throwing into gleaming brightness the moss-covered stones that lined the riverbed. The ground was spread with the fragrant cowslip, the marsh marigold. Isabel picked her way along a path overgrown with hazel and fragrant holly, deep in mud from the recent rains. Ducks and geese rustled among the thin reeds on the other side of the dense clumps of oaks and silver-white birches that separated her from the bogs.

In a grassy spot on the river bank she unlaced her slippers and splashed her feet in the rushing water. The scent of spring made her think about Brotton. She could imagine everything that was happening there. The animals born during the winter would be let outside for the first time. The lambs would be skipping across the new grass. Already the orchards would be pink and white, their fragrance sweetening the air.

As always, there would be a group of villagers standing outside the forge door gossiping, the favorite spring and summer place to gather. She imagined nobody there thought of her at all, except on occasion to marvel at the irony of her fortune. Who would have expected her to end up in a nunnery?

Laughter rang out behind her. Startled, she grabbed her slippers and ducked behind a hedge. There was a rustling in the thicket, and the sound of approaching footsteps mingled with a gay laugh. A girl, holding onto a man's arm moved into the shadow of a clump of thick shrubbery about fifty paces away. For a moment Isabel thought they were both from the entourage that had arrived that morning, but the girl appeared to be wearing the plain white linen of a nun's habit. Intrigued, Isabel crept closer. The man wore a scarlet mantle signifying nobility, black hose, and black shoes with long curling tips.

"Do you know what will happen if I'm caught here?" the girl said.

The girl was Clare. Isabel, stunned, shook her head, as if the vision would disappear.

"How could I leave England without seeing you again?" said the man.

"You'll be happy to be far away," Clare said.

"Clare, you know it wasn't my fault."

"I know nothing of the kind."

"Let's not argue," he said with a sigh in his voice. "We don't have much time, and we must figure out what to do."

They were quiet now, Clare's cheek pressed against his shoulder. Stepping as softly as she could, Isabel backed away. When she was far enough, she turned and ran toward the convent gates. At the guest-house she paused to compose herself, hurriedly lacing her slippers, brushing the twigs and leaves from her skirt and hair.

"Have you seen Tristin?" came the voice of a young man from the other side of the gatehouse.

"Not for an hour or so," was the reply. "Don't worry about him, he'll be back."

Because the speakers made no attempt to speak in hushed voices, Isabel knew they weren't residents of the convent or monastery. They must be from the noble entourage. They were standing just outside the main gates, so she would have to pass them to enter the convent. She decided instead to wait until they left. She stepped back to keep out of their sight, pressing against the gatehouse wall, hoping they would leave.

Soon came the sound of their approaching footsteps. She shrank inwardly as two men turned the corner and stopped at the sight of her.

Something about the taller man was familiar. His hair shimmered in the sunlight, almost white against his sun-bronzed skin. His tanned face had the swarthy look of a Norse pirate. He wore a white ruffled shirt. Despite his easy smile, there was a tension about him which gave him the appearance of a man to be reckoned with.

Then she knew who he was: The baron's brother, Edmund Decourcey.

He looked at her disheveled linen shift, first admiringly, then with puzzled interest. She knew he was trying to remember where he had seen her before.

Please, she prayed silently, *let him not remember.*

His smile broadened, and she knew he remembered. "What are *you* doing here?"

"You know who I am?"

"Of course. You were the girl in trouble for the interesting game you invented under the waterfall."

Remembering that day in the church, she felt a hot rush of embarrassment.

"Now, now," he said, "there's no need for such a blush. You weren't this shy at the time."

She knew she should turn and run, but as if she were a woodland animal in a trap, she was powerless to move. He stood with his feet slightly apart, his arms loosely at his side, the sharp, clear lines of his face catching the sun. She guessed he was in his mid twenties. In comparison, Jake seem like a harmless little boy.

A tremble worked its way through her limbs, weakening her legs. She concentrated on drawing herself to full height, lifting her chin.

"How proud she acts," said Edmund's companion, "like a duchess. Take her down a notch, Edmund."

Without looking away from her, Edmund said, "Back away, Robin."

Robin didn't move.

"Back away," Edmund said again. This time Robin moved back, out of earshot.

"I've wanted to talk to you again," he said, as if their meeting were the most fortunate of coincidences. "Come, walk with me."

The utter assurance of his manner stunned her as much as his suggestion. She stood still, genuinely not knowing what to do. He moved closer until he was close enough for her to smell the leather of his cape.

"Come," he said again, coaxing, taking her arm to lead her away from the convent gates.

She looked toward the convent. Nobody was there, but any moment someone could appear, and she would be in serious trouble. The last thing she needed was the scandal should she be caught talking with him. The scandals with Meg and Jake had been nothing in comparison.

"No, let me go." Like a colt caught in a trave, she sprung away, scooping up her skirts and hurrying through the gates.

She didn't stop running until she reached the dormitory, which, thank goodness, was empty. The other girls must still be in the schoolroom. She composed herself, changed into a clean shift, and went to join the girls.

All afternoon, she watched for Clare. At last in the refectory, shortly after the girls began eating, Clare entered. There was nothing about her to suggest that she had been in the river thickets with a man. Her face was set with its usual demure expression. Her hair was neatly tucked into her wimple, her gown neatly pressed. As always she moved with majesty, her chin high, her shoulders straight. Isabel marveled at the steeliness of her nerves. How long had she been meeting a man in the river thickets right under everyone's noses?

Late the following afternoon, Clare came into the copying room to supervise the girls. Isabel, leaning over her text, was aware that Clare had entered. Summoning her patience, she tried to concentrate on her work, but she found herself stealing sidelong glances at Clare, trying to learn her secrets from her face.

When the bells announced the end of work time, Isabel followed the other girls out. Clare walked behind. Isabel slowed until the girls were far ahead.

"You have something to tell me," Clare said, "I can see that you do."

Isabel felt embarrassed, as if she were prying. "I'm sorry," she said quietly.

"Why?"

"I saw you by the river."

Clare stopped walking and stared at her, disbelieving. She stopped and leaned on a pillar for support.

"Did anybody else see us?"

"No."

"You're sure?"

"Who else would walk through the river thickets? Elizabeth would be afraid she'd get her hem dusty."

"I just hope nobody else saw us. Anyway, I was going to tell you about him because I will burst if I don't tell someone."

"Who is he?"

"Tristin," she said, sighing again. "We wanted to marry, but our families were against it. I was promised to someone else, remember? Tristin and I planned to run away." She laughed bitterly. "But things didn't turn out as we planned. So here I am."

"What will you do?"

"He wants me to run away with him. He says we can be married in France and that nobody there will know I've taken vows."

"Will you do it?"

"It's a rash idea," she said, "and foolish enough for Tristin to have thought of. But it wouldn't work. Eventually we'd be discovered."

Isabel, who was accustomed to causing scandals, had never done anything approaching the magnitude of what Clare was considering. But it was fun to imagine how the residents would respond to the news that Clare had run off with a man, broken her vows, and gotten married.

"Maybe you won't get caught," said Isabel.

"Maybe. What would you do if you were me?"

Isabel smiled. "I'd want to run away with him, but I'd probably be too frightened."

"You know," Clare said, considering this. "I don't believe you'd be frightened. I'd believe you'd do it without fear. I wonder if I have enough courage. Anyway, I won't see him again for a while. He's staying at the Decourcey castle. He and a band of their knights are on their way to the king's court soon. When they return, they'll pass the night here again. I'll see him then."

They were almost back to the dormitory, so Clare stopped again. "When they come, I'll be invited to join them for dinner in the convent's banquet hall," she said. "I may need your help."

"Help with what?"

"I want to sneak out to be with him. At night."

Isabel let a moment pass before she allowed herself to ask: "Will Edmund Decourcey be with them?"

"Edmund has already taken minor orders. He'll soon be a full priest. Knightly adventures are not supposed to be for him. Not that that stops him, of course, so, yes, he'll among them."

A priest? It was impossible to imagine Edmund in somber priestly robes. "From what I know of him," Isabel said, "he doesn't seem like the cloistered type."

"He isn't. But then, who ever expected me to end up in a nunnery?"

"But a priest," Isabel mused aloud.

"He was supposed to finish two years at the monastery, but he left early. It upset his family, but they get tired of fighting him. He's been riding with Tristin ever since, and he's acquired quite a reputation with the court ladies. From what Tristin says, they don't leave him alone. You've seen him, so you can understand why."

Isabel had no trouble believing girls swarmed around him.

"Does he want to be a priest?"

"I guess so, but it's different for men. He won't be trapped behind walls like these."

CHAPTER 7

In late summer, a rumor spread among the girls that a witch had been discovered in the village of Brotton. Isabel knew that the witch was probably Alis. It could possibly be the cobbler's idiot son who flew into sudden seizures. Many times the parson had said he was possessed by demons. Or it could be Meg's elderly grandmother who had begun to mutter incoherently to herself. But Isabel knew better; there was no use trying to pretend otherwise. Alis would be tried for witchcraft.

When several members of the convent decided to attend the trial, it was assumed that Isabel would go, too. Brotton, after all, was her home.

"Do you want me to go with you?" Clare whispered.

Isabel nodded gratefully.

Sisters Agathe and Brigette, Clare, Isabel, and two other students stood together among the villagers who crowded in the open grass courtyard waiting for the trial to begin. Behind them rose the whitewashed bell tower of the church. The sky was a misty gray, the air damp and hot. The stake, surrounded by a mound of timber, had been erected near the platform. The executioner, a stranger who Isabel didn't recognize, stood ready, his black hood covering part of his face.

Isabel was so distracted by the stake and executioner that several minutes passed before she realized Meg stood nearby. For a long moment she and Meg looked at each other. With Isabel standing among nuns, looking almost like a nun herself in her crisp linen and soft bleached slippers, she wondered if Meg regretted having spurned her friendship. But Isabel had little energy for such thoughts. She looked back toward the side church door which led to the ironclad windowless room which was used as a jail when one was needed.

"I've known she was a witch for years," said a plowman, folding his arms across his chest, his long hemp smock still hitched up for work, his bare knees crisscrossed with fresh scratches.

"Wasn't hard to know that," said another, "with her strange ways, going off into the forest, chanting to the devil."

"I knew it from her eyes. Ugly."

Isabel's felt a surge of hope at this last remark. There was nothing ugly about Alis's brilliant blue eyes. Perhaps the witch was someone else after all.

"She'll be burned for sure," said another plowman.

"They say she sleeps with the devil, and flies through the night to his wild sabbaths." At the mention of a witch's sabbath, Sisters Agathe and Brigette crossed themselves.

The door opened and the parson, his rough woolen robes swishing, came out followed by the baron's bailiff, who would preside over the trial. Next came the jailer, leading Alis by chains attached to her wrists. The chatter of the crowd ceased at once.

"Do you know her?" Clare whispered.

A faintness came over Isabel. She managed to nod.

"They say she's lived in this village for years," said Sister Agathe, "but she's foreign born, and has no kin. No relatives at all, or none who dare claim her now."

Alis climbed the platform, the boards creaking and groaning under her weight. Her shift was torn and frayed, her hair tied behind her neck. Her expression was guarded and unreadable, but calm. She stepped carefully, holding herself erect with quiet dignity.

"She has the courage," Clare marveled, "to climb the scaffold like a queen mounting a throne."

Isabel nodded, but she saw what Clare missed: the slight trembling of Alis's hands and the unnatural whiteness of her skin making her face nearly as white as her hair.

"She expects the devil to rescue her," said someone behind Isabel.

"Or she would beg for mercy," said someone else.

Alis turned in her chains to look over the crowd. For the space of a heartbeat, her eyes and Isabel's met — not long enough to draw attention, but long enough for Alis's expression to soften. A dizziness swept over Isabel. The shouts of the villagers pounded in her ears and became the pounding of her heart.

The parson raised his staff to begin the trial. The crowd leaned forward, listening.

"We will put on trial today," he began gravely, "a woman well known for her sorceries and witcheries. For the heinous crime of heresy, and the unspeakable deeds her witchcraft led her to commit, we bring her to justice."

Someone in the crowd shouted, "Burn her before she brings the devil to us all!"

The parson turned to her. "How do you answer these charges?"

"I deny the charge of heresy," Alis said loudly and clearly. "I give the church its due respect."

The villagers hissed and stamped their feet until the parson again raised his staff for silence. "Let those who have witnessed the powers of her sorcery come forward and stand before us."

There was a movement in the crowd. A man leaning on a wooden crutch walked to the platform. He lived in a cottage near the center of the village. When he had fallen ill with the plague, his daughters had sought Alis's help.

"She practiced her magic on me," he shouted. "She pierced me with an instrument of the devil! My stomach popped open, there was a hole big enough to put a finger in, blood and vile yellow liquid poured out!" he paused for breath. "She called on her magic, made signs to the demons and chanted to the devil!"

Alis rattled her chains impatiently. "I made no signs to the demons, and I chanted nothing," she said wearily, as if addressing unusually stupid children. "He was swollen with the plague. I broke the carbuncle; that's why he lived. The barber had been pressing it, pushing the poison into him. It would have killed him."

But the villagers again hissed and shouted. The tempo increased until the air seemed charged with the energy of a lightening bolt.

"You travel by night to the devil's sabbath!" someone shouted.

"You lay with the devil!"

"You kiss him under the tail!"

The parson again raised his staff for silence. Alis waited until the shouting died down, and said, "I do no such thing."

In response came more hissing. The parson raised his voice to be heard, "A confessed witch in York explained the devil's ways. She spoke of a smelly green ointment that brings the devil. The potion is put on the forehead with a feather, and a fiery man appears who seduces the woman to all manners of perversions. What do you know about it?"

"I know that potion brings visions, not the devil."

"You've used the potion!" someone shouted. "You've slept with the devil!"

She shook her head as if the charge were too ridiculous to respond to.

The parson leapt forward, nearly shouting in her face, "You went into the forests, two witnesses heard you chanting to demons. That night was a hailstorm! A storm you brought to us with your evil magic!"

"Burn her now!" The crowd stamped and clapped. "Burn the witch!"

The parson, his face reddened from shouting, ordered the messengers to get the baron's signature on the death warrant. They waited until the bailiff nodded in agreement, then they spurred their horses and galloped away.

"The old baron would never have signed it," said someone behind Isabel. "Remember how queer he was? Maybe his son has better sense."

Isabel closed her eyes to shut out the stake that loomed over the crowd. She could almost see the flames and hear Alis's screams. Her heart jumped so wildly she thought she would faint. She could scarcely breathe past the strangling pain in her throat.

Sister Agathe saw Isabel's fright and said, "Quickly, say a prayer for Isabel. She's under the witch's spell!"

The students whispered the prayer to use against witches: "Sly sorcerer who attacks the soul, your spell shall be returned to you a thousand fold! In the name of God the Father, God the Son, and God the Holy Ghost, amen!"

Isabel leaned against Clare for support.

"Isabel will be all right," Clare said firmly, taking Isabel's hand in hers.

"Her cottage," came the deafening shout from the crowd. "Burn her cottage!"

The villagers stampeded down the street to Alis's cottage, trampling the neat rows of Alis's herbal gardens.

The flames started slowly, cracking at the timber frame, reaching toward the thatched roof. Soon the honeysuckle that framed the doorway was blackened with soot. The upper part of the house was enclosed in flames. The heat of the fire sent blood rushing to Isabel's head. Aching sobs rose in her chest as her terror grew. The villagers would see that she wept, and they would accuse her of sympathizing with a witch. They would believe she was in the grip of a demonic possession. Someone would stand up and denounce Alis as Isabel's kin. Then Isabel, too, would be thrown into the purifying flames. Isabel swayed dizzily. Then everything went black.

When Isabel opened her eyes, she was in the grip of a man's arms, the coarse hemp of his shirt scratching her face, the smell of his sweat stinging her eyes. For a terrible moment, thinking she was being lifted to the flames, she kicked and tried to shake herself free, a scream catching in her throat.

"We're taking you back," Clare whispered.

They were on the hill that led to the convent, the chants of the villagers far behind them. Isabel closed her eyes and tensed her limbs to make them stop trembling.

The great iron gate swung open. Once inside the cloister walk, Isabel opened her eyes to see the abbess approaching them. The man set her down and she reached out to the wall to steady herself.

The abbess turned to Clare. "What happened to her?" she asked, as if Isabel were another of the stone pillars that lined the cloister walk.

"She fainted."

The abbess turned to study Isabel, frowning. "Return to the dormitory," was all she said.

Isabel lay in bed staring into the darkness. Beside her, Elizabeth breathed steadily, deeply. The sandglass on the mantle told her that it was nearly time for the Matins bells.

The dim candle that burned all night beside the bed cast a warm glow over the bare stone walls. The tiny flame was meant to frighten away demons, and it was considered a bad omen if it went out. In the semidarkness, the crevices in the stone walls were too dark and deep, the shadows too long. Isabel knew every crevice in the walls. She knew which floorboards creaked, and which writing desks slanted enough that her quill would roll if she set it down.

The villagers had probably burned Alis by now. The thought made her feel as if ice were being poured down her back. The rhythm of Elizabeth's steady breathing didn't break as Isabel slid from the bed. She had to pass several beds, carefully stepping over the loud floorboards, to reach the window seat into which she collapsed, leaning her cheek against the cold iron of the window's casement, her mind strangely blank.

The bells clanged. Bed linens rustled and feet tapped across the rush-covered floor as the girls readied themselves for prayers. As was usual for that time of night, nobody said a word as they flocked into the garth. A light chill had come into the night air. In the rectangular grass court of the open garth, several nuns stood together, whispering, openly breaking the rule of silence.

Clare was among them. When she saw Isabel, she smiled. Encouraged, Isabel approached her.

"Do you feel better?" Clare whispered.

Isabel nodded. *What happened to Alis*, she wanted to ask, but she knew better than to ask with the other nuns watching and listening. Instead, she said, "I couldn't bear to watch the burning."

"She has been allowed to live," said one of them.

"Why?" Isabel asked in as off-hand a manner as she could manage.

"The baron's brother, Edmund, refused to allow the warrant to be signed," said one of the nuns. "He pardoned her."

"What possessed him to do that?" another of the nuns standing nearby asked. "Did he forget the Biblical commandment: Thou shalt not suffer a witch to live? If she is not destroyed, every villager may be condemned to centuries in purgatory."

"He said that her knowledge, however cursed, is too valuable to be lost."

"He is completely mad! What good can come from her knowledge?"

Afraid her voice would betray her great relief if she spoke, Isabel remained silent. All she could think was that Alis had not been burned. She pulled her cloak up around her face, as if to protect herself from the chilly air. The last thing she wanted was for anyone to guess how grateful and joyful she felt.

After Alis's trial, Isabel felt even more stifled in the convent. The days she could escape to the river thickets were too few. The ironclad dormitory window blocked so much of the light that even in the midst of summer she felt shrouded in oppressive shadow. The rule of silence had always irritated her, but now there were times she wanted to scream just to hear the sound of a human voice.

For what seemed like endless hours she sat on a low stool in the calefactory, gripping the drop spindle, trying to concentrate on her work. She preferred spinning to embroidering; spinning was a task to which she was more accustomed. Today her yarn was unusually thick and uneven, and she knew she would be reprimanded for it.

When she couldn't listen to the swishing of the wobbly wheel another moment, she threw the spindle aside. It clattered across the table and with a muffled tap, landed in the floor rushes. She dropped her forehead into her clenched fists, waiting for the rebuke that was sure to come.

Clare came to her rescue. "She needs fresh air. Come, Isabel," she said, leading her to the door.

"Her restlessness is her curse," one of the nuns muttered as they brushed past her.

Once at the far end of the cloister walk, Clare whispered, "Who is on your mind? The kitchen maid or the village witch?"

"The witch."

"I thought so."

"Have you heard anything else about her?" Isabel asked.

"She's been banished from the village. She built herself a hut in a part of the forest that the villagers believe is haunted. They're very upset about her living there. She chose a spot in a clearing near an ancient fairy ring, which they say is haunted by the worst of the demons."

"I see," said Isabel.

"You must have known her," Clare said.

For a moment she considered telling Clare who Alis was, but decided against it. Not even Clare could be trusted with so dangerous a secret.

"Nobody in the village really knew her," said Isabel. "She kept to herself."

"Yes," said Clare, "that's what everyone says."

That night, when all the girls in the dormitory were fast asleep, Isabel looked up at the window. The sky was black. Matins was over, and there were still a few hours until dawn. Beneath her pillow was a large metal key.

I am ready to eat meat, she thought.

She had to go under the protection of night. If anyone saw her emerging from the black forest, she would be in serious trouble. That alone could be enough to invite the accusation that she, too, was a witch. She remembered the kitchen maid and had a moment of such fear she thought she couldn't go. But she had to visit Alis. She should have gone long ago. Once she made up her mind, it had just been a matter of stealing one of the keys from the gatekeeper.

She drew a shawl over her shift, braided her hair, and crept from the dormitory into the open garth, tense like a cat about to leap or run. She locked the gate behind her.

She ran toward the village, pausing occasionally to catch her breath, until she saw, in the distance, the dimly outlined steeple, faintly silver in the moonlight, showing the village on the horizon. She stopped near the orchards at the far end of the valley and crept toward the whortleberry thickets. A dense cluster of oaks lay before her, and beyond that, a heavy blackness. She groped until she found the place where the brush parted and the path led into the woods.

In the shadows the trees took on unfamiliar and menacing shapes. Overhead bats flapped their wings high among the branches. Under her feet twigs cracked and she hit her foot on the sprawling root of an oak, nearly losing her balance. From the distance came the faint howling of wolves.

She stepped carefully, as if testing the ground. If she thought about what she was doing, she would lose her courage. Then, through the trees came the faint glow of firelight. She came to the clearing, and less than ten paces away was the hovel.

Alis stood in the open doorway, lit from behind by the glow of slumbering embers.

"I've been waiting for you," she said.

The ceiling of the hovel was low, and the mud walls slanted. On the earthen floor was a thin straw sleeping pallet covered by an undyed woolen blanket. Near the clay hearth were several pot-bellied jugs and baskets filled with nuts, berries, and roots. Cupboards were dug into the thick walls. A few utensils hung on the wall, and an iron cooking pot was suspended over the fire.

Alis sat on the floor and leaned back against the wall, hugging her knees in a curiously childlike gesture, tossing strands of white hair back from her weathered face.

"I was frightened for you," Isabel said. "I thought they would kill you, like the kitchen maid."

"You needn't have feared for me," she said, "and you needn't have feared for yourself. That wasn't the first time I was arrested in Brotton, you know. The last time was before you were born."

"Who saved you then? Not the baron's son?"

"No, he was just a young boy. His father had me released."

Alis must have seen the questions in Isabel's eyes because she smiled. "How that happened is a long, long story."

The firelight cast odd shadows over the walls. In the warm light, Alis's face was beautiful. Isabel suddenly knew everything said about Alis was true: she was a pagan with the ancient Sight.

"You're not a Christian," Isabel said, not knowing why she felt it with such certainty. "You said you are, but you're not."

"Does that matter?"

"No." How easily she uttered words for which she could be called a heretic. "But if you're not a Christian, why did you want the monks to choose me?"

"It was the best thing for you. You've learned to read, and you've seen what I could never describe. Your education will raise you up. I knew when you were ready, you would come to me."

"Why did you move into this glade, when you knew it would anger the villagers?"

"Because they will fear me enough to leave me alone. They won't bother me here."

Two lutes were propped against the wall. One was old and wooden, chipped with a broken string. The other was silver, shiny and new, like a jewel against the clay wall.

"Where did you get those?"

"My sister gave me the old one when we were in York."

"What about the silver one?"

"The answer will surprise you."

"Please tell me."

"It was a gift. From the Baron Decourcey."

Isabel felt confused. "Edmund's brother?"

"No," Alis said softly. "Edmund's father."

Isabel blinked, startled. Instead of asking the obvious question and inquiring how on earth Edmund's father came to give her a lute, she asked, "Can you play them?"

"Not any more," Alis said, spreading her thin and bony hands for Isabel to see. "My fingers have grown stiff and clumsy."

"Are you from York, like everyone says?"

"No, I was born on an island far to the north, many weeks journey from here. I was a young girl when my tribe was attacked by an army of crusaders. My sister and I escaped and hid in York. She died there many years ago."

"She was my grandmother?"

"Yes."

"What was she like?"

Alis smiled, her face was luminous. "She was beautiful and wise. She was a high priestess and would have been our tribe's greatest teacher and leader. My magic is very small compared to hers."

"Did my mother know who her mother was? Did she know she was related to you?"

"Yes, but Nan was timid and frightened. She kept the secret, and never wanted you to know. She would have been angry to know I gave you the amulet. When you wouldn't part with it, I knew it was an omen of your destiny."

The sounds of the forest whispered at the door of the hovel: the song of the crickets, the wind in the leaves, the distant howl of animals. Clare, the convent, and the village of Brotton seemed worlds away.

"Will you tell me about my grandmother?"

"Her name was Maya. She was lovely, and good, and—" Alis sighed. "How can I describe her? Nan was nothing like her."

Isabel didn't want to hear about Nan. She remembered her mother well enough. She wanted to hear about her beautiful and still mysterious grandmother

"I remember when your mother was born," Alis said. "She seemed like the last link to our old life. We named her Dana for the great goddess Danu. In public we called her Nan."

The mention of a pagan goddess frightened Isabel, but intrigued her, too.

"Your mother was born in York," Alis said, "but she grew up here. I watched her grow during the lonely years after Barnabe's death."

"Were you the older sister, or was Maya?"

"Maya was many years older, more like a mother than a sister. Our mother died shortly after I was born, and our father followed when I was eight."

"She took care of you?"

"Not just me, all the islanders. She was the high priestess of Eynhallow. As Nan grew, I kept looking for signs of Maya's spirit in her, but she had none. Nan was timid and frightened, like a mouse. I loved her, cared for her when she was a baby, and brought her to this village, but I was disappointed by what she became. She could never have been a priestess like Maya. She didn't have the life and spirit to know the goddess."

Alis smiled. "And then there came a child, a beautiful spirited girl, with hair and eyes like Maya but colored darker and richer, who faced the world unafraid, as Maya had done." Alis's smile deepened, showing a hint of dimples in her cheeks. "And who do you suppose that child is?"

Isabel smiled back.

"I will tell you Maya's story," said Alis, "which is also mine and becomes yours."

PART II

⚜⚜⚜

CHAPTER 1

Alis was born on Eynhallow, the Holy Isle of the Orkneys, northeast of mainland Scotland. At times in this far northern region, the sun seemed not to set at all. Summer twilights lingered on as the feeble blood-red sun, spreading a tangerine glow over the south western sky, crept to the horizon and appeared to rest there. In winter the darkness was complete and lasting but for the northern light of the goddess giving hope that the sun had not disappeared forever. On rare summer days when the sun shone brightly and the last wisps of fog cleared, the lush grassy mantle that covered the isle brightened to a brilliant emerald green.

There was nothing unusual about the foggy morning of what turned out to be Alis's last day on the isle. She had awakened long before the first light of dawn, and pushed aside the mat that covered the south-facing window of the hut she shared with Maya. She scanned the sky, searching for her star. When she saw that it was near the horizon, she sprang to her feet and pulled her woolen cloak about her shoulders, clasping it with a large pin of intricately wrought metal.

At fifteen, Alis was delicate and beautiful, like a woodland nymph. Her hair, softly spun and very pale, so blonde it was almost white, cascaded in soft waves over her shoulder. Her voice was musical, her body thin and fragile. Her mouth was delicately formed, and there was an appealing sweetness about her wide-set eyes.

Her fragile beauty was deceptive, for Alis was tenacious. Her decisions were often impulsive, but once she decided to do something, she threw herself into it completely. Such was her love affair with Kao. She refused to see him every morning, but a few days each week he paddled from his home isle of Westray and she met him in the glade before the village awakened. They had chosen a star, their own love-star by which they measured time, and when it reached a certain place in the sky, she crept to the glade where he waited for their stolen hour.

For a long time Alis, imagining that nobody knew of her escapades, worried that Maya would find out. Before she fell in love with Kao, she had never done anything of which Maya might not approve. Slowly she came to realize that Maya was aware of what she was doing, a thing which shouldn't have surprised her, for Maya possessed the ancient Sight. Still Alis hid their meetings from the other islanders.

Stealthily she crept from the hut. Once outside she took to her legs and ran toward the glade. The place where she and Kao met was surrounded by dense brush, scented with hawthorn and heather, near the southern shore where the soil was richest, the grass lushest. Here the sheep grazed and the finest vegetables were harvested.

Her bare feet tapped over the ground, branches snapping as she pushed past them. Now Kao would be paddling across the water. He would tie his canoe beneath the old oak which spread itself over a hidden corner of the northern cove.

Because the shores of Eynhallow were inaccessible to any vessel larger than a canoe, the isle received few visitors. Generations of invading yellow-bearded Northmen believed it uninhabited and thus left it alone. Viewed from the neighboring islands of Rousay or Evie it appeared rocky, desolate, uninviting, and too small to sustain even the tiniest of villages. The other isles in the archipelago were frequently raided by the Northmen, who claimed the isles as their own and collected what they called taxes but the islanders knew was plunder.

In the years of Alis's childhood, the yellow bearded men had come insisting that the tribal gods and goddesses didn't exist. In the beginning, neighboring islanders accepted the new religion out of fear, pretending to believe, but the new religion, which denied the great goddess of life and birth, was easily shrugged off as ridiculous.

Under the guidance of Maya, Eynhallow remained steadfast in the ancient religion. Even those of their neighbors who accepted the new religion continued coming to Maya when they needed remedies. Quite simply, the new religion's spells, which they called prayers, were not an effective cure for most sicknesses. The earth goddess had provided herbal cures for many illnesses, and her high priestesses understood how to use them. Maya had inherited all the ancient wisdom. She could induce seeds, roots, and plants to cure most maladies. Even their Christian neighbors thus protected Maya and her magic. In secret they came to the shores of Eynhallow when they needed her, and lied to the invaders about her powers.

Kao was in the glade waiting for Alis. First she saw Kao's tousle of dark hair, then his blinding smile as he rose to his feet. He held out his arms and she ran to him.

But something was wrong. She could feel it in the tension of his arms that wrapped around her and the urgency of his kiss

"Kao," she said, pulling back slightly. "What's the matter?"

"Nothing," he said, giving her a strange look which may have been anger or surprise. He then dropped his head to kiss her throat, burying his face in her hair.

She knew he was lying.

"Kao, please tell me.".

"How do you know something's wrong?" He said, drawing back, his voice surprisingly arch. "Are you a seer like your sister?"

"You know I'm not."

As if reassured by her denial, he resumed stroking her neck, softly brushing his lips against her. He lowered her to the cool grass, his hands already finding their way beneath her mantle. But oddly, his caresses left her unmoved. His sharp tone still sounded in her mind. She knew something was wrong.

She had known Kao all her life. When she was a child, he had teased her, telling her he would marry her when she grew up except that she was so headstrong.

"You'd drive a man mad," he had told her, tugging on her braid.

She'd felt annoyed by the way the girls had fussed over him. They pushed to be near him, simpering, touching him coyly. She especially hated the way Luda, a pretty Rousay girl, breathed his name: "Oh Kao."

"They make fools of themselves," Alis had snapped once, turning away from the sight.

"It's because he is beautiful," an older woman of the tribe had said, smiling knowingly at Alis.

Alis had tossed her head as if to deny it.

"Why does it bother you that they want him?" the woman had said. "Think about that."

But Alis didn't want to think about it. She often caught him staring at her, but then he would make a teasing remark and she would shrug the whole incident off. Then one day she came upon him in her favorite bathing spot, a hidden cove on the western shore. She had stood riveted on a rock that jutted over the brook, studying his lean body, golden in the shimmering sun, and his hair, water-darkened to jet black. The woman had been right, of course; he was indeed beautiful.

As if he had felt her presence, he turned to stare straight into her eyes, his direct gaze unsettling. Words were said but later she couldn't remember them. At the time they had seemed incredibly clever and she had thought him brilliant as well as beautiful. Somehow she had found herself in the water with him, his slippery body against hers. For those hours, all thought was suspended. Afterward they lay on the grass in a patch of sunlight to dry, her head cradled in the crook of his arm. He continued to kiss her, touching her hair. The afternoon turned to dusk, twilight becoming blackness before she realized that she would be missed.

"You're the prettiest girl on these islands," he said. "I love you, Alis." His words had seemed as natural as everything else, as if the correct response would be: But of course.

"How did this happen?" she had murmured, dazed and happy.

"It didn't just happen, silly girl. Do you think I just happened to be in your bathing stream?"

Next afternoon, the elders of the village set their marriage day. She and Kao would wed near the end of autumn. But Alis's body yearned for him hourly, daily, and she had no intention of waiting until her birthday to be with him. It was a game, trying to keep their meetings secret, ignoring the knowing smiles that greeted them when they returned from the woods.

Yet for all their stolen hours together, she didn't know him well enough to guess what was bothering him now. What could make him so tense and grip her so fervently? He acted as if he was afraid of something. She thought she would burst with the anxiety of wondering what it was.

"Tell me what's wrong," she repeated, then softened what sounded like a command with: "Please."

He sighed and pulled her into his lap to cradle her. "Alis, marry me today."

"We can't get married yet, you know that. Why should we, anyway?"

"There is going to be trouble soon. The invaders know about your sister. They say she is evil and her magic is blasphemous."

"Evil? She heals. She makes people well and helps them live. Everything she does is for the goddess. How can that be blasphemy?"

"They say the goddess doesn't exist."

"That's ridiculous, and you know it. What kind of god is theirs if he denies the goddess of life?"

"Please, Alis. Come back to Westray as my wife. The elders will understand that we married to save your life."

"I should desert my sister?"

"What can you do for her? She'll never give up the old ways."

Alis shrank away from him as the significance of his words crept up on her.

"Alis, listen—"

"No." She tried to shake her wrist free, but he held fast. "They're wrong," she said, "and you are, too."

"Am I wrong to love you and want to save you? I want you with me, that's all."

She knew from the look in his eyes and the way he stepped forward that he believed he could convince her to remain with him. But he misunderstood her reaction. She was weak with fright for Maya.

"Just let me think about it," she said.

"There may not be time. Come with me now."

His urgency made her know that she had to warn Maya right away.

"All right," she lied, "but there are things I need."

"There isn't time."

She held back stubbornly. "If I leave with you today, there are things I need to do."

"But how do I know you are coming back?"

"Because of how much I love you. Of course I'm coming back."

He tried to pull her close again. "I couldn't live without you," he whispered into her hair.

"I must go back now," she said.

"Stay a few minutes." His lips sought hers, his arms wrapping around her, pulling her close. She cringed from his touch, amazed by her own response. He suddenly seemed small and pitiful, but she had to hide her feelings. She had to get away and make him believe she was coming back.

"I couldn't live without you, Kao," she whispered. "I'll be back soon."

She tore herself away and ran back to the village. Once in the hut, she paused. How could she tell Maya what Kao had said?

"Wake up, Maya," she whispered, kneeling beside her. "Wake up."

Maya opened her eyes. "What's the matter?"

"I just spoke to Kao. There's danger."

Maya sighed, the sleep clearing from her face. "What kind?"

"The invaders know about you," her words jumbled together, "they say you are evil and blasphemous."

"Yes," Maya said, stretching.

"Yes what?"

"I've known for some time. They don't think I should be allowed to live."

Maya leaned back, dropping her arms onto the pallet. The calm in Maya's face set Alis back on her heels to stare in disbelief. Maya had a way of taking everything in stride. She was utterly self-assured and composed at all times, but that she could speak of her own death so calmly was chilling.

Maya was the oldest child, Alis the youngest, with two brothers and another sister ranging between, all three of whom had married and gone to live on other islands. Alis was said to be the most beautiful of the sisters, a thing that always amazed her, for she thought Maya lovely beyond compare. Maya's hair was a rich auburn, her eyes deep green flecked with black and gold, the luminous and expressive eyes of a seer. In the dusky twilight, the color of her hair deepened to a rich brown tinged with a glowing warmth. In the clear sunlight or early morning gray it seemed brighter, more vibrant. Maya was past thirty, no longer young, and despite the oils she used, her skin showed the slackness of her age, but her hair seemed not to have dulled at all. Next to Maya's dramatic coloring, Alis's believed herself pale and white.

Maya had been ordained as a priestess after a series of dreams she had when she was ten years old in which she was visited by the great goddess herself. The goddess gave Maya the gift of Sight, and their mother, who had also been a priestess, taught her the secrets of the herbs and forests. Alis often wondered what it would be like to understand the goddess's secrets. She wished she had been the one visited by the goddess.

"The invaders must be near Westray now," Maya said quietly. "That's why Kao knows what's happening. If he was that concerned for your safety, the raid will come any time."

"You will hide," Alis said. The week before, the elders had decided that Maya must hide in the caves on the north side of the island if the invaders came.

Maya looked away. A moment passed before she said, "That was what we said because if they come, as few people as possible must know the truth. The invaders have ways of making people talk."

"They have powerful weapons," Alis agreed. Who could stand against their steel lances and protective armor?

"Their words are their most powerful weapons. They frighten people by talking about hell-fire and divine punishment. Even the strongest soldiers can bend beneath such persuasion."

"What will you do?"

"I couldn't remain hidden here for long. The caves could hide me for a few days, maybe a week or longer, but they would find me. So I have a canoe hidden near the western bluffs. The elders have decided that if they come for me, I must escape. If I am gone, they will not harm anyone else."

"You're going to leave? Just like that?"

A gentle smile played at the corner of Maya's mouth. "Of course not. I was planning to speak to you."

"But you would have left?"

Maya smiled again. "Do you think I didn't want to bring you? When you see the canoe and supplies I have hidden you will see that you are included in my plans."

This was as perplexing as everything else. "How did you know I would leave Kao?"

"What happened this morning?"

Alis stared at the earthen floor, picking at the cracks, as she told Maya all that Kao had said. Maya listened quietly and then said, "Are you prepared to leave him now?"

Alis's chest tightened and for a moment she thought she would cry, but she whispered, "Yes." It was bewildering how quickly things had changed.

"And I knew you would be. He is beautiful, and you are young. It is easy to see why you wanted him. But he has no strength of character. He has no sense of himself or his own ideas, and will bend like a reed to any passing whim. In time you would have grown bored with him."

"Then why were you going to allow me to marry him? Why didn't you warn me?"

"I suspected you would discover for yourself what kind of man he is."

This quieted Alis. That she had stumbled upon a truth of Kao's character which Maya had already seen and understood gave her pause. Had she loved him for months without knowing him?

"What kind of man is he?" asked Alis, more to herself than Maya.

"He is not a bad person, but an extremely weak one."

Alis rocked back onto her heels and stared into Maya's face. Funny that she was only beginning to know Maya. Always she had adored her, but because of the great difference in their ages, and because Maya had the status of a tribal princess, she had always seemed distant and unreadable.

She and Maya had built their hut together shortly after their father died. With both their parents gone, they couldn't bear to remain in the larger family hut. Alis had helped gather the straw that Maya wove into thatch for the roof. Maya had done the heavy work, mixing the limestone with earth while Alis had helped smooth down the floor with a flat board.

"Where will we go?" Alis asked.

"South."

Alis knew what that meant. To the south, less than a three day journey by canoe, lay vast stretches of foreign lands. A few months earlier, Maya had announced her intention to see the foreign lands for herself to learn more about the ways of the foreigners. At first when Maya announced her intention to travel south, many tribesmen, including most of the elders, believed that she shouldn't go and tried to dissuade her. Perhaps it was unsafe in their lands.

"I must go," Maya had said, "and learn their ways. In knowledge there is strength, and we must become strong."

She had a way of speaking which was utterly compelling, enabling her to convince even the most skeptical tribes members. At last it was agreed that she should go. She left one morning in a canoe accompanied by a white-haired elderly man for an escort. The weeks of their absence dragged on until Alis was convinced that they were dead. Finally, after two months, they returned.

Everyone had gathered around to hear the fantastic stories. Maya and her escort had first visited a secluded Highland village that clung to the old religion, but understood the Christian ways. Perceiving that Maya was a holy priestess on an important mission, they gave her clothes so she could pass unnoticed among the people of the south, and provided them with two old mares. Maya and her escort then traveled south to see the foreigners for themselves.

"Far to the south are enormous towns where many hundreds of people live," Maya had reported to her silent and gravely attentive audience. "Most of the people are harmless enough, although they believe the life-giving goddess is evil. They call us pagans and say we practice black magic."

Now, remembering, an uneasy feeling rose in Alis's chest. "We are going south," she asked, "to live among the foreigners?"

"It's the only way. There is no place here to hide."

Alis couldn't imagine leaving Eynhallow. The island was her whole world, all she knew. She was familiar with every trail, every boulder and unusually shaped tree, each hillside and glade; she knew how the isle looked in the light of each season: the emerald green fields in summer sloping upward from the rocky shore, the deep purple heather of autumn, the black and white of winter. She knew all the best trees for climbing and the best pools for swimming. Here were the people she had known since infancy. How could she leave and find herself in a strange land among strange people?

"But what about the others?" Alis asked. How could they leave everyone they knew and loved behind? Their mother's youngest sister and only surviving sibling was surely too old for the journey, but what about their own sisters and brothers and cousins?

"We're the only ones in danger," said Maya.

"That's not true," Alis said. "What about Moury?"

A flicker of pain crossed Maya's face. "He hasn't returned from the mainland," she said.

Alis saw her pain, and understood it. Maya and Moury had been lovers for over a year and there was talk of marriage. Alis had never believed that Maya really loved him, but seeing Maya's face now, Alis thought perhaps she did. He enjoyed the special distinction of one of the goddess's few priests, yet he seemed utterly remarkable and plain. He was thin, wiry, and intense, and seemed no match for a woman as bold and courageous as Maya.

There came the distant tapping of drums. The sound grew louder, more urgent, the drums pounding the warning signal.

"They've come," said Maya, already on her feet.

Alis flung back the mat that hung over the tiny window. Villagers streamed from their huts, hurrying to the wide common area at the center of the village.

Maya was dressed; she seemed to have accomplished the task in an instant, was on her way out the door. Alis followed as the drums continued tapping the warning.

Everyone crowded around Maya.

"Who is coming?" someone asked. It was a ridiculous question prompted by anxiety, for everyone knew who was coming.

"What do they want?" someone else asked.

An older woman answered, "They want to collect taxes, you know that."

"Taxes!" spat one man. "They're here to rob us. They'll take our best sheep, the best of our crops."

"They want more than taxes this time," said Maya. "They want to destroy me and my magic."

Alis knew from the stillness that this did not surprise anybody. Maya had spoken their worst fears.

"We must do something," said a young man.

"There is nothing we can do," said Maya. "We cannot possibly fight them."

"So we're supposed to let them destroy you and rob us?" he asked.

"Hide as best you can," Maya said quietly. "If they find you, give them what they demand. If they ask about me, tell them that you last saw me in the caves near the northern bluffs."

"But they'll find you anywhere on the island," protested another.

The urgent warning of the drum came again.

"Don't worry about me," Maya said, "I will be all right." A strange quietness came over the group. They knew they should scatter and hide, but nobody moved.

"How will we manage without you?" someone whispered.

"Say what you must to save your lives, but in secret hold fast to the goddess. Quickly, go."

They did as they were told. Stealthily, silently, they crept into the hills, disappearing among the rocks and thickets.

CHAPTER 2

Alis followed Maya into the darkest part of the forest. They walked until they came to a large boulder that hid a damp mossy scoop of ground. They huddled together, buried beneath the damp leaves and musty pine needles. When they'd been sitting this way for so long Alis's knees became stiff, she shifted herself, stretched her legs, then curled them back beneath her. An eternity seemed to pass before the slant of stray sunbeams showed that it was midmorning.

Alis whispered, "I don't hear anything. Maybe they've gone."

"No, our people would tell us with their drums. We must stay here until nightfall."

It seemed much too long to crouch so uncomfortably. Alis laid her cheek against Maya's shoulder and waited. She knew they wouldn't be discovered as long as they could remain cramped this way. Their hiding place was a good one. Even those familiar with the island would have a hard time finding them. It would take the invaders several days to comb the island thoroughly enough, and after nightfall she and Maya would be gone.

Alis wondered what the southern lands were like. She had heard that the winters were much shorter. On Eynhallow, the winters were tiresomely long and dreary, but there was no comfort in this thought. She would miss the long evenings when she, Maya, and a friend or two huddled together in the hut, warming themselves around the low fire, sharing stories and speculation about who would soon marry, who had fallen in love, and who was becoming restless and would leave the islands in search of adventure.

Alis thought about the things she hated most about home, wondering if she would miss these things, too. She loathed gathering shell fish near the rocky north shore. As a child this had been her most hated task, but oddly, she found it sad to think she would never do it again. She particularly despised the game the boys played near the beach because it was forbidden in the village. Taking the bladder of a freshly killed pig, sticking a straw into it, blowing it up and tying it, they made a ball. After it dried in the sun it was perfect for kicking, but the boys were often too impatient to wait until it dried, so they batted the bloody thing around. Once it hit Alis's arm, soft, wet, and oozy. Did boys in the south play such repulsive games? Would everything be strange and different?

Alis closed her eyes and drifted into a dazed half-sleep. When she opened her eyes again, the shadows had grown long, the air cool. At last the sun set, sending a twilight glow through the forest. Alis tried to ignore the grumbling of her angry, empty stomach.

When she could bear it no longer, she whispered, "Maya, I'm hungry."

"Wait a while longer, then I'll go find something to eat."

Darkness came, and with it a heavy misty fog that covered them like a cool, damp blanket. At last Maya pulled herself to her feet. "Stay here," she ordered.

The silence that engulfed Alis after Maya left was suffocating and terrifying. The sounds around her intensified: the wind in the trees, the annoying buzz of insects. At last Maya returned with a handful of berries.

"There is nobody around," said Maya. "You can come out now."

It felt awkward to stand after having crouched for so long. Each of Alis's bones seemed to crack under the strain of standing and straightening her back. Walking made her feel light-headed and dizzy. As they walked to the shore, she leaned against Maya, whose arm was flung protectively around her.

The canoe, which was hidden in a narrow cave, was beautiful, rubbed with oil and polished to a shine. It was one Alis had never seen before. Maya must have worked on it and kept it hidden for a very long time. Supplies were neatly packed into bulging lambskin bags and secured to the bottom of the canoe.

The recent storms had driven in piles of seaweed, now shrunk to little stems crunching under their feet as they dragged the canoe to the water. Without a word, they pushed from the shore into the cove and silently slid through the darkness. They had gone several hundred yards when Alis felt an overpowering sadness. She turned to look back toward the island, shrouded in darkness.

"Do you think we will return some day?" she asked.

"It's nice to think we might."

Maya obviously thought that they would never go back, so they probably wouldn't, for the ancient Sight never lied.

"But," Alis nonetheless felt compelled to argue, "after the invaders take what they want, they will retreat, and maybe the old religion can be practiced in private."

"Maybe," said Maya.

"And then we can return home."

"Maybe," Maya said.

"But you told everyone to cling to the goddess in secret."

"Some will try, but eventually they will give up. The islands are changing. Soon nothing will be the same and our old ways will be lost. Maybe it's best that we leave before everything changes completely, with our memories intact."

Maya knew which star to steer by. She kept the unmoving star to her back, and watched the one that would lead her to her chosen landing spot. They had just enough supplies for the journey, so Maya carefully rationed the food and water.

Maya, like the stars, radiated strength and confidence, but the vast waters stretching out beneath the star-crested dome overhead made Alis feel very small.

After many days drifting south, they landed on a rocky shore near the mouth of a river. Maya showed Alis the clothes she had brought, saved from her previous trip south: a hemp skirt, woven shirt, leather boots vastly different from the heavy island furs and tanned leather. After they changed into the new clothes, Maya tied her silver amulets to a string that she could wear around her neck, keeping them hidden beneath her shirt.

They walked downriver for days, passing tiny fishing villages and larger farming communities. Alis had never before seen cottages made entirely of wood. By the second day, the leather of Alis's soles were so worn through that she felt the prick of every sharp stone. Her legs became heavy with weariness, with muscles she didn't know she possessed aching.

"Hold on a little longer," Maya said. "We're nearly there."

At last, when they paused on the precipice of a hill, the city of York lay before them in the center of a great plain. The distant roofline was a medley of dirty thatch and red tile punctuated by the bluish smoke of hundreds of chimneys and the rising spires of dozens of churches. Alis drew close to Maya for comfort as they stood looking at the city. Maya took her hand, and Alis sensed a twinge of excitement pass over Maya, as if at a new adventure.

"Wait until you see it," Maya said. "More people live within those walls than you can imagine."

They drew no attention as they passed under the arched gate into the city. The double-leaf iron gate flanked by two watchtowers opened through the thick sand-colored city wall. Inside they walked through the loud stinking confusion of narrow, twisting streets. The heavy donkey and horse traffic made the road as foul as it was congested. Alis felt sick from the heavy smell.

"Look," Maya whispered, and pointed to a troop of ballad-singers in an open square, surrounded by circle of listeners, their song rising above the backdrop of merchants crying their wares.

Then, from the other side of the square, Alis heard notes so lovely and delicate she felt transported. A woman with long graceful fingers sat plucking strings which were pulled taut over an opening in a pear-shaped wooden box. Alis had never heard a sound so exquisite, so unearthly, so utterly enchanting. The sound was like the song of a magical bird, or even the earth goddess herself.

"Come," Alis whispered to Maya, who reluctantly left the ballad-singers to follow Alis, who was then walking toward the woman. A few feet from the woman, Alis stopped, and as if caught by a spell, she stood transfixed, listening to the song.

"It's a lute," Maya explained. "Isn't it beautiful?"

"Lovely," said Alis.

When the woman finished, she gestured to her basket, indicating that Alis and Maya should pay her. After Maya gestured that they had no money, Alis turned away ashamed, and followed Maya. She glanced back once promising the woman with her eyes that when she had money she would return to pay for the privilege of listening.

Alis was struck by two beggars passing through the crowd, their open sores painfully red in the sunlight. She thought she could smell the stench of their puss-crusted flesh.

Maya put her arm around Alis and whispered, "They rub the honey from a buttercup bulb into the wounds to make them look like that."

"Why?"

"To excite sympathy. They're beggars."

Country girls wandered about with baskets of eggs, cheese, and butter. Nuns in violet silks trimmed with modest white satin sat in the shelters built beneath the great marble cross selling fine embroidered linen. At one booth, hung with crimson banners and huge crucifixes, churchmen sold indulgences. Plowmen, most likely from nearby villages, lined up to buy the indulgences that the churchmen assured them would get their loved ones out of purgatory.

Maya whispered to Alis, "They think their magic is better than ours."

When they passed merchants peddling medicines, Maya stopped to inspect their goods. As they walked away, she whispered to Alis: "That's how we'll earn our money. We can get herbs and roots from the forest we came through."

Workers in striped aprons stood before their stalls, grabbing the arms of passersby, pulling them into the shops. The street, just wide enough for a wagon to pass through, was dark from the overhanging upper stories. The housetops leaning against each other threw deep shadows over the narrow passageway.

A fresh stench drifted up from the piles of garbage that were dumped in front of a row of crudely thatched houses, no doubt to stay until the next rain washed them down the open gutter to the river. When Alis became used to the stink, she became aware of the more subtle tang of new bread, the salty smell of fish, and the sour fumes of the soap-boilers.

In the next open square was a juggler performing feats of magic. Alis and Maya stopped to watch. Then they continued on a crowded street that was no more than a passageway between two rows of timber-framed crudely thatched buildings. There they found an inn marked by a wooden sign painted with a yellow dragon. Once inside the narrow courtyard, Maya pulled the gong and the innkeeper appeared. Boldly she asked for a room.

He narrowed his eyes suspiciously. "For how long?"

"A few weeks, maybe longer."

"Two weeks is three shillings," he said

"In a few days," she said. "I will give it to you."

He started to close the door.

"Wait." She unfastened one of the amulets from the string, gesturing that he should take the largest. "Keep this until I give you the money," she said.

Alis watched him study the ring, knowing what his decision would be. The ring was a magical amulet, its floral, flowing pattern irresistible.

"It brings good luck?" he asked, looking at Maya with a new interest.

"Yes," said Maya. "But it brings death to sinners and thieves," she said, no doubt to prevent him from stealing it.

Carefully he tucked it into his waistband. Handing Maya a key, he led them through the inn courtyard up a flight of stairs to the first floor of a narrow wooden building. A door at the top of the stairs opened to a small room.

"You can have this room. It's all I've got."

Maya nodded her thanks, closing the door behind them. The room, no more than seven paces wide, was dusty, with faded white-washed walls and a frayed straw mattress on the floor. When Alis pushed open the shutters, peeling green paint came off on her hand. The window overlooked a narrow courtyard, separated from the street by a softly crumbling earthen wall. From the street came the steady clatter of hooves and iron cartwheels, pulsating like a heartbeat.

Even with Maya here with her, Alis felt utterly alone, and worlds away from home. Her eyes fixed on the crumbling wall, an emptiness rising in her. She was deeply tired, and at that moment, it seemed that this exhaustion would always be with her. She dropped her head into her hands, and leaned against the splintered window-pane. Tears came to her eyes, slowly at first, then gentle sobs racked her body.

Maya gently drew Alis to the straw pallet and laid her head onto her lap. "Cry, sweet Alis, cry," she whispered. The soothing nearness of her lulled Alis into a heavy, dreamless sleep.

The following morning, Maya and Alis passed back through the city gates to gather berries for breakfast, then the herbs and roots they needed for medicines.

Maya inspected the plants, examining the delicate underside of leaves, pulling roots from the ground, sniffing them, deciding which were the healthiest and ripest.

"The magic of this leaf is very powerful," Maya explained. "A single drop in a weak tea instantly eases troubled breathing. The perfect tea is made with these chamomile leaves when their smell is sharp."

She held up the downy grayish-green leaves for Alis to see, but Alis could only stare, astonished, at Maya. Why was she telling her the goddess's secrets? Only a high priestess was permitted to practice the magic of the forests.

"Pay attention," said Maya. "You must learn all the medicines. If something happens to me, you must be able to take care of yourself."

Obediently Alis squatted to look, but then she rocked back on her heels, continuing to stare at Maya. At last she said quietly. "I am unworthy."

"Later you will prove your worth. Now you will learn the recipes, so listen carefully."

Maya showed her how to chose the ripest candytuft leaves and extract the tincture. Maya worked busily, demonstrating each step of the process. When they gathered enough to fill the vials they had brought, they returned to city, passing back through the gates, making their way to the crowded market place. They stood awkwardly for a while until Maya imitated the merchants around her, crying her medicine as the others cried their leather, wool, metal buckles, and everything else from painted vases to carved crucifixes. Alis joined her, her own voice sounded timid and untried.

The nearby aroma of sweet, buttery tarts made Alis dizzy with hunger. She cried her medicine with a new energy, turning her back to the baker's display. At last when a customer frowned suspiciously but asked about Maya's potion, Maya told him confidently that the contents of one vial would sooth an aching throat, the other would aid troubled breathing. She sold their first vial, and handed the copper piece to Alis. Feeling jubilant with success, Alis ran to the nearest bakery and bought two buttery loaves. She handed one to Maya and together they sat on the stone steps of the cross at the center of the market place to eat.

By the end of the afternoon, they had sold the other two vials and were able to buy a chunk of cheese and pint of ale for supper. Wearily, they returned to the inn.

They didn't have a jug to fetch water from the well in the alley, so they had to wash from the well bucket.

When she at last fell across the mat, she felt an acute weariness. Maya's irregular breathing told her Maya was not yet asleep. In the darkness the room seemed distorted, and for a moment Alis imagined she was living through a strange and frightening dream. She would open her eyes and the sunlight would stream into their hut through straw flap that they left partially opened in the summer. She would hear the sounds of the village awakening. Maya would stretch to her feet and the day would begin like any other. Alis would awake as she had for months, light and happy knowing that Kao loved her.

But now everything was different. Alis wanted to talk about home. She wanted to ask Maya what she missed about home and what she thought about during their long silences. Instead, as she had done the night before, she fell into a deep dreamless sleep, comforted only by the warm nearness of her sister

CHAPTER 3

Two women living this way in the city could have attracted attention, but Maya worked to keep them inconspicuous. Never was Alis to go out without tucking her hair into a scarf, and she was to evade any questions. As the days and weeks passed, Alis came to know more of Maya's recipes. Soon she could recognize dozens of roots and berries and understand how to make use of each one's medicinal qualities. She knew how to prepare linseed oil for burns, and sweet cicely to sooth the stomach. She came to know the pale green egg-shaped leaves of the deadly henbane, and how to dilute the poison in a rich tea so that it would produce a deep, soothing sleep.

"A tea made from the elder root is the best cure for dropsy," Maya explained. "And a syrup made from the juice of fennel plants is best for coughs."

There were so many things to remember. The long spindle-shaped angelica root must be dug in autumn, Maya taught her, and dried rapidly. The pale purplish sicklewort was best gathered in June when the leaves were at their best. For every symptom there was a remedy: calamint tea soothed a cough, a sore throat called for periwinkle tea, lavender stopped dizziness, and tansy leaves slowed the cramps of dysentery.

"There is a city ordinance against selling potions that bring changes in the weather," Maya told her, "but I know no such formula."

Maya showed her how to prepare the vile liquid from the gum resin of the gale plant which brought miscarriages. "Never carry this with you," she instructed, "and never cry aloud that you possess this knowledge. Prepare it only if someone asks for it, and even then keep it hidden. The liquid is very dangerous. Any girl who swallows it will become violently ill, and some will die, but all will miscarry."

Alis had most of her lessons while they walked through the streets of York. Any time they saw a diseased person, Maya explained the malady and prescribed the best cure. Alis came to know from a sick man's eyes how close he was to death. She saw that the sick responded as much to Maya's manner, to her confidence and assurance, as to the remedy she gave them.

"I can cure you, if you have faith in me," Maya always said to her patients. "Do you have faith?" Only after they nodded and Maya believed them sincere would she continue with her work.

Alis learned the words, and to speak the tone that would reassure them enough to put aside their fears, trust her, and concentrate on regaining their strength.

"You have a gift," Maya said one day, "a gentle touch. You will make a good healer. Your deep appreciation of life will draw the goddess to you."

Her words proved true. Late one afternoon Alis went alone into the forest to gather herbs. In a glade some distance from the edge of the forest, a light transparent mist settled over the treetops touching the forest with a delicate loveliness. The sky was a luminous purple, the full moon just over the horizon. As if pulled by an unseen force, Alis was drawn down a gully and up the next hill, past a cluster of apple trees with tangy ripening fruit scenting the air. Her feet seemed to move of themselves, as if commanded by some higher power. She moved, absorbed by the lovely pale mistiness around her.

The forest opened and the sky spread out over her. She found herself at the gates of a monastery, a bell tower topped by an enormous crucifix rising behind the rambling red sandstone walls.

The sprawling building appeared to be sleeping. She backed into the trees to remain hidden from the gates.

The mist took on a heaviness, like a spirit with a definite form which seemed wise, all encompassing, and female. It was this spirit that had led her to these gates; it was this unseen force that had pulled her.

"The goddess," Alis told herself, recognizing her.

Maya had often spoken of her, but Alis had never imagined that she was so luminous and uplifting. She seemed to be part of everything, wise and understanding. Alis stood absorbing the wonder of the moment. Then she wanted Maya. Turning, she ran back through the forest toward the city gates. Pausing only once to catch her breath, she stopped within sight of the city walls.

The tiled rooftops and spires of the churches rising above the crenellated walls and towers were familiar enough, but the city seemed changed somehow: smaller, less significant, and entirely manageable.

She walked through the streets, feeling as if she carried a sweet and very special secret. At last her feet tapped up the stairs to the inn where she found Maya sitting in her favorite corner beneath the window's fading light, a weak candle burning beside her, a piece of basket-work in her lap.

After she breathlessly told Maya about the presence, Maya smiled and nodded. "Yes," she said. "You felt the goddess."

Alis sank onto the floor beside Maya, overcome with the thought that the goddess had come to her. "Does this mean that I'm worthy to know her secrets?"

"You are worthy if you respect and love her powers."

Alis wondered if she could ever possess the ancient power of Sight. After all, the Sight often passed through families. Their mother had been a seer, and after her, Maya. Alis began to look for signs of it in herself.

"Certain mixtures bring visions," Maya once told her, "and help develop the powers of Sight." As Alis came to know Maya's recipes, she knew that the mixture Maya spoke of was a brownish potion that she kept in a tiny vial. It was a bitter smelling salve, made from belladonna and henbane. Alis wanted to see the visions, and for a long time she fought the temptation to steal some and try it for herself.

One evening when Maya was out, Alis took a few drops, so little that certainly Maya wouldn't notice any missing, and went through the city gates to the forest. She hid herself deep in the woods on a bed of pine needles, resting her head against the softness of a partially rotted log.

For a moment she looked at the drops, hesitating. Then, closing her eyes, she rubbed the salve onto her tongue.

A shock of bitterness numbed her mouth, and her jaw locked as if she had bitten into a lemon. A tingling sensation started at the back of her head and slid down her body, making her lighter and lighter until she felt herself lifted onto the air. Her stomach was sick with dizziness as she drifted on and on. She opened her eyes and the branches reached down to her as if they would pull her to pieces. Her heart beat so wildly she thought it would burst from her chest as a wild throbbing rippled through her body. She tried to scream, but no sound came.

She closed her eyes again and drifted until she found herself among a crowd of laughing people, their faces wildly contorted. But they were not like any people she had ever seen. They were strangely colored, some with wings, others tails. She trembled until a weariness came over her, numbing her fright.

She shook for hours until she fell into a heavy sleep. When she opened her eyes, her terror was gone, and she was left dizzy and tired. The pale light in the trees told her it was early morning. She waited until she was certain the gates would be unlocked, then she stumbled back. The city streets seemed hazy and unreal with everything strangely out of focus.

In their room, Maya was waiting, watching, as Alis entered. Alis knew instantly from the strain in Maya's face that she had not slept all night.

"I lost my way," Alis said feebly.

As Maya looked closely into her eyes, Alis shrank under her gaze. What made her think she could hide the truth from Maya?

"You used the belladonna salve," Maya said, her voice quivering. Maya's face was tense and pale, her eyes hard and angry; never before had Alis seen her so angry. Alis turned away, the sick feeling rising again in her stomach.

"It is dangerous," Maya said. "Use too much and you die. If you are caught with the green salve, people will say you practice witchcraft."

"Witchcraft," Alis repeated stupidly.

"They say the salve's visions are brought by the devil. Never, never touch it again."

Alis heeded her warning. She never again used the salve and refused to sell it on the streets. Once a woman asked for it, whispering, calling it other names, but Alis pretended not to understand.

She and Maya often encountered citizens who were suspicious of them, backing away from their medicines as if from a leper. The bold ones demanded to know how they had learned such magic.

"From a wise-woman in Yorkshire," Maya always said. It was a good, safe lie.

They settled into a comfortable routine. With the crowing of the morning cocks at the first light of dawn, the church bells rang and the city gates were opened to mark the beginning of another market day. They now owned a jug, so each morning Alis fetched a jug of water from the well. She and Maya breakfasted on heavy barley bread, ale, and maybe a piece of dried meat. Before the morning bells played like music announcing prime, she and Maya were on the streets among the other peddlers crying their wares.

Alis learned to recognize and guard against poor quality in the market place: watered ale, stale fish reddened with pig's blood, or cheese made to look richer by having been soaked in broth. Justice in the city was harsh and direct. A baker caught cheating on the weight of his bread ended up in the pillory with one of his fraudulent loaves tied around his neck. A fishwife who tucked rotten fish in the center of the bundles she sold was forced to sit in the market place, her hands chained behind her back, her rotten herring tied around her neck.

One day, Alis approached the woman with the lovely pear-shaped lute who she and Maya had seen their first day in York. The woman sat to the side of a square, playing for passersby, her basket pushed forward for payment. Now that Alis had a few coins, she approached her. After dropping two coins in the basket, she settled herself to listen. Listening to the lute-player became her treat, her special reward after a hard day working.

There was a comfort in the anonymity of the city. Streets, corners, shop owners, and signs became familiar: a unicorn to mark a goldsmith shop, a bush for a vintner, and a horse's head for a harness maker. To all outward appearances, she and Maya became a part of York. They were a common sight in the market place. Their medicines worked, and customers sought their wares. Alis came to recognize faces, and built up her circle of acquaintances and customers.

But there was something wrong that she couldn't define. Her life was like a lute with a broken string played so skillfully that the missing notes went unnoticed. At times she became conscious of the water stains on the walls of her room, the moldy smell of the floorboards, and the sounds of mice in the walls. She longed for the misty, purple heather-covered hillsides of Eynhallow. She missed the sound of the sea which had been with her since birth.

One day as Alis and Maya sat on the steps of the great cross in the crowded Bull Ring market place, they noticed an older woman studying Maya's lovely silver amulet. They had learned to keep it hidden after several people had caught sight of it and whispered: "Pagan," but now its lovely floral pattern peeked from Maya's shirt.

This woman gazed at it without fear. She had a rounded face, hair which had once been dark but had become a lively black and white, and very fair skin.

"That is a holy token," the woman said quietly.

"Yes, I know," Maya answered, matching her tone.

Alis knew from the way the woman spoke, the slight lift of her vowels, that she was from the north. As Maya and the woman looked at each other, Alis sensed a connection from which she felt excluded. It was almost as if they had known each other for a long time.

"I'm Vivianne," the woman said. "I've been here on the mainland for many years."

"We arrived a few months ago," Maya said, "from Eynhallow."

"The Holy Isle," Vivianne said, studying Maya with new interest. "I heard that the high priestess and her sister had fled to the city. I had hoped to find you. I'm from Bressay, a long way from Eynhallow, but there is a woman newly arrived from Duncanby, and many others from the isles. You must meet them."

"The woman from Duncanby may have news of Eynhallow," said Maya. "I suspected there were islanders here, but I'd lost hope of finding them."

The connection Alis sensed between the two of them made her feel they had forgotten her presence even though she sat near enough to brush Maya's arm.

"There are many of us," Vivianne said. "There's a woman from Evynrue, and a man, a holy priest, from Evie."

Alis felt rather than saw the change that came over Maya at this, for the priest could only be Moury.

Vivianne must have noticed the change in Maya, too, because she said, "You both must came to supper with me. I'm sorry that the priest will not be there tonight. Later you can see him."

Vivianne lived in a back room of a brothel on a crowded street several blocks from the inn where Maya and Alis lived. Her street, lined with large houses with fragrant orchard and gardens behind high walls, was wide and spacious, making the street on which the Yellow Dragon Inn stood seem old and crowded.

"I once earned my money in this brothel the easy way," she said. "Now I'm a kitchen maid."

"You don't sell medicines?" Maya asked.

"Not on the streets," said Vivianne. "It's too dangerous because people are afraid of our magic. They call us witches. And you must stop. Only people who I know and trust can come to me when they are ill."

"How shall we earn our living?" asked Maya.

"There are harmless things to peddle," Vivianne explained. "Scented soap made from plant oils, dyes, or berries gathered in the forest."

Twenty people crowded into Vivianne's room for supper, more than Alis thought could have fit into the tiny room. They drank barley beer and ate bread sweetened with honey. The tiny room resounded with laughter. Maya looked happier than Alis had seen her for months. The way they laughed and made fun of the local religion made Alis grow nervous and apprehensive.

"The invaders planned to destroy the village on Eynhallow," said the woman from Duncanby when Maya asked for the news. "They believed there were too many superstitions connected with the Holy Isle. But the villagers pretended to accept the new religion, so they were left in peace."

"Do you know anything about Kao from Westray?" asked Alis.

"He married a thin girl with bright red hair."

"Luda," murmured Alis, turning away. She felt a pang of jealousy, then resolutely pushed it away. After all, she had loved him without knowing him.

Later, when she and Maya were back in their room, Alis said, "Visiting them frightens me. I think it's dangerous. It's better with just us two."

"And how safe is that? If something happens to me, you're alone. And what kind of life is it? We need people, Alis, people to love. Everyone does."

The next day Moury came to find Maya and they talked a long time. After that, Maya took to eating supper each evening in Vivianne's room. Occasionally Alis joined them.

Once each month, on the full moon, Vivianne, Maya, and the others went into the forest where they found a fairy ring of large stones. "Such rings are all over Britain," Maya told Alis. "All Britain used to be inhabited by people like us." In the fairy ring on the full moon, they danced and celebrated. Hearing that they did this, Alis was horrified. She pleaded with Maya not to dance in the forest this way. It was dangerous. They would be seen as foreigners and sorcerers, but Maya insisted on going.

So Alis spent time alone. She wove baskets or mats, or made clothing for herself and Maya. At first she was bored and restless in the room, frequently pacing around, wondering where Maya was, thinking she should perhaps go out and find her. Then, as she became accustomed to the silence, she came to enjoy its solitary comfort.

She learned to live with the strange isolation that had come over her since leaving Eynhallow.

CHAPTER 4

One day Maya told Alis that Moury knew how to read and write. He had first learned from a Highland priest who had befriended him. After arriving in York, he had found work as a scribe for a wealthy banker, a position which honed his skill. This news didn't interest Alis much, but she could see that Maya thought it important.

"We must learn, too," said Maya, who had always been intrigued by the written word, viewing it as a form magic that she didn't understand.

"Why?"

"We must learn all their secrets," she said. "We must study anything that might help us."

Few people could read, and the citizens were suspicious enough of their knowledge of herbs and medicines. The ability to read alone wouldn't have frightened Alis, but the thought of adding to the things that would set them apart and direct suspicion against them terrified her.

To please Maya, Alis agreed to study with Moury. The work was tedious and dull, but Alis lost herself in it, busying herself copying the letters Moury taught her, repeating aloud the sounds they stood for. Because candles were expensive, they sat near the window, and when the sun sank too low to study, they set aside their work and talked, usually about strange religion of these southerners, and their strange ways.

"I can read their books," Moury said. "I know their ways. They think everything to do with our bodies, including love and marriage, are sinful. Their god merely observes the world from a faraway heaven, occasionally interfering."

His face changed when he spoke, his face becoming animated, his eyes bright. Alis thought him interesting, perhaps a bit eccentric, but as he spoke, Maya became riveted, gazing at him as if at a god. She knew Maya was in love with him. She felt jealous, and believed Moury wasn't nearly good enough for Maya.

Alis returned to the woman who played the lute. She listened for a long time, and dropped some coins in her basket.

"It must have taken years to learn," Alis said.

"It's not difficult, if you feel the music inside of you."

Later, Alis thought about her words. Perhaps, if she worked a few extra hours each day, selling two or maybe three bottles of remedies in addition what she already sold, maybe she could pay the woman for lessons.

To her delight, the woman agreed. Each day toward sunset when Maya went to have supper with Moury, Alis joined the woman, whose name she learned was Liza. At first Alis's fingers were clumsy and the music fell so flatly upon her ears that it was difficult to believe it was the same instrument that came to life under Liza's expert hands. All through that winter, she kept the secret of her music lessons from Maya. Not that she was afraid Maya would disapprove; quite the contrary for Maya was fascinated by any kind of knowledge or magic, but until she could bring the music to life the way Liza could, she wanted nobody to know.

One day in midwinter, with a luminous smile, Maya told Alis that she was carrying Moury's child. After taking vows according to the tradition of Eynhallow, they went through a Christian ritual, "for the baby's sake," Maya said. In return for saying vows in front of a priest, they received a piece of paper saying they were married in the eyes of the church.

"We will baptize the child also," Maya said. It was far too risky to be thought anything less than a good and devout Christian.

During the months they waited for the baby, Alis saw less and less of Maya. Often she would be gone for days. She always invited Alis along, but Alis preferred to pass the time alone.

When the baby came, Vivianne was there to help. Alis was glad Maya had chosen their inn room for the baby's birth place. The birth was easy, taking less than an hour. Maya remained awake only long enough to hear that her child was a girl. The child's name had been decided in advance. If a daughter, she would be called Dana in private, after the great goddess Danu. In public she would be called Nan, a common name among those native to York. While Maya slept, Alis washed the tiny baby from head to foot, then cradled it in her arms.

After Dana was born, Alis's loneliness disappeared. She fell in love with the infant, and Maya was content to allow Alis to care for her. Alis wanted Dana to have one of the fine linen blankets stuffed with down which the nuns sold at their booth in the cool shade of their canvas tent. She also wanted to buy real cotton diapers, for she couldn't bear the thought of dressing Dana in the crudely woven fabric from which she and Maya made their own clothes. But the blanket was expensive, and Alis knew she shouldn't touch their precious hoard of silver savings. Instead, she saved a bit each day, selling a few extra bottles of goods, buying nothing for herself, until the day she had enough silver pieces for a fine blanket for Dana.

The baby's coloring was so unlike Maya's that she seemed not her child at all. Her hair was mouse-brown like Moury's, and even her eyes were an ordinary blue-gray. But she was Maya's own baby, Alis's niece. They may call her Nan in public, but when Alis was alone, stroking and petting her, she whispered the goddess's holy name, knowing it made a difference. Despite her birth in York, she was a child of Eynhallow, the daughter of a high priestess. Some day she would understand the greatness of that.

During the three weeks Alis spent saving for the blanket, she had no lessons with Liza. It was worth it, though, when she had cotton diapers and a luxurious blanket for Dana.

One morning, Maya surprised Alis by taking her hands, turning her palms upward, and saying, "You have not been playing the lute. Why?"

"How did you know I was ever playing the lute?"

"First, I can see the strange calluses on your fingers. Second, you have been humming to yourself for months, and third, how could I forget the way you gazed at that lute-woman with your heart in your eyes."

"Of course you would know," Alis said. How had she expected to hide something from Maya?

"You wanted to buy a blanket for my baby, so you have not been playing the lute. It is impossible for anyone to have a sweeter and kinder sister. So I had to think of a way to thank you."

From a hemp sack, Maya took a wrapped package and extended it to Alis.

"What is it?"

"A gift for you. Open it."

Inside was a lute. The wood was old and chipped, but the strings were gleaming and new. Alis held the instrument in her hands, speechless

"It's yours," Maya said.

The following spring, the king announced a campaign against the pagan tribes in the west. In the distant reaches of Wales there still lived in the dense forests those who clung to the old religion and practiced magic. The time had come to conquer them, the king's heralds told the gathered crowds in the marketplace.

It was early and Alis had already returned to the inn room after a day in the market place. Dana slept, wrapped in the gray down-filled blanket. Alis sat by the window, practicing her writing, when trumpets sounded in the street. Alis scooped Dana up and hurried outside.

The marketplace was crowded with people eager to hear the announcements. In the open square, standing high on a wooden platform, one of the king's heralds read an announcement: "We have captured, right here in our midst, a coven of witches — witches who pray to a pagan god and practice black magic."

There was a cheering. Alis didn't wait to hear more. Holding Dana close to her chest, she hurried to the street where Moury lived. She could see from the street that the building where Moury lived had been taken over by men dressed in royal livery. She turned and hurried to Vivianne's brothel.

On the step just outside the brothel stood a man she had never seen before, a man with gray eyes and a yellow-beard streaked with white. He stood on the step looking disoriented.

Seeing her approach, he said, "Do you know where Vivianne is?"

"She's not here?" Alis asked

"Nobody will tell me where she is," the man said.

Alis entered the brothel. Inside, the walls were softly crumbling, the floors strewn with rushes. A woman whispered to Alis, "Vivianne has been arrested and charged with witchcraft. You must leave at once."

Alis couldn't move. The woman dropped her voice even lower and said, "I saw your sister. She may have been arrested, too. Go now, and take care."

Dazed, Alis went outside, feeling as if she were about to stumble.

"Where is she?" the yellow-bearded man asked again

"Who are you? Why do you need her?"

"My name is Barnabe." He showed her his red forearms. "I need some of her ointment."

She looked at his arm and knew right away which ointment he needed

"Can *you* help me?" he asked. "Is a healthy chicken payment enough?"

He carried a half-dozen living fowl slung in a bag over his shoulder. As if on cue, the chicken began to squawk.

For a frightened moment, Alis wondered if this was a trick. Was this man trying to trick her into admitting she understood the magic of the forests?

From the distant marketplace came the sounds of more trumpets

"There will be another announcement," Alis said to Barnabe. "I must go listen."

"I'll come with you," Barnabe said.

She stood with Barnabe in the market square. Four arrested women were taken in chains from the Toll Booth prison to the wooden platform where stakes had been hastily erected for their executions. Vivianne was chained with the other women beneath the statue, wearing nothing but short ragged smocks tied at the waist with rope. Her hair was clipped short, her eyes swollen, her skin covered with open sores and bruises. One of the women had a great purple slash reaching from her temple to her neck, another's hand was mangled with several fingers hanging limp, broken.

Maya was not with them.

Like Alis, some people in the crowd watched in silent horror but most stamped their feet, chanting, "Burn the witches, burn them." When a blare of trumpets came from the steps of the Toll Booth, the crowd quieted. A small procession of men wearing royal livery came down the steps. One, who seemed to be the leader, climbed the steps and turned to face the crowd.

"You see before you," he said gravely, "vile sorceresses and heretics. Listen, and their guilt shall be proven to you."

The law required that all confessions made under torture be confirmed before sentence could be passed.

"Repeat after me," the torture master commanded the first woman. "I, Jean Barnes, of free will, admit to despising the church and practicing pagan magic."

"I Jean Barnes—" she repeated obediently. If she dared deny her guilt, she would be taken back to the torture chamber. Few did anything so foolish. It was better to die quickly in the flames.

When Vivianne's turn came, she uttered the required words in a voice Alis would never have recognized as hers. When the confessions were finished, the man wearing royal livery said,

"We are called by duty to submit these witches to the purifying flames." He held up a scroll of heavy parchment. "For the protection of our city, we have obtained from these vile and wicked heretics the names of their fellow conspirators."

Maya's name was one of the first on the list. For a terrible moment, Alis thought she would faint. A wave of blackness came across her vision, clearing only at the center, leaving a ring of darkness blocking out the crowds. She swayed precariously, then caught herself. She mustn't faint.

She was only vaguely aware that her own name had not been called. She turned and pushed her way through the crowd, clutching Dana, who had begun to fuss. She hurried back to the inn, although she knew she shouldn't return to her room. If they knew she was Maya's sister they would perhaps look for her there. And how could she endure the loneliness of the bare, stained walls? Dazed she wandered into the empty courtyard. Everyone must still be at the trial. The only noise was the cackling of fowl in the yard behind the tavern.

Alis sank onto a wooden bench, and rested her head against the earthen wall. Maya was in the Toll Booth, caught like an animal in a trap. Nothing could save her now from torture or a horrible death. No, Alis's mind screamed silently. She couldn't let Maya face the torture master, the executioner, and the flames. The thought struck her that there was something she could do for Maya. She could, at the risk of her own life, save Maya from a cruel death.

She felt she was being watched. She turned, and there was Barnabe. The breath rushed from her lungs in a sickening gasp. He must have followed her.

"If you are staying in this inn," he said, "you'd better not go back to your room."

"Do you know who I am?"

"Of course not. But I can see from your face that you are in danger."

"I have no where else to go. I have things I must get from the room."

Leaving him there, she walked up the steps. Alone in her room, she put everything from her mind except the task of saving Maya from torture. She prepared two vials, one for Maya, and one for herself should she get caught. Her three silver pieces she tucked into a pouch at her waist; the rest she sewed into the hem of her cloak.

Dana slept all afternoon. Toward twilight, she gave Dana a mild sleeping potion to keep her quiet. Then, many hours after the tolling of curfew, she covered her head with a dark hooded cloak, slung the baby across her chest, and slipped into the dark street. At the slightest sound she went cold, expecting hands to grab her from the darkness. Staying close to the buildings and avoiding the streets where she saw the yellow lanterns of the night watchmen, she walked stealthily to the Toll Booth. Behind the prison was a stone wall with a low row of tiny iron clad windows, each the size of a fist.

"Maya?" she whispered at the first opening.

There was no answer.

"Maya?" she tried at the second and third. From the fourth came the groan of a stranger. Finally from the shadows of the fifth cell came Maya's voice.

"Who is it?"

Alis knelt at the tiny window. From the clanking of heavy chains, Alis knew that Maya was moving.

"It's me, Alis," she whispered into the darkness.

"What are you doing here? Get away! Save yourself, and Dana."

Alis's heart beat so wildly she could scarcely speak. Then one of the vials was in her hands.

"Hemlock," she whispered.

"Bless the gods," Maya whispered, "and bless you, my sweet and beautiful sister."

Alis tossed her the vial. It struck the floor with a muffled thud. Alis heard the stopper pop from the bottle.

"Now listen to me," Maya said. "You must leave the city at once. You're in great danger. Some people arrested know your name, and who knows what they'll say under torture. The moment the gates open in the morning, you must take Dana and leave. Promise me that you will."

"I promise," Alis said.

"Barnabe from Brotton is in town," Maya said. "He has been looking for Vivianne. Vivianne saved his life once, long ago. You can trust him. Now listen carefully. His wife has been dead for many years, and because of his great age, not a marriageable village girl will have him."

"What are you talking about?" Alis asked, too stunned to take in Maya's meaning. How could she speak of such unimportant matters at a time like this? A thunder pounded in Alis's ears, and tears stung her eyes. She was almost angry at Maya for remaining so cool. Did she feel none of Alis's terror?

"I'm talking about you marrying him," Maya said.

"I can't," she said, thinking Maya had gone mad.

"Don't argue. You must save yourself and my baby." After a short pause, she said, "They have Moury."

Alis swallowed; she had guessed as much. "Dana is here," she said. The baby was quiet from the sleeping draught, and Maya couldn't see her for the darkness.

"Alis, you must marry Barnabe. He is a good man: simple, steady, and honest. Even with his help, you'll be lucky to get out alive. There is no time to waste. Do you understand?"

"How do you know he wants to marry me?"

"I know he's looking for a wife," said Maya. "Of course he'll want you."

"But how can I go without you?"

"Do you think I won't be with you? Where do you think my spirit will be, if not with you and Dana?"

Maya didn't understand. "I can't be without you," Alis said. She needed Maya to guide her, to tell her what to do. She dropped her head, her forehead striking the iron bar. The impact unleashed the tears that had been stinging her eyes and they rolled hotly down her cheek.

"That is not true," Maya said. "Your destiny was set the day you chose the harder route. You could have stayed on the islands with Kao. You didn't, because you are braver than you know. Now listen to me. Do not claim Dana as yours. You will always be in danger, under suspicion wherever you go. Make the villagers believe she's a foundling. Leave her on the steps of a nearby church. A family will take in an infant, and she will grow up without the kind of suspicion you will always face, particularly if Barnabe forgets and says something to give you away. Do you understand?"

"Yes," Alis whispered. Something broke in her voice, which she knew Maya heard. She thought about marrying Barnabe and she thought about the hemlock in Maya's vial and both horrifying images blurred into one, throwing her thoughts into a confusing spin.

"I will make a prediction for you," Maya said quietly. "You will love again, one day. The love you wanted but could not have with Kao, and the love you envied me and Moury."

"Barnabe?"

"I believe there will be someone else, later, someone who *you* will help. You will help him heal and nurture him, and he will love you far more than either of you will realize."

"He will be sick?"

"His heart will be sick, and you will nurture his spirits, and you will love him. Unlike Kao, he will have a spirit to match your own. But by the time you meet him, much of his spirit will be broken."

Guilt came over Alis when she realized how closely she'd been listening to Maya's prediction. How could she think about herself at a time like this, with Maya about to die? In the horrible moment that followed, she heard Maya sucking the contents from the bottle, gasping from the sharp bitterness.

"I feel it working," Maya said. "Go."

Alis wanted to say something more, but no words came. When Maya gave her chains a tired rattle, Alis turned and, holding Dana tightly, hurried back around the marketplace, staying in the shadows. She ran back toward the inn, dizzy from the pounding in her head.

In the inn courtyard she stopped. There was a light burning in her room where she had left no light. Her fingers closed around the second vial of hemlock. Keeping her back to the courtyard wall, she crept down the darkened corridor of the overnight guest rooms. Miraculously Dana still slept quietly.

A door opened and Barnabe put his head out. "Come in quickly," he said, opening the door just wide enough for her to slip in. "They're looking for you." He slid the metal bolt into place, locking her in. Her knees went weak, and she leaned against the door post.

He looked at the vial in her hand. "What's in that?" he asked.

"Hemlock."

His eyes widened. "Where were you?"

"Saving someone from a cruel death."

"Your sister?"

"Yes." Their words, hazy and unreal, came to her as if from across a great distance.

"I'm sorry," he said. He looked at the vial in her hand. "You're very brave."

She drew in her breath. "I must get out of the city." As she said the words, an overpowering sadness came over her.

"You'll come home with me," he said.

"Why would you risk your life for me?"

"You know why."

She turned away so as not to see the way he looked at her, so eagerly and tenderly. In a desperate attempt to widen the distance between them, she pulled open the pouch attached to her waistband and let the three silver pieces fall into her hand.

"Thank you for helping me," she said. "Take these for payment."

"I'll take them, but you come with them."

A weariness came over her. He must have seen it in her face, for he said, "It'll soon be morning. Come, sleep for a few hours. When the streets are crowded, no one will notice you."

She realized how close she had come to being arrested, and dead from her own hemlock. He dropped onto the straw mat on the floor. Trembling, the strength gone from her body, she lay Dana down and sank to her knees beside him on the mat.

"Thank you," she whispered.

"You will come with me."

What choice did she have? She had no place else to go. But, strangely enough, the sinking feeling of dread left her. She thought perhaps the ancient power of Sight might be hers, because she knew it would be all right. Life in his village would be hard, but no worse than life in York without Maya. She might not find happiness, but she might possibly find peace. The thought made her feel very old, although she was not yet twenty.

"What about Maya's baby? Can we bring her?"

"She will be ours."

"No," Alis said. "Maya said she should be raised by another family. We should leave her on the church steps and tell nobody who her parents are."

"All right. Come. We must sleep for a few hours."

In the darkness she became aware that she had not stopped trembling. Ever so lightly, the tension in her limbs spread throughout her body, making her quiver. None of what had happened seemed real. She felt too empty and stunned to cry. That would come later, she knew. Now she needed to sink into the oblivion of sleep.

He seemed to know how she felt, for he put his hand out only to brush the tears from her cheeks and rub her shoulder reassuringly. For the remainder of the night, he lay beside her without touching her. Soon he was breathing steadily, deeply. Once she woke up because Dana cried. Another time she woke up to find Barnabe's arm carelessly thrown over her, the rough hemp of his shirt scratching her cheek. The smell of dirt and stale sweat came to her, but an instant later she was sleeping again.

CHAPTER 5

Alis awoke to the pealing of morning bells. Hazy sunlight seeped in through the cracks in the shutters, turning the rough plastered walls a dull, murky gray. She shifted on the lumpy straw pallet, pulling the sheepskin blanket up under her chin to keep out the morning chill.

Barnabe rolled onto his back and looked at her. With the dazed look of sleep in his eyes and his graying hair rumpled, he seemed much older. Coughing first to clear his throat, he said, "The gates open soon."

She nodded. They must get out of the city as soon as possible. She closed her eyes, remembering Maya's dank and smelly cell. Quiet sobs rose in her chest.

She buried her face beneath her arms, her cries stifled in the mattress. Her tears were not the soothing, comforting kind, but bitter and burning, stinging her eyes. Barnabe touched her neck and hair, gently and soothingly.

When Dana awoke and wailed for milk, she gave Dana the last of the goat's milk from the pouch. She smoothed her shift and splashed her face with water from the basin. Barnabe quickly dressed and tied his things into bundles. Comfortably slung across Alis's chest, Dana at last quieted.

"My lute," Alis whispered, suddenly remembering the instrument in her room. The lute, and the amulets tucked into her hem, were the only possessions she cared to take with her. But after she said the words, she realized how childish they sounded.

"Your what?" asked Barnabe.

"Never mind."

"Please tell me what you said."

"I remembered the lute that Maya gave me in my room."

"I'll try to get it."

"No, it's silly." How could she care about such a thing, with Maya lying dead in a cell and Dana's life in danger? The only thing that was important was getting Dana out of the city.

"Stay here," Barnabe said, taking her key. He returned several minutes later, carrying the lute. Thank you, she wanted to say as she watched him tuck the instrument into his already heavy sack, but the words caught somewhere deep in her throat.

They were on the street as the town awakened. Pigs scavenged freely through the piles of garbage as the blacksmiths and butchers were rattling their shutters open. The streets were muddy as usual. The city gates were already crowded as they passed through unnoticed. After they climbed the first hill, just before York disappeared from sight, Alis turned and looked back, remembering the twinge of excitement and adventure Maya had felt when they had stood looking at the roof line for the first time.

"Good-bye, you vile, wicked city," she said. Swallowing hard to keep back the tears, she turned and matched Barnabe's steady, even pace. They walked along a gently curving road that wound along the hills, bordered by hedges and trees. By early afternoon a thick hoar of dust has accumulated on their shoes and garments, making Alis feel thoroughly shabby. She walked, dazed, feeling as if she were in a strange dream, her deep weariness numbing her. The movement soothed Dana, for she slept soundly.

Once they were in the forest, she found the purple leaves to put on Barnabe's rash. They walked on. Some time later, he said, "My arm feels better already. Thank you."

At midday they came to a hamlet consisting of no more than a half dozen cottages. At the second door upon which they knocked, they found someone willing to sell them a pouch of cow's milk in exchange for one of Alis's copper pieces.

"Careful further west," said the housewife. "The plague is at Threshfield."

Barnabe sighed heavily at this news. "We can't stop for milk near there," he said, "or sleep anywhere nearby."

They walked on. Barnabe had a relaxed, easy-going manner that she found comforting. Soon she came to feel that she had known him a long time. Only at rare intervals did he break the silence.

"What is the child's name?" he asked once.

She paused, then said, "Nan." She would have to remember to call her Nan from then on.

At times Alis caught Barnabe looking at her with a mixture of pity and wonder. She should have tried to guess his thoughts, but she was too wrapped up in her own heavy feeling of melancholy.

At another farmhouse where they stopped to buy milk, Alis borrowed a needle and thread, saying she had mending to do. She walked a short distance off by herself, sat beneath a sprawling oak, and quickly stitched "Nan" onto the down blanket. She would leave the child on the church steps, but she wanted her to keep the Christian name Maya had given her. How strange and plain the name "Nan" looked when printed in letters, not nearly good enough for Maya's daughter.

When night came, they made a bed in a pile of pine needles hidden from the road by a deep bank. The low quarter moon lit the sky behind the spread of branches. She laid Dana beside her on a bed of pine needles, and became painfully aware of Barnabe, moving closer to her.

She would be his wife, she told herself. Maya had said it was best, so it must be. She could not question Maya's wisdom now, when she had no energy for thoughts of her own.

His hands were awkward, fumbling. He wasn't intentionally hurting her; there was nothing malicious about him, she knew, but his calloused hands felt like sandpaper. She closed her eyes, remembering the thrill she had felt at Kao's touch, and the joy of his beautiful body next to hers.

No, she mustn't remember. She must look ahead, not back.

Clumsily he pushed away her skirt and removed his own trousers. After a few more awkward caresses, he entered her. She tried to stifle her moan of pain.

"I'm sorry Alis," he whispered later. The weak silver moonlight bathed them in a feeble light. He propped himself on his elbows, looking at her. "How beautiful you are," he whispered, "like an angel. I'm sorry for all that's happened. You don't want to marry me, I know. But I'll be good to you."

She smiled. Maya had been right, he was a good man. She lifted her hand to pat him, feeling she must respond, but her hand fell back to the ground, too weary for even the feeble gesture. He seemed not to mind. She sighed, and drifted into a restless sleep.

The following morning they began walking again. That afternoon they approached Barnabe's village of Brotton. All that day Alis had doubted the wisdom of abandoning Dana to be raised by a strange family. Had Maya not instructed her to do so, she could never have brought herself to even consider the idea.

"There is a monastery on a nearby hill," Barnabe said as they neared Brotton, "with an adjoining nunnery. If we leave the baby there, the nuns will bring it into the village."

She had to do it. If Maya had said it, it must be for the best. She felt she could trust Barnabe completely, and he seemed completely kind — but he knew her dangerous secrets.

Taking care to remain out of the gate-keeper's vision, they found a back entrance to the nunnery. After carefully wrapping the lovely down blanket around Nan, she tucked the silver pieces she had offered Barnabe into the diaper.

Nan was just over a year old, big enough to sit up on her own and crawl a bit. Alis would have to wrap the blanket tightly around her and fasten it securely to keep her from crawling away.

Barnabe said, "She will be cared for. The nuns will think her parents from a nearby village were killed by the plague."

"Yes." Alis followed him down the gently sloping hillside toward Brotton. The village was unremarkable, looking exactly like every other village they had passed. The fields, surrounded by ditches and thorned hedges to protect the plantings from the animals, spread out past the pastures. The slow, steady teams of oxen in the yellow fields created an air of stillness, as if nothing here ever changed.

The village was centered around a hill upon which stood a wooden steepled church. As she and Barnabe passed the open door of the forge, a group of women turned to stare at them. Barnabe waved to them, and they nodded in response, their harsh and stubborn eyes fixed on Alis.

"They don't much like strangers," Barnabe whispered. Aloud, to the women, he said, "This is Alis, from York. She's come to be my wife."

"Pleased to meet you," one of the women muttered, as if she was anything but pleased.

After they walked on, Barnabe said, "Don't worry. They're always like that at first. Take for instance Sarie, wearing the blue shawl. She came here years ago as a bride all the way from Pickton. You'd never know it now the way she gets on with everyone, like she's lived here all her life."

Alis said nothing in response. His reassurances did nothing to take away her uneasiness.

Barnabe's cottage was just like the others, a gabled, half-timbered structure with walls of baked brick and a thatched roof covered with bright, springy green moss. In front of the fence that encircled the yard was a dung heap swarming with swine, crowned with a thick mass of flies. Behind the cottage was a cattle shed for hay and straw.

Barnabe lifted the wooden latch of the cottage door and led her into the cold and uninviting two-roomed interior. There was a large central room, divided into two sections, one for them, and one for the animals. The oaken furniture was sparse, the walls blackened by soot. Beside the clay hearth were tongs, a meat hook, and a large copper kettle. The floor, made of earth mixed with limestone, was as dark and musty as the walls. Very little light seeped past the overhanging thatch eaves. The sound of the nearby brook was low and mournful, like a whispered dirge.

Gingerly she set down the bundle she had been carrying, and looked around. The cottage smelled musty. She thought perhaps if the walls were white-washed and painted, like the inn walls, the rooms would be cheerier. The kitchen was in a separate rickety lean-to. She wandered into the sickly garden, turning over leaves to inspect them. There was much work to be done.

That afternoon she and Barnabe were married by the village parson, who turned out to be Barnabe's uncle. The parson was a kindly elderly man with a shiny bald head and a lean, slightly hunched body.

"You're from York?" he asked Alis. When she nodded, he said, "You've worked in the fields?"

Barnabe said, "She'll do fine."

Soon the wooden church was filled with people. Barnabe introduced his elderly aunt and his two grown daughters and their families. Barnabe was well liked, Alis could see that right away. He smiled at everyone with easy warmth. For Alis the villagers put on a show of welcome, but she sensed they were cautious and distant. A few of them seemed to have the attitude that if Barnabe had chosen her she must be all right. Many of the villagers came to their cottage with wedding gifts. She was determined to do nothing to create suspicion, but she was unprepared for the way they inspected her things. Before she could hide away Maya's amulets, one of the village men caught sight of them.

"What kinds of charms are those?" he asked. "Do they bring good luck or bad?"

"Good luck, of course," Alis said.

"You have unusual eyes," another said. "And your hair is the color of the northern barbarians."

"Lots of people have hair that pale," said Barnabe.

"And most of them are pagans," said someone else.

"You have a strange way of talking," one of Barnabe's daughter said to Alis.

"Everyone in York talks that way," Barnabe said. It was a lie, but his daughter had to believe him. How could she know differently? Few villagers had ventured past the fields surrounding the village.

Barnabe's son Jon found her lute. "Can you play this?" he asked, his tone as heavily suspicious as the man who had found her amulet.

"A little," she said. How strange their reactions were to everything.

A village woman took Alis aside. Alis had been introduced but had forgotten her name.

"You're lucky, you know," the woman whispered confidently.

"Of course I am," Alis said.

"To be marrying a Huron," the woman went on, as if Alis had not spoken. "There have been Hurons here as long as there has been anybody. Good solid folks. And Barnabe is a good man."

"Yes, thank you."

All that day she wished she had taken Dana and returned to Eynhallow. Then she thought better of the idea. *Soon nothing will be the same and our old ways will be lost,* Maya had said. *Maybe it is best that we leave before everything changes completely, with at least our memories intact.*

Night came, supper was finished, the bowls washed in the bucket outside. The fire on the hearth was low and very warm, crackling softly and comfortingly, throwing long shadows across the main room.

Once they were in bed, Barnabe clumsily pushed aside first her clothes then his as he had done the evening before. Within seconds he was rolling on top of her, but she stopped him.

"Wait, Barnabe," she whispered. "Not yet." Very gently she pulled him close to her, but kept him from entering her. "Kiss me here, like this. May I show you?"

With her hands in his hair, she kissed his throat and neck, pushing her hips against his thighs, all the while preventing him from entering her. "It feels nice when you touch me here. Gently, gently —" In the darkness, feeling just his gentle touch and tender kisses, a warm, contented feeling filled her.. Slowly, surely she felt herself becoming aroused. A heat, like a tingling in her groin, stirred her. No it wasn't the same as with Kao. How could it be? There was no such intensity, no such excitement, but her body was responding. She wrapped her arms around him and caressed his neck and shoulders and back.

Later, as they lay together, breathless, he held her tightly against him, touching her as if she were a fragile, precious vessel.

"My lovely, lovely Alis. You *must* be a pagan to know such pleasure."

She felt frightened until he said, "The angels sent you to me."

She smiled to herself, knowing she would find peace in this marriage.

CHAPTER 6

✠✠✠

Next morning, Alis and Barnabe ate a chunk of black bread and cheese for breakfast washed down with watery ale. Before sunup he was in the fields. Shortly after he left the cottage, Alis was in line at the well, bucket in hand, feeling awkward among so many strangers.

They began speaking of the child found on the monastery steps.

"A baby, about a year old," one woman told another, "probably an orphan from Threshfield. The plague hit there."

"What did the nuns do with it?" someone asked.

"Brought it here, of course. The blacksmith's family is taking the child in. Ellie doesn't mind another daughter."

Alis tried to act as if this news only vaguely interested her. She wanted to know all about the blacksmith's family, but she knew better than to ask questions that might make people wonder. Not until early afternoon did she catch sight of Nan in the arms of a very thin young woman with wispy brown hair who Alis guessed was Ellie, the blacksmith's wife. Ellie was showing Nan to a group of admiring women outside the forge.

Alis watched, knowing Ellie would make a suitable foster mother for Maya's daughter. She didn't draw to near for fear that Nan would reach toward her.

For the first time, she was glad that Nan had not inherited Maya's striking and uniquely northern coloring. Her hair was brownish like Moury's. Her eyes, too, were an unremarkable blue-gray, nothing like Maya's deep swirl of luminescent green, gold, and black.

There were a thousand tasks for Alis to ease the painful memory of Maya and the nagging worries about Nan. The garden plot needed tending, there were roots and berries to gather and livestock to care for. She threw herself into her work with a furious desperation.

She had fully intended to hide her knowledge of herbs and medicines, but a few days after her arrival, a plowman fell ill with the plague. The man was in the field near the orchards when he began howling with pain. Around him stood about a dozen villagers. Someone was pushing the carbuncle, trying to flatten the boil. Horrified to see them forcing the poison back into his body, Alis said, "No, that will kill him."

"What should we do?" asked his wife.

"We must break the carbuncle," Alis said firmly, pulling out a small knife. "It is the only way to save him." She had watched Maya perform this operation many times. It never failed.

"She's mad," screamed the man. "Keep her away!"

Barnabe said, "Leave her alone and let her work. She understands medicine." With a gesture of authority out of his character, he pushed the people away to make room for her.

She suddenly felt awkward, at the center of attention, but she no longer had any choice. Gritting her teeth and turning her attention to her work, she cut a gash the length of her thumb in the boil. Blood mixed with a greenish yellow oozed out, filling the air with a nauseating stench. After a pitiful moan, the plowman passed out from the pain, but Alis, with her hand firmly on his wrist, knew that he lived. She pressed the skin around the broken boil to force the liquid out. Minutes passed. As the plowman writhed and moaned, the villagers who could bear the sight watched without a sound.

Within the hour everyone could see that he would live. When he opened his eyes, they were clear. His face was no longer pasty white and he had the strength to move his hand.

Alis nearly collapsed with relief, realizing how serious the consequences could have been. Had he died, she could have been accused of murder.

The plowman's wife knelt beside her husband's body, pressing her cheek to his chest.

"How did you learn such magic?" one of the villagers demanded.

"It isn't magic," she said as firmly as she could.

"But where did you learn it?"

"A wise woman who wanders through Yorkshire," she said, giving Maya's standard story. "I met her in York."

"Medicine is evil," he said. "God alone must decides who lives and who dies."

Alis didn't respond. What should she have done, let him die?

"There's a medicine woman in Bridgeton," Barnabe said, "a three day journey. For some remedies we must travel all the way to York. Now we can save ourselves the journey."

"The woman in Bridgeton is a witch," said another woman

"That has never been proven," said Barnabe.

"What proof is necessary?" said one of Barnabe's daughters. "She is a magician."

At that, the plowman's wife stood up and said, "Someone help me carry him home. And leave Barnabe's wife alone. She helped, that's all. She deserves thanks, not scorn."

Back in their cottage, she told Barnabe she had made a dreadful mistake. Never should she have demonstrated her knowledge. But even as she said the words, she knew she couldn't have let the plowman die.

"Nonsense," he said. "The woman in Bridgeton isn't very good. The villagers will be happy to save themselves the journey."

Alis sighed, knowing that the damage had been done. It wasn't that Barnabe was stupid — quite the contrary — but he was too trusting. *Simple,* Maya had said. *Simple and good.*

After that the villagers were suspicious of her, but when any of them fell sick, they came to her for a cure, secretly in the night. Alis and Barnabe became accustomed to opening their door to a furtive knock to find a distraught neighbor begging Alis to visit their cottage and heal a family member, or a mother carrying a sick child.

"Please make him well," the visitor would beg, and Alis didn't dare refuse.

Barnabe would always be in the background, ready to help. For a few hours, until dawn or the patient recovered, Alis and the neighbor would share a special intimacy. Sometimes the feeling lingered, and the neighbor would later defend Alis in the face of the whispered accusations that she practiced black magic.

There were, of course, patients who Alis couldn't cure, often because they waited too long to come to her. She learned to sense the presence of death, accepting when there was nothing she could do to help. As gently as possible, she would tell the truth. Because of this the villagers listened in dead silence when she spoke, fearing her words, her verdict, as if she were the goddess herself.

The villagers of Brotton had many peculiarities, but the one that most intrigued Alis was their fright of the dark forest that stretched west from the village.

"Demons live there," Ellie told Alis, in a moment of rare friendliness, "and elves, too. But the demons are the worst."

"Is there no protection from them?" asked Alis.

"Church bells scare them away," Ellie explained. "So does the sign of the cross and the whispering of the Lord's name. But stay far away. There is an ancient fairy ring which attracts the worst of demons."

The forest, Alis soon learned, was beset with real dangers in addition to the ones Ellie listed. Boars came out of its depths and trampled the crops, hares ate the cabbages of household gardens. But it was their fears of demons and spirits that most fervently gripped the villagers' imaginations.

If a calf died unexpectedly, the villagers believed the death was the fault of demons. A hailstorm was either a sign of God's wrath or the work of witches. The villager's fears were so easily aroused that the slightest thing could create near hysteria. She had hoped to find peace in the village, but now she knew there was none here. No longer did she even have the precious quiet time she had in York. How luxurious it now seemed to shut the door to her inn room and be entirely alone. Here she was always at work amid a group of people: in the fields, threshing grain, at the well. Her solace came from her lute playing, which she did late at night before falling exhausted into bed.

During the day, she and Barnabe seldom saw each other, except when they worked their strip of land together, for their duties were neatly divided. Alis tended the gardens and harvested the flax and hemp for rope, sacks, and linen, and because they had no cow, she traded eggs for milk and butter. After the sun set, they scraped together something for supper.

Then, during the second year of their marriage, Barnabe fell ill with the plague. He was in the fields when the carbuncle swelled, or she would have been able to save him. The plowmen with him hadn't broken the carbuncle to release the poison because just touching the carbuncle made Barnabe scream with pain.

By the time she reached him, his eyes were bright with fever, heat poured from his skin as if from hot coals, and his breath stank. Within hours he was dead.

The entire village came to his burial. Alis felt their eyes on her. She wished she could cry, but she felt only a deep sadness and dread for the future. She was aware of Ellie and her family standing nearby, with Nan among their other children. Nan was old enough to stand by herself, but soon she whined to be held. With a tired, absent-minded gesture, Ellie scooped her into her arms, and Nan quieted. Barnabe's family was nearby, his daughters sobbing loudly. Occasionally a sympathetic hand touched Alis's shoulder.

When at last the prayers were finished, Barnabe's brother John and his wife Kate invited her back to their cottage for the evening. She was grateful for the invitation, feeling for the first time that someone was reaching out to her, letting her into their world, as if they knew that she would never have had the strength to face Barnabe's cottage alone that night.

Kate, John, and Alis sat on straw mats in front of the fire, telling stories about Barnabe. Except for the addition of a sleeping loft, the cottage was no larger than Barnabe's, but because young children lived there, the place had an alluring vitality and warmth. The tiny clothes strung by the fire, the rag dolls on the floor, and the pattering of feet up and down the loft ladder stirred a longing in Alis, not for the children, not for Barnabe and not for Dana, but for Maya.

During the days following Barnabe's death, Alis's neighbors brought her gifts of food, fresh baked bread and biscuits and meat pies. She accepted their gifts graciously, but not without some fear.

The house and yard were strangely quiet and empty without Barnabe. For many a confused moment, she forgot he had died, and would expect to hear the latch rattle and the sound of his footsteps.

Then she remembered he was never coming back and his cottage belonged to her. It was very bewildering.

CHAPTER 7

One evening a few weeks after Barnabe's death, Kate knocked on her cottage door.

"Please come in," said Alis, "I have stew ready."

Kate shook her head. "I haven't that much time. I just want to talk to you."

Alis pulled a bench near the fire and waited while Kate settled herself onto the bench.

"I say this for your own good," Kate said. "You must remarry."

Alis studied the worn lines of Kate's face. Kate seemed incurably tired, her frown permanently etched into her forehead. She was not pretty, her features too harsh, her nose too prominent, her face angular and sharp, but her eyes were intelligent, her expression betraying a strength of character. Alis knew that her warning was prompted by kindness. Yet Alis had no wish to marry again.

"But who is there for me to marry? The only widower is now pledged to Annie, and the unmarried men are too young."

Kate nodded sharply as if she had already thought of that. "You must ask the parson or the baron's men to send to another village for a husband for you."

Alis swallowed, and tried another tactic. "Who will want me, Kate? I'm from York, and I've never borne a child."

Again Kate nodded. "It will be hard, I know, but you must find a man. Few men will want a barren wife, but perhaps you can find a man like Barnabe who already had children. And maybe you're not even barren. Maybe with the next husband — "

"I will think about it," said Alis, "but it's only been a few weeks. I need some time."

"No," said Kate, rising, "you must remarry soon."

As it turned out, Kate was not the only person thinking about the consequences of Alis's newly widowed status. The following day, a bailiff who she had never seen before approached her as she returned from the fields.

"Are you Huron's widow?" he asked abruptly.

"Yes. Why?"

"Barnabe Huron holds a strip of land in the baron's name."

"I'll continue to work it," she said.

"You'll be allowed to work it, if you can meet the obligations and pay the rents." His tone indicated that he didn't think she could meet the obligations and pay the rents.

"I'm sure I can to it."

"If you don't, you'll lose the strip."

The immediate need to work the strip and meet her rents pushed all other thoughts from her mind. Each morning she was in the fields by sunup. When the barley came up, she tended the plants. By the end of the harvest, she paid her rents and tithes like everyone else and the bailiff left her alone. Kate never again mentioned the need to remarry, evidently feeling that she had done her duty in warning Alis.

Survival, she soon learned, depended upon the length of the winter and the success of the summer growing season. A long winter and poor crop could mean death. Had life on Eynhallow been this difficult? It was hard to remember. She remembered only the nearness of her family, the comfort of Maya and all that was familiar.

Life would have been much easier had she been able to collect payment for the medicines she dispensed, but she dared not. If she asked her neighbors to pay, their resentment would grow that much faster. Instead she bore the extra burden of providing medicines. She planted and harvested the necessary herbs in her gardens, for she dared not venture into the forest to search for them.

One afternoon, making sure that nobody was watching, she crept westward through the dense thicket, fighting her way through the tangle of branches and shrubs. Less than three hundred paces from the start of the forest she came to a rich grassy glade with a ring of large white stones. The sunlight turned the stones a beautiful, gleaming white.

No sooner had she found a comfortable place to sit near the ring when a strange sound in a nearby tree made her turn. Several feet above her head in the thick trunk of the oak, a white owl emerged from an opening. She caught a glimpse of him for just a moment before he ducked into the darkness, but she understood the omen. A white owl in an oak could only mean the nearness of Maya's spirit.

For a long time Alis held perfectly still, her eyes closed. Maya was near enough to almost feel her touch and hear her voice. What could Alis say to her? What could she tell her that she didn't already know? All had gone as she had instructed. Alis had escaped from York with her life, and Dana was safely with a foster family.

A peace descended upon Alis which carried her through many days that followed. She returned to the glade as often as she dared, and the forest glade became hers as no place had before. She came to treasure the time she spent in the glade, basking in its loveliness. In winter the forest was black and white with a sparkling layer of ice on the delicate silver-white birches, and in the spring the sunlight turned the bogs a bright emerald green. Here she revived her spirit and regained her strength.

Autumn was hardest for Alis because the harvest required the villagers to work closely together. Harvesters worked in teams, one worker swinging the heavy, two-handed sickles and others catching the armfuls of wheat, lifting and dividing the bundles, and with a quick twist of a few strands, binding them together and letting them fall to the ground. After the wheat was cut and the cattle were herded into the fields to eat the stubble, the women turned to the grain-threshing. The women worked in groups of two, with one woman beating the grain with a flail, the other fanned the chaff. Alis worked alongside the others, and always felt out of place.

From afar, Alis watched as Nan grew up in the fold of her adoptive family. She looked for a spark in Nan to show she was Maya's daughter, but there was none. Nan grew into a meek, quiet and unadventurous girl.

One day, the king again announced war with the western pagans. The village gossip turned away from the usual matters of who was marrying who, and whose babies had been born. Instead they concentrated on the excitement generated when Lord Decourcey, the local baron, joined the king's armies.

"They say he didn't want to go," said the cobbler's wife early one morning as she drew her water. Several other women, their water drawn, lingered about the well.

Alis stood back, awaiting her turn, listening. Mostly what she did in the village was listen and watch.

"He doesn't want to fight the pagans," said the cobbler's wife. "Maybe he's a pagan himself."

"How can you say such a thing about our own baron!" said Ellie. "For shame."

The baron was gone a long time, so long, the villagers lost track of how many years. Then something happened, a scandal of some sort. The baron did something disgraceful and he lost his lands to the crown. Nobody in the village knew what the baron had done. Nothing changed in the daily lives of the villagers other than the king's men came to collect their rents and tithes instead of the baron's men.

One morning, after church, the parson announced that the king was sending a messenger with special news. So the villagers gathered in groups, lingering about the church yard, waiting, their chatter filling the air like the steady buzz of swarming bees.

The messenger never came, so they dispersed to the fields and their daily tasks.

Alis returned to her cottage to dress for her day's work. She emerged, with her skirt hitched up to mid-calf to keep it out of the puddles, and was on her way to her garden plot at the edge of the crofts at the far end of the village. The crystal blue morning sky without a trace of cloud was unusual for Yorkshire, even in summer.

The church yard was deserted. The door of the church stood slightly ajar, and on the stoop was a herald's discarded parchment. He had left it, no doubt expecting it to be posted on the church door as were all public notices, but because none of the villagers, even the priest, could read, it was left rolled and tied with a piece of twine.

Curious, she scooped up the parchment and unrolled it. It had been many years since her lessons with Moury, and she was surprised and pleased to see that, although slowly and clumsily, she could read the written words.

"His Lordship Curan Decourcey," the announcement declared, "seventh Baron of Norton returns today with the full pardon of the archbishop and the full pardon of his Majesty the King. The village of Brotton will welcome him shortly before noon on this day, the second of July."

She was still gazing at the announcement when she heard approaching footsteps. Glancing up, she saw the parson rounding the corner with her neighbor Kate's son, a lanky youth of about sixteen years.

Flustered, feeling as if she had been caught stealing, she stepped back, and the parchment crackled angrily. The parson and the boy appraised her coolly, disdainfully.

"You can't read, can you?" asked the boy.

"Of course not," lied Alis.

Alis hastily rolled the parchment, left it on the stoop, and walked away. She set to work pacing the freshly plowed field, taking fistfuls of seeds from the pouch and flinging them over the ground. Her lambskin shoes, dampened from the muddy soil, squeaked as she worked.

The sun was well over the horizon, but there were no other workers around. They were all off somewhere, probably greeting the returning baron. She didn't care. She enjoyed being alone in the fields. The only sound was her footsteps, and the cawing magpies. Ignoring the scarecrow she had built earlier, a flock of magpies swooped down on the field. She billowed her apron like a sail to shoo them away from her seeds. Concentrating on her work, she broke up the clods of earth with a barrow, covering the seed.

When she stood still and listened, she heard the distant sound of trumpets and fifes. The noises in the distance grew louder with dogs barking, children shouting, and people clapping and cheering. She slung her empty pouch over her shoulder and walked toward the noise.

The villagers were assembled along the broad lane that led past the church, dressed in their Sunday bleached white shirts and smocks. The cottages facing the lane were hung with banners of blue, gold, and scarlet. Alis guessed the banners had been provided by the baron's bailiff. They were acting as if the king himself were coming to Brotton.

Six mounted knights in linked mail appeared around the bend. The baron came next, on a gleaming white horse hung with richly embroidered scarlet cloth and silver plumes. A mantle of purple silk draped over his shoulders and a falcon perched on his wrist. He had the kind of hair that had been blond in childhood but had darkened to the color of wet sand. His features were stern, his sullen eyes shadowed by heavy brows.

He rode with the easy grace of a well-trained horseman. When he pulled at the reigns, his shoulders swelled, muscles rippling against the plum-colored satin of his well-fitted doublet. He had the insolence of a lion stretching in the sun, alert, ready to spring and strike, exuding a frightful kind of power. There was a hard, angry tension in his face. His eyes were defiant, his jaw strong, the skin across his cheekbones pulled taut. The features of his face were sharp and angular, giving the impression of one who seldom smiled. She wondered what he had done to require the pardon of the king and archbishop. Something about him made her think he was capable of anything.

The villagers seemed not to notice that his mood was far from joyous. They cheered him as if he were smiling happily at them and their banners. He had caused a scandal, but he had been forgiven and was after all their rightful baron. The young village girls turned wide eyes and blushing cheeks toward him.

When the Baron Decourcey turned to study the crowd, his eyes narrowed and he refused to smile. Perhaps it was because Alis stood apart that he turned to look at her. She stood alone and did not cheer, as if she were not one of the villagers.

Something like curiosity enlivened his face as he studied her. The intensity of his face would have wilted her, but she was too entranced by the mystery of his expression. She wondered if it was true that he had not wanted to go on the crusades. He seemed like a fighter.

The crowd shifted about, agitated, as the baron and Alis stared at each other.

The moment was broken when the parson leaned forward and whispered something to the baron's squire, who in turn said something to the baron. The baron listened quietly, and then said aloud, "Nonsense."

A bit of life came into the baron's eyes, as if he took delight in shocking the villagers. His smile was slight, but the jarring whiteness of his teeth and the sudden brightness of his eyes provided an unsettling contrast to the dark melancholy of his face.

He spurred his horse lightly and approached Alis.

"The good parson here tells me that you have the power to cure," he said. "Some think you are a sorceress who practices black magic."

"I am not a sorceress," she said evenly.

"You are not from this village, are you?"

"No, my lord," the bailiff answered for her. "She's a stranger from York. She's here because she's our neighbor's widow."

From the way the baron nodded, Alis knew that he understood her position in the village. After a long moment, he turned away. When he gave the signal, three heralds wearing scarlet doublets and gold embroidered emblems mounted a stage which had been hurriedly erected. After a ceremonial flourish of trumpets, one of the heralds began reciting a list of routine amendments to the laws of the barony.

When he finished, the baron himself said, "Let it be added to the proclamations, that it is hereby forbidden to execute any witch or sorceress without my signature on the warrant." He turned to the bailiff. "See that the law is put into effect throughout the barony."

"But, your lordship," stammered the bailiff. "That's not the way it's done. Witches must be burned the moment they prove themselves a hazard —"

"Enough," Decourcey snapped. "I'll not have it on my barony." With an impatient snap of his reins, he turned to lead the procession out of Brotton.

The villagers shifted themselves to stare at Alis. There was the cobbler's wife who had warned her against venturing into the forest stood nearest. Beside her was Kate, who had warned her to remarry and whose son had been amazed by her ability to read, and Rickart, the plowman whose son she had been unable to cure of the pox. Just to his left stood Ellie, holding her daughter with one hand and Nan with the other. Nan watched her blankly. Only Ellie's face seemed not to be as stern and accusing as the others.

"I am not a witch," Alis told them calmly. She turned and returned to her cottage.

CHAPTER 8

One evening in September Alis's exhaustion was so acute and the sack of wheat she carried so heavy that she leaned far to the right as she walked, walking in a curve instead of moving straight forward. The sun slanted low over the hills, the tall woods looming darkly in silhouette. Soon the leaves would turn, but now they were deep green, heavy black masses against the sky. The air, misty and gray added to Alis's feeling of heaviness.

As if it were the most natural thing in the world, Ellie fell into step beside her. "It's a good apple crop this year," she said. "Even the storm last night didn't do much harm."

Alis nodded in agreement, "The picking will start soon."

With Ellie matching her pace, they walked in perfect step. But in their exhaustion, they seemed to lean together.

"Did you see what the storm did to the forge roof?" Ellie said. "When will the men have time to repair it? With apple-picking time almost here, and corn to be harvested."

Alis sighed heavily to show she sympathized. She let a few minutes pass before asking as casually as she could, "How are your children?"

Ellie had long grown accustomed to the question, and seemed to think nothing of Alis asking it. "Everyone is managing. Jack's leg is better, and Liza — you already know — will be married next month."

"Hmm. And Nan?"

"Nan's a good, quiet girl. Soon we'll start thinking about a husband for her."

"A husband?" Alis felt startled, even though Nan was almost fourteen, the standard age for girls to marry. The thought of Nan marrying made her slightly dizzy.

Alis became aware of Ellie watching her, her face curious and intent. She thought Ellie suspected more than she let on. Surely Ellie thought it a strange coincidence that Nan had been found at the same time as Alis's arrival.

"She seems too young to marry," Alis said, feeling that she must say something.

"Finding a husband will be difficult," Ellie said. "After all, we never learned who her parents are."

"Oh yes," Alis agreed, even though it seemed to her it couldn't be that hard to find Nan a husband among the village youths. After all, Nan had been raised with Ellie's family and had lived here all her life. The villagers seemed to believe Nan's parents were natives of Threshfield who had been killed during the plague. Although in the eyes of Brotton this still made her a foreigner — Threshfield after all was many miles away — she was nonetheless believed to be a native of Yorkshire.

It was easy enough to imagine Nan as a Brotton wife and mother, and the thought saddened Alis. It seemed that there should be something better in store for her. After all, her mother had been a high priestess and tribal princess. She should have a brighter future

They approached Alis's cottage. Ellie nodded and continued on her way. Soon Alis had a low fire crackling comfortingly on the hearth, chunks of bread and cheese on the table in front of her, her mug filled with watered ale. The evening passed like any another: quiet and lonely. After supper, she sat near the fire and mended her clothing. As the sun set, she used the last of her water to wash. In the morning she would draw another bucketful. Before the sun set completely leaving the cottage dark, she was on her pallet tucked beneath her heavy sheepskin blanket, sinking into sleep.

In the dead of night, long after she had drifted to sleep, a loud tap came at the door. She sprang to her feet, clutching the blanket around her shoulders.

"A moment please," she shouted, as she oriented herself in the darkness. Someone must be ill. It had been an exhausting day, and now there was a long, sleepless night ahead.

She reached the door just as there came another impatient rap. "A moment," she repeated wearily as she fumbled in the darkness with the latch.

She creaked the door open, then blinked with surprise at the figure of a slim youth splendidly dressed. The bright orange-yellow light of his lantern turned him into a glittering spectacle. A quick appraisal of his costume of brightly colored linen stamped with the baron's heraldry told her that he was a messenger from the castle.

"Alis Huron?" he asked abruptly.

"Yes, that's me."

"The baron has summoned you. His wife's ill."

She was too surprised to answer. She was accustomed to being awakened to practice her medicine, but this summons put her mind into a complete spin. Why should the baron call for her? Surely he had his own physicians and apothecaries.

When she remained motionless, he said, "You'll have to come with me."

"Of course," she said. "What are her symptoms?"

"I don't know."

She looked at her vials and jars, with no idea of what to bring. Because she hadn't seen a case of the plague or whooping cough for months, she had no guess what the illness could be. She decided not to bring anything. When she saw the symptoms, she would request what she needed.

The cold night air cleared her mind. A heavy blanket of mist shrouded the sleeping village in silence.

She was surprised to discover that the messenger intended her to ride with him on his enormous, gray dappled horse. When she stood feeling stupid and bewildered, staring at the enormous and suddenly frightening beast, he asked: "How did you think you'd get there? Walk?"

That was, in fact, exactly what she'd thought. She concentrated on getting onto the horse. It took several tries before she was behind him in the saddle, clinging to him in terror as they galloped away, sure she would be thrown to the ground.

"Stop squeezing!" he shouted over the pounding hooves. "I can't breathe."

But she refused to loosen her grip as they flew on at a dizzying speed, her heart pounding like the hooves. The entire village would be awakened by the thundering noise as they galloped down the road, no doubt about that. The rider held the reins in one hand and his lantern in the other. If anyone looked out and saw it was her on the horse, she would be the talk of Brotton, but she was too frightened by their breakneck pace to think about the consequences.

The steep hill seemed to ascend forever before flattening out and spreading into a wide grassy meadow, glowing in the misty moonlight. Ahead was a bewildering mass of towers, walls, and battlements dimly outlined against the sky. A row of torches on the battlements lit the area surrounding the outer wall. A broad lane led to a wooden bridge then into an open ground with a tourney ring and several sheds. Through a stout palisade they came to the massive gateway flanked with bastions set with enormous blocks of worked stone.

Beside the gate hung a heavy metal rung, but the messenger didn't ring it. The guard who was posted at the wicket inside the gate recognized the rider, and when the guard shouted, "He's back with the village witch," several men hurried to pull open the gates.

One of the men peered up at her and said, "Why the baron thinks a village sorceress can do what the physicians can't, I don't know."

She was too distracted to answer, for she had to concentrate on getting off the horse. Dismounting proved as difficult as getting up in the first place. Even with four men to help her, she was too terrified to lean over and slide down, certain she would tumble to the ground. When at last, after a dizzying descent, she stood on ground, she felt as wobbly as if she had long been at sea.

"She doesn't look much like a sorceress," observed the younger of the men.

"That's because I'm not a sorceress," Alis said.

The younger man laughed. "Well, you better learn some magic in a hurry. You're expected to perform a miracle."

The messenger led her through an arched stone entryway. At the far end of the courtyard was an enormous hall that resembled the nave of a church with a vaulted roof carried on two rows of columns. The room was lit by several blazing torches set in metal holders on the wall. A fearsome display of antlered heads with gleaming tusks mounted on heavy spikes adorned the interior. Several sheaths of arrows lined the far wall. Heavy tables on trestles were arranged about the room. The room smelled faintly of herbs and spices.

On the near wall was a portrait of a stiff lady draped in sumptuous plum-colored robes who Alis guessed was the baroness.

"When did the baron marry?" she asked the messenger.

"When he came back from the western crusade."

Alis wondered why there had been no announcement, much less fanfare and a procession.

"Is his wife English?"

"No," he said, his quick glance betraying his surprise at her ignorance. "She's the king's cousin."

They entered a narrow passageway ornamented with carved moldings and gilded traceried panels. A stair tower wound its way up to a double door.

"Enter," came a woman's voice after the messenger knocked.

Inside was an anteroom with two wide doors leading to a bedchamber.

"Go on in," the messenger said to Alis.

Alis was stunned by the magnificence of the room. Three of the walls were hung with long crimson and blue tapestries embroidered with gold and silver threads. The small windows were set with glass panels glazed with lovely muted colors and covered with trefoiled tracery. The room was dominated by an enormous bed with carved posts and carefully draped crimson, blue, and silver and curtains.

A young woman lay stretched out on the bed, a thin linen shift covering her sweating, swollen body. A priest bent over her, chanting.

"This is the villager who's to cure her," one of the handmaids said to the priest.

Very slowly and deliberately, the priest lifted his head to study Alis. His eyes held unmistakable hostility, and he made no motion to move.

"The baron's order," said the handmaid.

Alis approached the bed. Astonished, she laid her hand gently on the baroness's belly.

"I didn't know she was about to have a baby," Alis said, looking up.

"Any time now," said the handmaid.

"Is there a midwife?" Alis asked.

"The midwife says the baroness is too weak from her illness to give birth."

"What are her symptoms?" Alis asked, bending nearer to the sick woman.

"She's been coughing blood."

Alis knew from the fetid smell of her breath and from the way her limbs were swollen that she had the dropsy. This would be easy enough to cure. She needed only bit of sicklewort potion to rid her stomach of the blood, and elder roots for the swelling.

"I must go into the meadow to gather a bunch of elder roots," she said, "and several sicklewort flowers."

"See," said the handmaid to the priest. "She's a medicine woman."

"It's magic," said the priest.

To Alis, the handmaid said, "Tell us what you need. We'll send someone to get it for you."

"Sicklewort leaves," she said. "Be sure they're pale green and moist. Also elder roots, which must be thick and square. And I'll need a pot of boiling water."

The handmaid gave the commands, but Alis paid little attention to the flurry of activity behind her. She fully understood the danger of her position. If the baroness died, she would be held responsible. If she lived, she would be called a sorceress.

The baroness would survive the dropsy, of that Alis was confident, but she was so small and slight, and would be so weak from her illness, she would have a hard time with the birth. When the baroness moaned softly, the handmaid pressed a damp cloth to her forehead. The baroness was thin, pale and very young, her limp hair clinging damply to the sides of her face. She was no more than sixteen or seventeen; she could even have been as young as fifteen. She'd had a severe case of the pox, probably in childhood, and her face was scarred with the hideous marks. It was impossible to tell if she would have been pretty without the disfigurement.

"I may be able to cure her dropsy," Alis said, always cautious in her predictions, "but I cannot help with the child. I know nothing about midwifery."

"We have a midwife," said the handmaid. "Just make her strong enough."

When the messenger returned with the sicklewort and elder roots, Alis set to work preparing the potions. The sicklewort worked quickly, causing the baroness to vomit the blood. Alis held her head over the basin, whispering comforting words as she coughed up the last of it. Within minutes the baroness's eyes cleared and her breathing deepened.

"More water," she gasped.

The handmaid jumped to obey.

"No," said Alis, "more of the sicklewort tea first."

"But she wants water."

"No," said Alis. Only after she satisfied herself that the girl's stomach was emptied of blood did she permit the maid to give her the water. The baroness gulped it thirstily, then dropped her head back onto the pillow. Soon her breath settled into a steady rhythm.

Realizing that she, too, was exhausted, Alis sat on a nearby bench and leaned back against the wall. She told herself that she would just rest for a few minutes, but her eyes soon closed of themselves and she slipped into a restless sleep.

She awoke to the handmaid tugging on her sleeve. "The baroness is waking up," she whispered. "Look."

The handmaid pulled Alis to her feet as the baroness sat up, stretching her arms as if arising from a routine sleep. Her eyes were clear, and her skin had lost a bit of its pasty whiteness, but no sooner did she open her eyes when she let out a low, pitiful groan.

The handmaid opened the anteroom door and spoke briskly to the messenger. "Run get the midwife," she said, "and tell the baron his wife is cured of her malady and will soon give birth."

Alis felt weak with relief. She had done all she could do. She was not a midwife. Nothing more could be expected of her.

The midwife arrived, a stocky woman with graying hair, wearing the rough undyed skirt and shawl of a villager. Alis guessed she was from another village on the barony. Expertly, with a brisk and competent manner, she set to work.

"She will have a hard time," Alis whispered, but the midwife didn't answer.

Alis watched silently, then became aware of a presence behind her. She turned to see a splendidly dressed man who stood just inside the anteroom speaking to the handmaid. They were too far away and spoke too quietly for Alis to hear what they said.

Alis recognized the Baron Decourcey from the leanness of his frame and the lift of his chin. From across the enormous chamber, he seemed every bit as forbidding as he had the day of his procession when he had looked down from high upon his horse. Now she could see how thin he was, his body long and angular, hard like the lines of his face. High on his horse he had given the appearance of a more bulky frame. He was so tall that his head nearly touched the arch of the entryway. He was older than she had at first guessed, for his youthful body contrasted the deep lines about his mouth and eyes. A gloomy air hung about his stern features, and there seemed a sharp cynicism in the narrowed slant of his eyes.

He walked toward Alis and asked, "She's cured?"

"Of her malady, your lordship," the handmaid answered for Alis. "The village witch cured her."

"What about the child?"

"The pains have started," the handmaid said, "and the midwife is here."

He looked directly at Alis and actually smiled. "The witch," he said. His smile, so startling against the deep melancholy of his countenance, disarmed her. It was a melting smile.

Just as suddenly, his smile slipped away. "Will she live?" he asked.

"Her fever's gone," Alis said, "and her strength is returning. She will not die of the dropsy."

"Will she survive the child's birth?"

In her peripheral vision, Alis noticed the handmaid bow and back away. Curan Decourcey had not taken his eyes from her.

"I don't know," Alis said. "I'm not a midwife."

"Please don't lie to me," he said. "Will she live?"

"She'll have a hard time," she said. From somewhere came a rush of courage and she said, "There's nothing more I can do, so I want to return to the village."

The handmaid sprang forward. "Forgive her, your lordship," she said. " To Alis, she said, "I believe his lordship wishes you to stay and help as best you can."

"I know nothing about midwifery," said Alis.

"You mustn't answer back that way," she said to Alis. To the baron, she said, "Forgive her, your lordship. She doesn't know how she should speak."

"She seems to do all right," he said. "I don't believe she needs any coaching at all." With that, he turned and left the room.

When he was gone, the handmaid said to Alis. "You're lucky he's not in a foul mood."

For a long time after he left, Alis felt as if he were still in the room. She continually glanced toward the anteroom, feeling as if he stood there, watching her. The thought of him unsettled her.

The midwife began giving commands, and soon the room was in a flurry of activity, with a half-dozen serving girls making preparations for the lying-in. The handmaid joined them, but Alis had no idea what to do. She backed against the wall, hoping nobody would pay attention to her. It seemed absurd for her to be there.

In the dim light of the scented candles, the room had a strange eeriness despite its opulent luxury. I'm dreaming, Alis thought, I'll open my eyes and be back on my pallet in my cottage. The morning bells will ring and this will all have been a dream.

When the midwife and her assistants huddled around the bed, the handmaid indicated that Alis should sit on a bench with her against the back wall.

"You must take care with the way you speak to the baron," the girl cautioned as they settled on the bench. "Since his return, he's been moody and queer."

"We heard no announcement in the village of the baron's marriage," said Alis.

"The baron hasn't been happy about it. I don't think he cares much about what happens to her now," she said, glancing about to be sure they weren't being overheard.

This took Alis aback. Her one guess had been that his love for the baroness had prompted him to summon Alis for a cure. The messenger had said that the baroness was the king's cousin, and she remembered the announcement she had read the day of his return.

"What had he done to need the king's pardon?" Alis asked her.

"Nobody knows," the handmaid said, "but whatever he did, it must have been terrible. The king took his lands and titles, and the archbishop excommunicated him. For a long time he was in the far west part of Wales among the pagans."

"The pagans?"

"They say," she went on, "that he rescued a pagan sorceress on the eve of her trial and ran away with her."

It took Alis a moment to absorb this highly unlikely rumor. "Really? Why did he return?"

The girl shrugged. "One day he begged the king and archbishop's pardon. Everyone says it's because he's ashamed of his behavior. The pardon was granted on the condition that he marry the king's cousin."

The handmaid yawned and soon fell asleep, her head dropping onto Alis's shoulder. Alis could see from the rim of light at the crevices of the sealed window that the sun shone brightly. Overcome with weariness, Alis laid her head on the girl's shoulder and, despite the distressing sounds of the baroness's groans, sank into sleep.

CHAPTER 9

Alis was awakened by a piercing scream. The handmaid, leaning on Alis's shoulder, still slept, despite a second scream, which was more excruciating than the first. How she managed to sleep through those blood-chilling screams and moans, Alis couldn't imagine. Curious and frightened, Alis moved the handmaid so she slept leaning against the wall and went to the bed to see.

When the next scream came, Alis tapped the midwife's shoulder and whispered, "Should I get something for the pain?" Juice from the ripe nightshade berry would ease the pain without hindering the ability of her body to function naturally. It was senseless for her to continue in such agony.

"No," the midwife snapped, "be off with you."

Alis recoiled, wanting only to get far away. Maybe she could slip from the room. Perhaps she could even get away from the castle. Leaving would be disobeying orders, but she had to get out of the room. If anyone asked, she could say that she had to get fresh air.

Her legs seemed to move with a will of their own as she walked from the chamber and through the anteroom. Before leaving, she glanced back, but nobody paid attention to her. Once in the narrow corridor, she found herself with a dizzying choice of directions. Before her was a spiral staircase leading steeply downward. To the left, the corridor wound around a bend; to the right it seemed to lead to another anteroom. She couldn't remember how she and the messenger had come. A glance through a small arched window cut in the thick stone told her she was high above the ground, so she opted for the staircase and walked down. The stairwell was strangely quiet. This should have relieved her, but instead made the place seemed haunted and frightening. At the bottom of the stairs she found herself in a wider corridor, which she followed, thinking perhaps she could find a door leading to the open courtyard.

"Ho, there," came a quiet voice.

She spun around. Reclining on a seat carved into the thickness of the wall sat the Baron Decourcey, one leg propped comfortably against a foot rest, the other dangling to the floor.

"Where are you going?" he asked. Gone from his tone was the air of command. He asked as if he were merely curious, as if she had every right to wander about the castle without permission.

"I'm trying to find my way out," she said.

"Has the baby been born?"

"No, but I can be of no use. The midwife told me to be off."

He swung both feet to the floor, still leaning against the cushion. His stare made her uncomfortable. As she had done in the baroness's chamber, she looked down, wishing she had the courage to meet his eyes. Maya, who would have had the spirit to face anyone, would never have dropped her chin.

"Stay a minute and talk to me," he said.

Now, startled, she looked directly at him. "Why?"

"You interest me. Why shouldn't the village witch be of interest? My bailiff tells me that you have no family in the village, and you are from pagan lands."

"I am not from pagan lands." How did these rumor start when she had been so careful?

"Tell me where you're from," he said.

Instead of answering, she said, "I have lived a great many years, and seen many things. I am past thirty."

This surprised him. He had evidently guessed her younger. "We are almost the same age, then. Your magical powers keep you young looking, I suppose?"

"I have no magical powers."

"You use oils on your skin."

"Not because of vanity. Because dryness bothers me."

"I am not a priest," he said. "I see nothing wrong with vanity. Isn't vanity a woman's birthright?"

He wasn't smiling, but she could see he was teasing her.

"You haven't told me where you're from," he said.

"York," she lied, "but I don't know why it matters."

"It matters because I want to know," he said, no longer playful. His face, and even his brows, seemed to darken. How strange this man was, so moody, with a brooding air of melancholy.

"Where are you from?" he asked again

She couldn't change her story now. "York. My mother was from somewhere in the north."

"That's closer to the truth. How did you come to live in York?"

Why was he drilling her this way? Suddenly overcome with exhaustion and fright, she said, "It's been a long night. Why are you tormenting me?"

He looked genuinely puzzled at that. "Tormenting?"

"May I please go home? I'm weary." To emphasize her exhaustion, she lifted her hand to her throbbing temples.

After considering her words for a moment, he waved his arm. "Go," he said. "Tell the gateman to find a horseman to take you."

Before he could change his mind, she turned and walked briskly in the direction she had been going, still not knowing if it was right. At the end of the corridor she recognized the passageway leading to the large hall through which she had come when she had entered the castle.

At last she saw the glow of weak morning sunlight at the main arched doorway. Once in the courtyard, she found the gate, marked by the tall watchtower. Just past a row of stables she came to the outer wall. Beyond the stables were the orchards and gardens encircled by trellises.

She stopped at the sound of a child's laugh, shrill yet merry, like delicate bells. A little boy, perhaps three years old, was playing beneath a spreading oak, his nurse sitting near on a bench. The child was lovely, his gold-colored hair seemed alive in the hazy sunlight, his smile sweet, yet disarmingly bold. There seemed to be a halo of light around him.

After several minutes, the child's laughter ceased, and he turned to stare at her, as if he had sensed her presence. His round eyes were deep blue, almost violet, his curly hair infused with light.

She walked on, not stopping until she reached the gatekeeper. "Who is that little boy?" she asked.

"The baron's ward, Edmund."

"Is the boy his son?" she asked.

The gatekeeper started at the suggestion. "Hilda is his only child," he said. "That boy arrived a few months ago."

Alis passed through the gate. She had no intention of asking for a ride, as the baron had suggested. Who was she to put on such airs? The village lay at the bottom of the hill. She would be home within a half hour.

Before she reached the village, she had constructed a story of Decourcey's life based on the unlikely rumor that the handmaid had told her: He had fallen in love with a non-English pagan girl, having indeed rescued her on the eve of her trial, and the boy was their child. Something had happened to the girl, perhaps she had died, leaving him alone in unknown lands. Grieving and broken-spirited, he had begged the king and archbishop's pardon, married the king's cousin, and brought his son back to his castle. No wonder he was so filled with pain, no wonder he was so confused and changeable. This was perhaps why he was intrigued by the stories that Alis was from pagan lands.

Whether or not the details of her invented story were right, she knew she was close to the truth about him. It came to her that perhaps he was the man Maya had meant, the man she would love again, the man she would help heal.

What an imagination I have, Alis told herself. It had been a long and harrowing night, and she wanted only to close her cottage door behind her, put aside all thoughts of the baron and his household, and sleep.

"You were at the baron's castle," said Kate, when Alis later emerged from her cottage

"The baron summoned me. The baroness was ill."

"You cured her?" Kate drew back slightly.

Alis shrugged. "She's better, but I didn't do much."

Becka, Kate's daughter, who had come up behind them said, "What's the castle like?"

Alis described the luxurious interior, grateful to talk about such details instead of answering questions about the things that had happened.

When she finished, Becka said, "They say he is a queer man."

"He is, indeed," Alis said, testing what she had heard on them. "They say he rescued a pagan girl before her trial."

"I've heard that, too," said Kate, lifting her chin. "I believe it."

"Remember he hadn't wanted to go on the crusades in the first place," said Becka.

"Queer," said Kate.

Alis wanted to know whether the baroness survived the baby's birth, so at the end of the work day she walked up the hill to the castle. A different gatekeeper sat in the watchtower, watching her approach with idle curiosity.

"Could you tell me sir," she asked, "if the baroness is well?"

"She's well," he said.

"And the child?"

"A boy," he said, his face brightening. "An heir. They've named him Albert Curan Decourcey."

She nodded her thanks and turned back toward the village.

Next Sunday, after church, Ellie's husband rose and addressed the villagers.

"I have a happy announcement," he said. It seemed to Alis that many people knew what he would say, for there was a visible relaxing, like a sigh and smile that passed through the crowd.

"I'm ready to announce the engagement of my foster daughter Nan to Garth Cole."

There was clapping and murmured congratulations. Alis blinked, stunned. Garth was many years older than Nan, and one of the more unsavory men in Brotton. Not Garth, Alis moaned to herself. She disliked his face, which was usually without expression. He rarely had anything to say, and his smile was oddly vacuous, giving the impression that he was stupid; but this was not his gravest shortcoming. His first wife had left him with five sons, all of whom seemed as odd and distant as their father.

If all that wasn't bad enough, he was poor, even by Brotton's standards. He was one of the few plowmen without his own plot of land, and had to hire himself out as a day-laborer to his more prosperous neighbors.

Alis looked over the crowd until she found Nan. Nan stood near Garth, both of them smiling stiffly. Next to him, Nan appeared a timid and frightened child.

It was time to tell Nan who her parents were. She shouldn't have waited this long, but she had always carried the hope that a change would come over Nan. She had watched long enough for a spark of courage, life, or spirit. There was none, and never would be. But if Nan was old enough to marry, she was old enough to know that her mother had been a beautiful and bold priestess, the leader and teacher of her people, and her father had been intelligent and learned.

Alis's first opportunity to speak with Nan came the following week. Nan sat alone behind the forge, whittling a broom handle. Alis hesitated, making sure that nobody was near. There were voices coming from inside the forge, but should someone come out, she and Nan would be hidden from view.

"Nan," Alis said softly.

Nan looked up without interest. Her expression didn't change as she watched Alis approach and sit down on a broad tree stump.

"I'd like to talk to you," Alis said.

"What about?" Nan asked, resuming her whittling.

"Do you ever wonder who your parents are?"

Nan's knife stopped in midair. Slowly she turned to face her. "I used to," she said.

"Not anymore?"

Nan shrugged.

"What has Ellie told you?"

"She says what everyone says. I was found on the monastery steps with my name stitched in a blanket. My parents were probably from Threshfield because they were hit by the plague."

Alis wondered how to continue. Nan surprised her by saying, "I never thought that was true, though."

"Why?"

"One of my foster uncles' brothers passed through Threshfield just after the plague hit and found out that no child had been orphaned. Ellis tried to keep that secret so nobody would worry about my origins, but I think other people figured it out. Threshfield isn't that far away."

"What do people guess."

"Someone pointed out that you showed up at the village shortly after I was found. Ellie says no, you came later."

So Alis's guess was correct. Ellie suspected the truth, but sought to protect Nan.

Nan said, "I used to wonder if you were my mother."

"I'm not your mother."

"I know," Nan said.

"How do you know?"

"I feel you're not."

Alis reflected upon this for a moment. Did Nan perhaps have undeveloped vestiges of the Sight? Had Maya not died, had things not happened as they did, could Nan have been a different kind of girl?

"I knew your mother well," Alis said.

Nan let a moment pass, then said, "Was she a pagan?"

"Do you want to know?" Alis asked, but she already knew the answer from the way Nan drew into herself.

"Let's not talk about it anymore," Nan said, suddenly taking a keen interest in her whittling. "Please go away now."

"All right."

Alis left, but she didn't go home. Instinctively she walked toward the glade. Once there, she sat in the ring of stones. "Maya," she pleaded silently, "tell me how this happened? Why is your own daughter so lifeless and frightened?" She waited, searching her heart for Maya's response.

Slowly Maya's answer came to her, in the form of a powerful feeling. A peace, like a deep contentment, crept over her, relaxing her limbs. A light air of delicate mist hovered about the trees and Alis stared into it, as if in a trance.

"Patience," the feeling seemed to say. "Just wait."

Wait for what? Alis demanded silently.

Just wait, came the answer.

CHAPTER 10

Nan and Garth were married by the parson on a Sunday after church. The day was damp, and gray. Afterward a feast was set up in the church courtyard. The gloominess seemed fitting because Garth hardly said a word and Nan equally quiet. Alis couldn't bear to watch, and as soon as she could she escaped to her cottage.

That evening she took a loaf of freshly baked honey bread and her fattest chicken to Garth's cottage as wedding gifts. She knocked, unsure about how her gifts would be received.

One of Garth's sons opened the door but didn't invite her in. Garth came behind him and stared at her until she spoke.

"I brought wedding gifts," Alis said, shifting uncomfortably.

"We don't want them," he said.

Alis took a step back, too surprised to speak.

"Nan is not to be friends with you," he said, and muttered. "We don't want your witchcraft here." He slammed the door shut.

Her disappointment in Nan's marriage gave Alis the idea she should leave Brotton and search for a better life. What was there here for her? She wondered if anyone could be left on the islands who would remember her. No — a new generation had grown up there. The old ways were probably completely lost. She considered trying again in a city, York or maybe London. But however hard things were in Brotton for a widow, surely it was worse in a strange place. Or was it? Perhaps she would be better off where nobody knew her, where she could begin again.

For solace she went often to the glade. Sitting in the magic stone ring, she could feel close to Maya. Here her sadness was bearable because she could visit her sweet memories.

One day she brought a piece of basket work, but she rested her head against the stone and closed her eyes, and the basket fell aside, forgotten. Sometime later, she was startled by the crunching of leaves and twigs. Her eyes flew open as a figure moved among the trees. Believing one of the villagers was approaching, she scooped up her basket-work, astonished. She had believed them all too frightened to venture into the black forest.

A man came into the glade, blinking against the sudden glare of the sun. She could see that he wasn't a villager. He wore a plum colored doublet fringed with gold, and he carried a fine hunting bow slung over his back. A startled moment passed before she realized she was looking the Baron Decourcey.

"The witch," he said when he saw her, in exactly the same tone he had used in the castle. He shrugged and let his bow fall ground. "I thought I'd find you here, in this circle of stones."

She didn't answer. She had no idea what to say.

His face was as solemn and gloomy as before, but there was a light in his eyes. She smiled because she suddenly felt no fear.

He said, "What does your Sight tell you about me?"

"I don't have the Sight."

"I think you do. There is something in the blueness of your eyes that tells me you see more than others. What does your Sight tell you about me?"

"Hmm," she said. "You have her beautiful son, but you keep the secret that you're his father."

The surprised arch of his brow told her that her guess was correct

"The boy's mother was pagan," she said. "You rescued her before her trial."

"I knew you were a seer," he said. "Or perhaps you've heard the rumors."

"I have seen the boy. His parentage wasn't hard to guess. He has your looks, but none of your melancholy."

He smiled at this. "Is it true that you have no family in the village?"

She decided to tell him the truth, so she said the words she'd never before spoken aloud. "I have a niece."

"Then you must also have a brother or sister," he said.

"My sister died in York."

"What happened to her? How did she die?"

"It's not a pretty story," she said.

"I've been here before looking for you," he said. "My bailiff told me it's rumored that you visit this place. This circle of rings frightens the villagers, you know."

"They're easily frightened," she said.

"You must worry that they will accuse you of black magic."

"Of course that is a worry. Ever since I came south into this kingdom, I have lived under threat of death."

"Why did you come?"

A moment passed, then another. She decided to answer him with a question: "Why did you return from the west?"

"That's not a pretty story, either."

You will love again, one day, Maya had said. *You will help him heal and nurture him, and he will love you far more than either of you will realize.*

A flutter came into her chest, growing until her stomach tightened with the sensation. She felt embarrassed because she knew what their future held. She had it from the best source, a high priestess with the gift of Sight.

Suddenly it was all too much. She had to get away so she could make sense of what was happening. She was on her feet. "I must go back."

"I don't even know your name. Everyone just calls you the witch."

"I'm Alis."

"Stay a moment, Alis. I keep thinking about how you looked at my procession, standing alone away from the others, as if you don't belong."

"I don't belong." She said it simply, without self-pity, without reproach

"Are you afraid of me?" he asked

"Not here," she said, and it was true. Here in the glade, he appeared almost humble. "But I don't understand your interest in me."

"What isn't interesting?" he asked. "You're supposed to be a witch. I find you here, in a glade with an ancient stone ring. You have the power to heal. Nobody knows your family. After your husband died, you showed no interest in remarrying. You've managed to pay the rents and tithes yourself. You're as beautiful as an angel and as mysterious as a woodland spirit. Who wouldn't be intrigued?"

Again gripped by the desire to flee, she backed away, feeling like a cowering little girl.

"I really must go," she said.

"I want to see you again," he said, "here, where I don't frighten you."

The following Sunday after church, a herald from the castle announced that the baron was acknowledging that Edmund, the foundling in his castle, was in fact his son.

All that day the villagers discussed the announcement.

"The child is probably the son of that pagan girl."

"He's a queer man, next to a heathen himself."

"Acts like he's proud of his pagan bastard."

Later that day the bailiff took Alis aside as she was walking home from the fields.

"Which cottage is yours?" he asked.

Startled, she pointed to it. "Why?"

"His lordship wants to know. My official message is that you are to be released from your rent obligation on the grounds that the burden is too great for a woman alone. So that your neighbors do not become jealous and resentful, you will pay with the others and later your goods will be returned secretly. And if you need anything, you're to ask me."

The bailiff had delivered his little speech to her as if the whole matter was of little consequence. He waited until she nodded and murmured her thanks, then he turned and walked away.

About a week later, on a warm rainy night, she was sitting beside the fire making thread for cloth. She was weary of her work, tired of gripping the distaff, tired of winding the taut thread onto the spindle. Winter was the time for cloth-making, and she had an enormous pile of flax to spin, but she longed to throw the spindle aside and reach for the lute which was propped against the nearby wall.

When a quiet knock came at the door, she thought perhaps Kate had come to fetch her. She knew that Kate and a few friends gathered on such nights to spin together.

She opened the door and there was the baron standing on her threshold. The absurdity of his presence as if he were just another neighbor paying a call, brought a bubble of laughter into her chest.

When he swept off his cap and bowed low, she thought he mocked her, but when he said, "May I come in?" his voice was serious and humble.

She looked about for his horse, but didn't see one. He must have come on foot. As she stepped aside to let him enter, he looked around the interior. Near the hearth was a lambskin rug. He moved to the rug, and she followed. She sat a short distance away, hugging her knees.

"I've been looking for you," he said. "You haven't been in the glade."

"I try not to go often. It makes the villagers suspicious of me."

"You've still never told me exactly where you're from. Please tell me now."

"Eynhallow, the Holy Isle."

"An island off the coast of Wales?"

"No. It is far to the north, near Pictland in the Orkneys."

"It sounds beautiful, and far away. Please concoct a witch's potion so we can fly there together."

"I can do no such thing."

"Then how did you get here from Eynhallow?"

"In a canoe with my sister." She told him the secrets she had carried for years as easily as if she spoke of them every day.

It was hard to get used to the sight of him sitting on the floor of her cottage. He seemed so out of place, in his lush mantle trimmed with miniver and his black velvet cap with a deep violet plume. She almost expected him to vanish any minute, like the wisp of a dream.

"Hmm," he said. "And how did you come to marry a villager?"

"I met him in York."

"I see." Then: "What was he like?"

"Barnabe was very kind. Now you tell me *your* secrets. What happened to Edmund's mother?"

"She is dead. She died when Edmund was very young."

"You loved her, didn't you?"

"Yes," he said quietly. "Very much."

"Edmund cannot inherit your barony." She stated it as a fact instead of a question.

"Of course not. His birth is considered illegitimate, even though I married Linel. But we were married according to local Welsh customs. When I claimed Edmund as my own, the king issued an order that Edmund must become a priest. There was nothing unusual in that. Younger sons who cannot inherit often become priests. Edmund's case, though, is different. The king wants to make sure he never has military power because his mother was a foreigner and the king is afraid he may grow up to be an enemy of the realm."

They held each other's eyes, and a look of deep understanding passing between them. Alis felt the tension leave her body. She felt light and free, laughter welling inside her, bubbling in her throat, fighting to free itself.

What was it about his face that seemed so harsh and stern even when he smiled?

He leaned forward and reached for her. She accepted his embrace and he kissed her sweetly and deeply.

The rightness of how she felt in his arms made her know this was the love Maya had predicted. Later, after he was gone, she remembered the way he looked at her, with kindness mixed with gratitude, and she knew he would come to her again.

CHAPTER 11

One stormy day about three months later, there came a loud rap at Alis door. She opened the door and found Nan standing there, her hair dripping from the rain, her face hard and angry.

"They say you're a witch and can read the future," Nan said. "Why didn't you warn me not to marry him?"

"Would you have listened?" Alis asked.

Nan seemed to recoil into herself. She looked at Alis through narrowed, frightened eyes, as if at any moment Alis would lift a hand to strike her.

"Come in," Alis said gently.

Alis unrolled her pallet and indicated that Nan should sit. Nan huddled in a corner, pulling her knees up to her chin in a protective gesture.

"Just who are you?" Nan asked. "Why are you interested in me?"

Alis chose her words carefully, not wanting to alarm or upset her further. "I took care of you when you were a baby."

"Why did you leave me on the church steps?" Nan asked curiously, without malice or anger.

"Because your life would have been harder if anyone guessed our connection."

Several beats of time passed before Nan asked, "Just what is our connection?"

"Your mother was my sister."

Nan blinked, but her expression didn't change, as if this didn't surprise her greatly. She sat still for a very long time. Alis waited.

At last Nan asked, "What was my mother like?"

Maya. How easy it was, even after all these years, to conjure up a clear image of her. But how could she find words to describe her?

"Your mother was beautiful, bold, and courageous," Alis began, but stopped. It didn't sound right. She was all these things, but she was more. "She was a leader. People gathered around her, sought her advice, and loved her."

"Was she a pagan?"

Alis sighed and turned away. How off-hand and condemning the question was.

"In a way she was, I suppose."

"In a way? What do you mean? Did she believe in Christ or not?"

"Of course she did," Alis said, "but she called him by a different name."

This seemed to satisfy Nan. Then she asked, "What am I to do?"

"About what?" Alis asked.

"You're supposed to be a seer, a witch with the power of Sight. So tell me what to do. I am married to a brute."

"You cannot undo your marriage," Alis said. "You know that."

"Before we married, he said nothing about me being an orphan. But someone has been talking to him, telling him that I am probably a foreigner."

"That's how he justifies the way he treats you," Alis said. "It's an excuse. He would act the same had you been Ellie's real daughter.

"I will have a child," she said. "With his five, this baby will make six." She dropped her head onto her knees, her face turned toward the wall. It was the gesture of a very old woman, and Nan was only fifteen years old.

Alis had to pause to absorb the fact that Maya would have a grandchild. What she felt was deep joy.

"I must go now," Nan said, rising. "I just wanted you to know."

The light pitter-patter on the roof told them that the rain had slowed. Alis rose and followed her to the door. As Nan hurried through the rain using her shawl to shield herself, Alis stood on the threshold leaning against the doorpost, watching her disappear into the gray mist

"Dana," she whispered, "come back and talk with me again, my dear Dana."

That winter was the harshest the village had seen for many years. Livestock that usually survived until the spring died before Christmas. Alis's fingers became so raw and reddened that they cracked and bled when she gripped the axe handle to chop firewood.

The baron, whose first name was Curan, visited her often. One evening in early January, as Alis sat shivering by her fire, she was startled by the sound of hooves clicking up to her door. She opened the shutters a crack and watched as Curan dismounted. In the light of the unclouded moon that hung low in the sky, his hair was bright and silvery. He cut an image like an ancient god chiseled against the broad starry sky. Instead of tying his horse to the nearby low-hanging branch as she expected, he walked to the door, leading the horse by the bridle.

She opened the door and for a confused moment thought he would bring the horse in with him, but instead he said, "Come with me."

"Where?"

"To the castle."

Her surprise must have shown in his face, for he said, "It's much more comfortable there."

Yet she hesitated. He seldom spoke of his family, except to repeat what others had said about his marriage, that it was purely political, ordered by the king. He told her nothing about the child that had been born the night she was summoned to the castle or his daughter Hilda.

"Come," he said.

She looked at the horse, a giant beast, and shook her head.

"It will be all right," he said. "We will ride slowly."

Compelled by curiosity, she nodded and allowed him to help her onto the horse, wondering if her neighbors watched as he swung himself onto the horse in front of her, and flicked the reins with a casual gesture. The night was too dark for anyone to see their features, but if someone saw the horse stop in front of her cottage there would be difficult questions and more uncomfortable gossip, but as she held tight to his waist, pressing her cheek to his back, it didn't seem to matter.

As they approached the gate, several men sprang forward to open it as if they had been waiting for him to return. Alis lifted her shawl to cover her hair and face, but it proved unnecessary, because none of them looked directly at her as Curan helped her dismount and led her through the courtyard. The house servants in his private quarters did the same thing, keeping their faces carefully turned away.

"Do they know who I am?" she whispered.

"I don't think so," he said.

Alis assumed they knew she was a village woman, and felt they needed to know no more. The details of her name, which village she was from, and what she looked like were unimportant. A flush of humiliation crept up her neck, burning her cheeks. She felt less than human, like an inanimate object unworthy of even of curiosity.

Curan led her into his private rooms. He pulled off his gloves and tossed them onto a high table just inside the doorway. If possible, this room was even more luxurious than the baroness's chamber. Sumptuous tapestries of red, blue, and silver hung over the walls, delicately scented candles were set in brass holders around the room, and the furniture gleamed.

Then she caught sight of a pale-haired woman who turned to face her. She stared at the woman, who stared back, her face blank and startled. A moment passed before Alis realized she was looking into a small, round mirror mounted in a wooden case. She had caught glimpses of herself in the dark waters of the well but she was unprepared for the unclouded image of her own face. How old her skin was, soft, slack and tired, and how faded was her hair.

"I am an old woman," she said aloud, "and ugly." She turned away, ashamed, from both the mirror and Decourcey

"No." He took her hand and led her forward, toward the mirror. "Not at all. Look at your eyes."

She looked into a pair of clear, slanting vivid blue eyes fringed with bristling golden lashes. Such a bright and merry blue, without a trace of green or gray. They were intelligent eyes, alert like a woodland animal's, piercing and cautious.

He watched her in the mirror.

"You are lovely," he said, pulling her into his arms. She leaned against his chest, enveloped by his cloak, feeling warm and safe.

The first flash of lightning lit the room just as they fell back onto the bed. For hours thunder shook the room, preventing sleep. Alis lay beside him in his luxurious bed as the room flashed with lightning, turning the stone walls as bright as daylight but eerily silver-gray.

When morning came, she had slept only fitfully. Awakening in his room, with the pale sunlight streaming in bathing the walls with a misty gray, made her feel she was in heaven as the Christians described it. The lovely peacefulness of the room contented her.

The monastery bells sounded different from the castle, as if they were much smaller and very far away. In fact, everything except Curan and his room seemed small and far away.

His arms were around her. In his face, she thought she saw own tranquility. She pulled back, allowing her question to form itself in her mind. Knowing it might be uncomfortable or shatter the lovely mood, she felt she had to know

"Where is your family?"

"Soon the household will gather for breakfast. They won't expect me. I take my meals separately. I try to see the children every day, but Catherine leaves me alone."

"Catherine is your wife?" she asked.

"My wife was Edmund's mother. She's dead. I don't even know who Catherine is, except that she is the king's way of keeping me from leaving, keeping me from remarrying, insuring that my estate is left to someone he can control."

His expression hardly changed as he spoke, but a deep sadness filled his eyes, making her want to comfort him. She wanted to ask about Edmund's mother, but her questions could wait for another time. She pulled him close, and he buried his face in her hair. Suddenly she felt immensely powerful and strong. Not since the days of Nan's infancy had she nurtured, and the feeling was intoxicating. How good it felt to reach outward, lost in the wonder of something new and beautiful outside herself and the closed and narrow world of Brotton. Curan stirred feelings in her that she had forgotten were possible. He was the answer to a wish she had forgotten she had.

A sharp knock at the door shattered the stillness.

"What?" Curan muttered, rolling from the bed, pulling a robe around himself.

The knock came again.

To Alis's horror, Curan said, "Enter."

Curan stood near the door. Alis pulled the blanket over her head, then lowered it to her temples so she could peek out. Again the precautions proved unnecessary because the steward who entered and bowed to Curan didn't look at the bed.

"A messenger just arrived," said the steward. "His majesty is on his way. His retinue will stay here tonight on their way to Newcastle."

"Fine. Tell Christopher he has work to do," he said. "The west tower must be opened and made ready."

"There's other work for Christopher," the steward said. "The storm did damage in the one of the villages."

"What kind of damage?"

"Lightning struck a bell tower in Brotton."

"Call for Christopher's assistant. I'll meet him in the main hall."

For a moment her head spun with all the things she didn't know. How could she hope to understand this man when his entire world was so strange and alien?

When the steward left, Curan returned to the bed. "Tell me again," he said, "where were you born?"

"Eynhallow, the Holy Isle."

"Does such a place still exist?"

"I don't know."

"That's where I want to be now, instead of attending to the work I have to do."

The weariness that had come over him infected her, too.

"I'll send someone in with breakfast for you," he said. "I am sorry I have to leave now."

After he was dressed and left, she looked around the room and found it neat and elegant, and luxurious, but impersonal. The white porcelain jug on the dressing table, the embroidered unicorns on the tapestries, the inlaid chest, could have belonged to anyone. She touched the cold metal of the comb and the softness of the tooth-cloth, but again, there was nothing that spoke of Curan. This, she realized, was a clue in itself. He seemed not to live here at all.

The door opened and a serving woman entered with a tray. She expected the woman to be curt and haughty, refusing to look at her as the others had done, but this woman looked directly into her face.

"Breakfast, ma'am," she said, setting down a tray with a chunk of white bread, a piece of cheese, and a glass of ale.

After the woman left, Alis picked at her food, uncomfortable in the castle without Curan. Pulling her shawl over her head and shoulders, and keeping her head bowed, she crept from the room into the stair tower. She crossed through the pantry. The door that she knew led into the main hall had been left carelessly open. Pulling the door nearly closed so that she could peek through the crack, she peered into the main hall, now swarming with people gathering for breakfast. Servants were carrying large trays, dogs of every breed scouted beneath the tables, picking at the scraps of food from among the rushes.

Seated on a carved chair on the dais was the thin woman who Alis instantly recognized as the baroness, Catherine.

Alis's first feeling was pity for this woman whose husband didn't love her. But then a feeling of humiliation crept over her when she thought of what Catherine might say about her, if she knew anything about her. She pulled herself away from the sight, vowing never to return. Let Curan visit her if he chose, but never would she return to the castle.

As she descended the hill toward the village, she noticed right away that something was wrong, even before her conscious mind registered what was different. Of course, the church steeple was gone.

The church yard was so crowded Alis thought every villager must be there. She saw Nan, Garth, and his children. Nearby were Ellie and her family, and hundreds of others. She walked toward them.

The parson stepped forward. "Where have you been?"

"Where?" Alis froze where she was, her voice caught in her throat. "The baron's castle."

"Liar," he said in his high-pitched, irritatingly squeaky voice. "What were you doing there?"

She thought quickly. "Someone was ill. I was summoned for medicine."

"Witchcraft! You were practicing witchcraft! You were probably in the black forest."

This caused a sensation. Everyone seemed to be saying something, but she couldn't catch a word. Only Nan stood silent, watching her.

She willed herself to remain calm. "You can plainly see that I was not coming from the forest. I came from the castle hill."

"You're under arrest for practicing witchcraft in this village," the parson said.

"Witchcraft?"

"You caused the lightening to hit the bell tower."

"Ridiculous!" she snapped.

Two ploughmen whose cottages stood near Alis's came forward and bound her arms. A few children threw stones which stung her skin. Again, everyone seemed to be speaking, but their voices meshed into one and spun round and round her head confusingly. Nan was looking silently, in horror, as was Ellie.

The village had no jail, so she was pulled to the windowless room attached to the church and locked inside. She sat, shivering at first, then numb to the cold.

If they left her here for long she would die, even before they could hold a trial, before Curan might learn of what happened. With her hands bound behind her back she couldn't even use her hands to try to warm herself.

She tried to remember if she had seen the bailiff in the crowd. If he had been there, if he knew what was happening, Curan may learn in time to save her. Then she shuddered. Could he save her? If enough of the villagers wanted to see her dead, what protection did she have?

She couldn't have been in the shed longer than half an hour, just long enough for her limbs to become numb from the cold, when the door opened and blinding sunlight streamed in.

"Untie her," came a gruff command, "and let her go home."

Not until her wrists were unbound and she stood on wobbly legs could she make out that the speaker was Curan's bailiff.

"Thank you," she murmured shaking her wrists and stumbling from the shed. Because she kept her head down, she didn't even know who was watching her as she hurried to her cottage. Only after her door was safely latched did she breathe a sigh of relief. A long time passed before she stopped trembling.

CHAPTER 12

The following summer, Nan's child was born. The lying-in was attended by many of the village women. She stopped thinking of Nan as either a link to the past or a hope for the future. She had no hope for her child, either. What hope could there be for a child of Nan and Garth?

Nobody invited Alis to the lying-in, but she couldn't stay away. It was Maya's grandchild, after all. Nan was thin and weak, and if anything went wrong with the birth, Alis wanted to be there to help as best she could. She made herself as inconspicuous as possible, in a corner of the room with a few of the older women, waiting until at last the infant's gasping cry pierced the room.

"A girl," someone said.

"Her name is Isabel," said Nan.

When Alis saw that the child's wispy tufts of hair were deep chestnut with glints of red, her heart rose in her chest, bringing an involuntary smile to her lips.

During the first years of Isabel's life, Alis watched her grow as she had watched Nan. To Alis's delight, Isabel was a spunky child, energetic, healthy, vigorous, and a bit wild; nothing like Nan.

Meanwhile, she and Curan fell into a routine as comfortable and predictable as her marriage to Barnabe had been. He came when he could, and they sat quietly together, offering each other solace.

Because she refused to return with him to the castle, he came to her cottage, and in the warmer months, they met in the glade. If any of her neighbors knew of his visits, nobody ever said a word.

For the first time, she cared nothing what the villagers said or thought.

One day an idea came to her like a vision. She would build a hut in the glade. She would continue to live in the village of course, and nobody would know about the hut except Curan. She needed a place to escape and be alone. The villagers, she knew, feared her and the forest too much ever to venture there. The hut would be her secret refuge.

During the hours she could escape from the village, she worked busily in the glade. She propped the timber frame up against a huge gray rock that jutted out of the sloping earth. The walls were woven twigs stuffed with moss and overlaid with an earthen plaster made from clay, water, and lime. Her hut would have a low clay hearth, which she would carve with images remembered from Eynhallow. She dug cupboards into the thickness of the mud walls, and along the walls carved an earthen ledge to sit on. She wove mats for the floor, and made earthenware pots and bowls. Her bed was a raised plank set near the fireplace for warmth.

Soon there were touches of luxury everywhere because when Curan came, he sometimes brought something: a delicately painted bowl, a fur blanket trimmed with miniver, a lambskin rug, a long carving knife, a brass poking-iron for the fire.

She understood that he came to her to escape from his world, just as she wished to escape from hers. The forest glade belonged to another place, and another time.

On an autumn day, she met his son Edmund for the first time. She was sitting on the threshold of her hut in the glade, whittling a knife handle when, from the direction of castle hill, branches snapped and cracked. Moments before the figure appeared through the trees, she knew her visitor was not Curan. The steps were different, lighter and quicker.

A young boy appeared, blinking as he emerged from the path that led through the dense thickets. He was now ten years old and she had not seen him since he was a little boy in the castle courtyard — but she recognized him immediately.

He came to an abrupt halt at the sight of her, lifting himself triumphantly. "I came to find you," he said. "I am not afraid of witches."

"I am not a witch," she said.

His features were fine and straight, like his father's, but more animated. His coloring, too, was similar to Curan's, but his hair was a lighter, more vibrant white-gold. His eyes were bright and alert, his chin held high.

"What are these stones?" he asked.

"A magic fairy ring," she said. "They have been here for thousands of years. The people who used to live here, a long time ago, worshipped the goddess in this ring."

At this explanation, he looked at her suspiciously. "I think you *are* a witch," he said.

"I am not a witch."

"I'm going back home now," he told her. "Nurse will be looking for me."

She smiled. "I hope you'll come back to visit me again, Edmund."

Alis learned that Nan was ill when she overheard one of Ellie's daughters telling a neighbor at the well. The news tormented Alis more than she could have predicted. All that day she was plagued with questions: How ill was she? Why had nobody summoned her? Perhaps her illness was of no consequence since nobody had come seeking her medicines.

The following morning, Nan died. Alis knew from the black cloth hung in Garth's windows. She would attend the funeral, that would draw no suspicion — most the villagers attended all funerals — but her mourning would be done in private.

She sat in a chair in front of the fire; she had not gone out all day, when a knock came at the door. "Come in," she called.

It was Ellie. Slowly Alis rose to face her

"I have sorry news to tell you."

"Yes, I know," Alis said. "Nan has died."

"How did you know?"

"I heard she was ill, and I saw the black cloth. I'm very sorry."

"I just wanted you to know," said Ellie. "Nan always seemed to like you. She never said anything because that wasn't her way, but I know she liked you."

"Thank you for telling me that."

Ellie turned to leave. After the door had closed behind her, Alis whispered, "May the gods bless you." Nan couldn't have had a kinder foster mother. Tears of gratitude came to her.

Alis now watched Isabel the way she used to watch Nan. The child looked so like Maya it was frightening, except that her hair was richer and darker, her eyes deep brown instead of brown flecked with green and gold. She had a way of tossing the hair from her eyes like a restive colt. She's beautiful, Alis thought. Maya's granddaughter. The thought filled her with such happiness she thought she would burst.

Alis watched for the day she could ease Isabel's burden, for her life was hard, far harder than Nan's had been. Garth for a father and a flock of half-brothers who followed his lead would have crushed the spirit of a less resilient child. Yet Isabel grew bolder and more determined with each passing year. She had a way of standing with her feet slightly apart, her hands on her hips, gazing about defiantly. She was what Maya would have become in such a family.

Several months after Nan's death, Alis came down the road just as Isabel's brothers were gathered around Isabel, teasing her.

"Pa says your mother was a queer foreigner."

With a gesture of utter exasperation, Isabel jerked out of his grip, then pushed him with such force that he was sent sprawling in the dirt.

He staggered to his feet and made ready to attack when Alis stepped forward. "Enough of that," Alis snapped.

They all turned to her. She glared at each of the boys with a stare that she hoped would frighten them. "Go, be off," she said, stamping her foot.

They turned and ran toward their cottage. Garth, Alis knew, was in the fields. The boys would likely close themselves in their cottage and later discuss the fact that the witch had interfered.

Alis turned to Isabel, who was staring at her.

"Pay no attention to them," she said. "You're better than they are. And your mother was not a foreigner. Everyone knows she was born right here in Yorkshire."

"She was an orphan on the church steps."

"That only means her parents died."

Isabel stared at Alis with the kind of intensity of which only a child is capable. Then she said, "Why do you watch me?"

This surprised Alis. She had no idea Isabel was aware of the interest she took in her. She was equally surprised that there was no fear in her voice, merely curiosity.

"Because you're a very special, and very beautiful child."

Alis tore the hem of her shawl where she kept one of Maya's amulets. She had tucked it into the shawl that she always wore. At first she carried it, waiting for the day she would give it to Nan. Now she understood the amulet was meant for Isabel.

"This is for you," she said, offering the lovely floral shaped amulet.

Isabel took it eagerly, studying it for a moment, then closing her fist around it. "What is it?"

"It's magic, but you must keep it to yourself and not show anyone."

"How do I know it's magic?"

"Keep it safe, trust what I say, and you will know it's magic when good things happen to you."

"Thank you," Isabel said.

From that time on, Alis carried a special feeling with her. Isabel was like a single, golden thread stretching back to the days of Eynhallow, her only link to her old life. The goddess had given her no children of her own, but had made her the sole guardian of Maya's granddaughter.

For the first time she knew that the Sight was indeed hers, for with absolute certainty she knew that good things lay in store for Isabel.

CHAPTER 13

"How are Edmund's studies progressing?" one of the king's officials asked Curan. Curan sighed, weary of the endless questions. Already the king's representatives had inspected his accounts, and finding them in order, checked the records of his tax collections. Ever since he'd been pardoned for deserting the king's armies in the west, a careful watch had been kept on all that happened in his barony. Royal officials reported on everything from the skill of his knight-attendants to the relations between himself and Catherine, which was, to his amusement, considered state business.

The subject of Edmund was of particular interest to the king's men. Certain tribes in the far west, in the farthest reaches of Wales, had still never been tamed, and the king viewed his son as a rebel waiting to grow up and cause trouble.

"Edmund's Latin is effortless," Curan said. "Greek gives him a bit more trouble, but his tutors are pleased with his progress."

"At age eighteen" said one of the officials, "he will enter Fountain's Abbey for two years."

Curan nodded wearily. The order for Edmund to complete his education in that faraway and notoriously strict abbey seemed unusually cruel, but Curan was powerless to argue.

"Did he keep these books?" the official asked, pointing to the large account books which were still opened on the table.

"He checks them," Curan said, unable to keep the pride from his voice. Edmund, a talented mathematician, had been checking the work of the accountants since his thirteenth birthday.

"How is Albert's training progressing?"

"He works hard, but tires easily. I suggest you watch his exercises for yourselves."

It was not for Curan to speak to these strangers about how slow his youngest son was, both with his physical training and in the study of more abstract lessons. His sons were so different that strangers wouldn't know they were brothers. Edmund was tall and lean, with swarthy, easily tanned skin. Although Edmund spent the vast majority of his time indoors with his tutors, his face glowed with a healthy sheen. Albert was pale and thin, although his knightly training involved endless hours outdoors, learning to wear mail, riding for hours fully armed, and practicing with bow and arrow. Edmund would wander into the courtyard where his brother was practicing, put on partial armor, and leap onto a running horse, a feat which Albert, after months of practicing, still couldn't do. Albert hated those hours in the stables and courtyards, returning at night miserable, smelling of horses, almost too tired to drag himself to his bed. Although he would always have attendants to clean his armor and tend his horses, a good knight had to know how to do such things for himself, which he may have to do in an emergency.

Both Edmund and Albert were unsuited for the lives they were destined to live. Edmund should have been the baron, Albert the priest. The irony of the situation was that Albert would have gladly changed places with Edmund. It seemed to Albert that Edmund was destined for a life of leisure and ease. What could be easier than a contemplative life, studying and copying texts?

But Albert would have had just as hard a time training for the priesthood. He had never learned to read. A few times the chaplain had tried to teach him, but he became impatient and frustrated with the letters. Even Hilda, who had no interest in learning, quickly mastered the alphabet.

At times Curan thought it must irritate the king that his cousin's son and future baron was weak and dull and would never amount to much. But it was just as likely that the king would be happy to have an easily led royal puppet. Not that the king himself would bother much with so small a barony; it would be overseen by his administrators.

At last the king's officials closed the account books and rose to their feet. "We shall leave in the morning."

"Make yourselves comfortable in the meantime," Curan said. "Rooms have been prepared for you."

They strode from the room with the haughtiness of ownership. Left alone at last, Curan wandered to the window. All morning it had rained, but where the heavy gray storm clouds broke, a broad beam of sunlight slanted across the sky, lighting a patch of the dense forest. It seemed to Curan that the sun shone on the exact spot of Alis's glade, beckoning to him. But it was still too early to go to the glade; better to wait until after sundown when fewer questions would be asked about his whereabouts. Even with the king's officials about, he planned to visit her. Where he spent his nights was not among the things they concerned themselves with.

Alis would be in the fields for another few hours. It bothered him that she worked as she did, but time and again she had refused to move to the castle.

"What would I do there?" she had asked.

"I'll have a post created for you," he had said. Plenty of villagers came to work and live in the castle."

"Enough people will guess your interest in me, and they won't like it. If something happens to you, I'd be at their mercy."

She seldom referred to Catherine by name, but Curan knew she was thinking of his wife, and she was right, of course. Should something happen to him, Catherine would never permit her to remain in the household, and she would have lost her cottage in the village.

Although Alis showed no interest in Hilda, Albert, or Catherine, she was tirelessly intrigued by Edmund and stories about his mother Linel. At her subtle prompting he sometimes spoke of her.

On the surface, Linel and Alis seemed to have much in common, but in truth they were nothing alike. Linel had been a child; seventeen when he fell in love with her, eighteen when she bore Edmund, and nineteen when she had been executed for witchcraft. She was as young and wild as the Welsh countryside, and he had loved her exuberance and youthful beauty. Alis, in comparison, made Linel, for all her appealing energy and lightness, seem childish and silly. The difference lay partly in Alis's greater age and wisdom. The lines in Alis's face and haunted light of her eyes spoke of the great pain she had endured

Curan always carried the image of her as he had first seen her the day of his procession, standing erect and apart, watching everything through piercingly intelligent eyes. He was drawn to her quiet dignity and evident strength. Her eyes, for all their intelligence, were lovely, gentle, and kind; and her expression, for all its lines of weariness, was caring and full of love.

He worried about her in the village. His bailiffs understood their orders were to watch and protect her without incurring the villagers' suspicion, but still he worried.

So a few weeks earlier, he brought her a sack of gold pieces. "If something happens to me," he said, "you can go to York."

She had accepted the gold, hiding them beneath a stone in the floor of her hut with the silver pieces she and her sister had saved in York. "I have quite a hoard now," she had said. "What it will buy me, I don't know."

When at last the sun began to set, throwing the dusky glow of twilight across the hills, Curan watched the oxen teams returning to the village. When darkness fell, Alis would be in the glade, waiting for him. He drew his cloak over his shoulder, and rang for a page giving orders that his horse was to be made ready.

First he climbed the stair tower over the main living quarters to visit the nursery. The night candles were being lit when he arrived. The nurse was braiding Hilda's hair and Albert was sitting on a nearby bench.

He scooped each up in turn, hugging first Albert than Hilda.

"Mother says a lute arrived today from London," Hilda said. "Who is it for?"

He was surprised that Alis's lute had already arrived. A few weeks earlier, when one of the strings of her old lute had broken, she had asked if he could find her another. He sent for a new string, and also a beautiful new silver lute, hoping it would please her

"It's a gift for a friend," he said.

"Who?"

"Nobody you know," he said. The door to Edmund's room was open, but the room was empty. "Where's Edmund?"

"He's still with his tutor," Hilda said.

"Tell him I said good night."

Hilda was very much like her mother, already giving airs about her close kinship to the king. Curan had been afraid Catherine and her children would attempt to make Edmund feel inferior, but they never did, perhaps because they knew they would incur Curan's harsh disapproval. Or perhaps because Edmund so excelled at everything he did that he was an unlikely object of scorn. Or perhaps because his future had been decreed by the king so he posed no threat to Albert inheriting the barony.

How well he remembered the night Edmund was born, the night Linel had gone off into the forest with the women of her village and returned the following morning with the infant who had seemed too tiny, red, and helpless to be real. Curan had not been able to get enough of the miracle of looking at him and touching him, afraid, for the first weeks of his life, to hold him. Not surprisingly, since Edmund had inherited his mother's fine chiseled features, he grew into a beautiful child.

Curan found the lute in his private chamber, wrapped in linen sack, set in a wooden crate. He checked to be sure the extra string was also inside.

His horse was saddled and waiting for him at the castle gate, but because of the crate tucked beneath his arm, he decided to walk.

Alis had a fire burning in a pit she had dug near the stone ring. She sat near it, whittling. Her eyes grew wide as he drew the lute from the crate.

"It's lovely," she said, turning disbelieving eyes from the lute to him and back again. "All I asked for was a new string."

She took the lute into her lap, bending over it as lovingly as she might bend over an infant, and plucked delicately at the strings. He sat back against one of the stones and listened.

She played for a long time. When she stopped, darkness had descended over the forest, then set the lute aside.

"I heard something," she said, "but I couldn't believe it was true, about your son Edmund."

"What about him?"

"Is he going into the church? Will he become a churchman?"

"It's not a bad vocation. For clever boys without land, it's the easiest way to a comfortable position."

"The church?" her entire body tensed as she said the words, her face clouding with what could have been anger. "Curan, you can't be serious."

The intensity of her reaction surprised him. Thinking she didn't understand what it meant, he explained, "He'll receive a good education and the chance of a good position."

She grew silent, absorbing this. Then she said, "Knowledge is good thing."

"The decision is not mine, anyway. When I acknowledged him as my son, the king took a personal interest in his destiny. His mother, after all, was a convicted witch of foreign birth. The king has decreed that he must enter the church or face banishment."

"What if he refuses?"

Now she had succeeded in astounding him. Did she have no idea what a drastic thing it was to defy a royal order? "Why would he?"

She leaned forward and absent-mindedly plucked at the lute strings.

"Only one son can inherit," he said." The church is a good place for the son who cannot inherit."

"Usually it is the oldest son who inherits," she said.

"The oldest *legitimate* son."

The wind that rustled the leaves was warm and balmy. Quietly she said, "Edmund came again to visit."

"I'm not surprised."

"He knows very little about his mother," she said gently.

"I haven't told him much; he's still young. Now come here. All day I have been waiting to hold you."

She settled in his arms, but he could tell she was distracted. He supposed she was still thinking about the degree that Edmund must enter the church, so he said, "The church will do fine for Edmund. You'll see."

It was a bright day in August, just before Edmund's eighteenth birthday, when the first bout of fever came over Curan. He took to his bed, soaking his sheets with sweat, at times trembling with cold, slipping into delirium. By that afternoon, his physicians had given up diagnosing him.

"They don't know what to do for you," Edmund whispered to his father.

"Of course they don't." Curan hadn't meant his voice to snap the way it did. He tried to soften his tone, but his words came out just as raspy and angry when he said, "What do they know about medicine?"

Edmund surprised him by saying, "Nothing, of course. I'll call for Alis."

Thank you, he wanted to murmur. *How did you know?*

Then he remembered Alis hated coming to the castle and had told him she would never come again, he added, "Tell her I'm very ill."

When Edmund sent a page to the village to fetch her, Catherine summoned Hilda and Albert from the room saying, "That woman makes me uncomfortable. With all the stories they say about her, to think she was here the night Albert was born—" instead of completing her sentence, she shuddered for emphasis.

Curan closed his eyes and lost himself in a feverish swirl of colors and strange thoughts. If he could be cured, Alis would be able to do it, but he felt no fear of his illness, or death. It seemed that he was floating, and the sensation lulled him.

"Tell me how my mother died," Edmund asked.

"I told you, Edmund." Curan didn't open his eyes. "She was accused of witchcraft."

"Why?"

"Because she practiced a different religion. She appeared to have a strong magic which people considered evil."

"You rescued her," Edmund said.

"Yes."

Edmund didn't say anything more. Curan waited, gathering his strength, then said, "For two years we lived in the woods, moving from village to village where she had friends and kin." The memory of those days came back to him like a beautiful, long forgotten dream. The forests had provided all that they need, and Linel had been as lithe and sure-footed as a mountain goat, as resourceful as a chipmunk.

"Then what happened?"

"Several months after you were born, she was caught. A trap was laid in one of the villages we frequently visited. She was brought to trial for witchcraft, and among her crimes, she was accused of bewitching me. While in prison awaiting her trial and execution, she was so carefully guarded that there was nothing I could do."

Edmund held his hand and they waited. When he opened his eyes again, Alis was bent over him, one hand on his chest over his heart, the other on his forehead. How out of place she was here, as if she belonged only to the glade, which like her seemed unearthly.

"In my cottage in the village is a jar filled with orange berries," she said to Edmund. "Have someone fetch it right away."

Curan thought there was indeed something magical about Alis, as if a light radiated from her. How white was her skin, like delicate porcelain, how pale her hair, how lovely and blue her eyes.

"You're beautiful," he whispered.

"Hush now," she said. "Try to sleep."

"Will I live?"

A moment passed, and then another before she said, "Don't ask me questions that I can't answer. I'm not the goddess, after all."

"That's what you are," he said, "a goddess." She had a calming effect on him. There was a dreamlike serenity about her. Had it not been for her, the years since his return from the western campaigns would have been utterly hollow and empty. It seemed to him that the man who had returned from the western wars was an empty shell, a shadow of his former self, unworthy of her.

She drew on her shawl, as if to leave.

"No," he said, "don't go."

"I'll be back soon. Now sleep."

Before his eyes closed, Curan caught a glimpse of Edmund, who had been watching them. He understands, Curan thought. He knows what she means to me. He forced his eyes open again, wanting to see what was in his son's eyes. He braced himself for disapproval or disappointment, or both. But instead, Edmund's eyes were clear, his worried frown for Curan's health. Contented, Curan started to lose himself in a cloud of darkness, but forced his eyes open.

"Edmund," he said, "there's something I forgot to tell you."

Edmund leaned over, listening. Curan wondered at his stupidity in almost forgetting the most important thing he had to tell his oldest son.

"You must see that Alis is protected," he said.

Edmund patted his hand reassuringly. "You didn't have to tell me that."

PART III

CHAPTER 1

After Isabel's visit to Alis's glade, she carried with her a vivid image of the firelit hut, its smells and sounds. She needed time to absorb the stories Alis had told her about her grandmother Maya. Gone now was the restlessness she had suffered after Alis's trial. Now she welcomed the quiet work, the embroidering or spinning that occupied her hands but kept her mind free. She was almost grateful now for the somber gray walls so conducive to thought.

After that first visit, she returned to the glade on each of her free afternoons. Their time together was limited, so Alis told her, in sketchy detail, about her grandmother's life and how Alis had come to live in the village. There was still much she didn't understand. She didn't understand, for example, Alis's connection to the baron. Isabel had heard rumors in the village that because Alis possessed the ancient Sight, even the baron himself had visited her for advice. She suspected there was more to the story.

For the first time she felt peaceful and content, so peaceful that she was able to keep her voice entirely passive when an excited whisper came from the other side of the convent dormitory: "Have you heard? A noble entourage has arrived!"

The speaker was Mary, a quiet, mousey girl who slept in a bed near Isabel and Elizabeth. Never had Isabel seen her so animated.

"I saw them when they arrived yesterday," said Elizabeth, in her superior, knowing voice. "No guest quarters for these visitors. A suite of rooms is being prepared in the abbot's own house."

"I wonder who they are," said another girl.

"I couldn't see who was with them," said Elizabeth, as if she personally knew all the persons of rank in Yorkshire. She loved to put on airs because her father was a knight. "They were too far away for me to see."

"I know who is with them," said another girl. She paused as if braiding her hair suddenly took all her concentration.

"Well," said Mary, "tell us!"

"The party is returning from the king's court. Tristin of Northumberland is the highest ranking knight with them. Next is Edmund Decourcey, the local baron's brother. His sister Hilda will meet the entourage here tonight. And, I happen to have heard, that Tristin of Northumberland is a personal friend of Sister Clare's family, and she has been invited to dine with them. The best part is that she will choose one or two students to join her."

This last sent a flutter of excitement through the room.

"Some of us might dine with them?" one of the girls repeated.

"That's what I heard," Mary said.

Isabel turned and busied herself straightening her trunk. *I may need your help*, Clare had said. She suspected Clare had concocted the excuse of bringing a student to give her a reason to have Isabel there for whatever Clare needed her to do. It was a plausible cover story, and made her wonder what Clare was up to. The very thought of joining them for dinner sent a shiver of nervous excitement through her limbs.

Perhaps Clare had changed her mind and planned to run away with Tristin after all. At that very moment she might be with him in the river thickets. The thought made Isabel smile, but she checked herself. It would do no good to have the girls wondering why she was smiling.

"The question is," said one of the girls, "who will she chose?"

"She should pick Elizabeth," said Mary, "because her father is a knight in the king's own retinue."

"Yes," said Elizabeth, "But she may not chose on the basis of rank."

"On what other basis should she chose?" someone asked.

"She may take the best scholar," said another girl. "That would be Isabel."

Nobody said a word to this. Isabel knew what they were thinking: It was one thing for Clare to show kindness to a poor village girl, it was quite another to present her to noblemen as a specimen of the convent.

"Wouldn't that be exciting, Isabel?" Elizabeth said, her voice oozing with false sweetness.

"It would be nice. But really, Elizabeth, she should pick you. I believe she will."

"You must tell us all about it afterward, Elizabeth," said one of the girls, as if the issue were settled and Elizabeth the chosen student.

Footsteps came down the hall, and the girls hushed. It was Sister Agathe to hurry them along.

Late that afternoon the girls were back in the dormitory, bent over their embroidery hoops. With so much practice, Isabel's stitches had become neat and competent. She still disliked embroidery, but at least she had learned to guide the needle and master the stitches.

The hazy sun slanted through the window casements, throwing wide beams across the room in which danced lively bits of dust. Isabel knew from the sinking sun that the supper bell would soon ring.

The door opened, and one of Clare's handmaids entered. On her arm was a cream-colored gown.

"Which of you is Isabel Cole?" she said.

Isabel set aside her hoop and stood up. Everyone in the room stared at her. "I am."

"I'm here to help you dress. You're to be Sister Clare's guest this evening."

"Thank you," Isabel said quietly, knowing her voice betrayed nothing of her own excitement. She avoided looking at the other girls.

The bells clanged, but, as if stunned, nobody moved.

"Well, what are you waiting for?" the handmaid snapped. "That's your bell."

When the last of the girls had shuffled from the room, the handmaid helped Isabel get ready. Isabel sat on a stool as the girl unbraided and combed her hair, dampening the ends to make them curl. She pulled it into a long tail and tied it in several places with a soft creamy ribbon.

"How pretty this color looks against your hair," the handmaid said. "You do have nice hair, such a deep, rich color. You're a lucky girl. Sister Clare told the abbess that you are the most brilliant student and the convent should show its model scholars to such distinguished company."

After Isabel's hair was combed and braided with the braids wrapped demurely around her head, the handmaid helped her into the gown. The gown was gathered in front with a delicate needlework pattern, the waist dropped low, the sleeves full and cuffed at the wrists. There was a strange softness about the material as it shimmered in the hazy afternoon light. The fabric moved as if alive.

"It's real silk," said the handmaid. "One of Sister Clare's own."

"It's beautiful." Isabel felt delicate and lovely, utterly transformed by the gown. She was seized by the impulse to open Elizabeth's trunk and look at her self in the mirror, but there was no time for such vanity. The handmaid walked from the room, expecting Isabel to follow.

Isabel felt as if she floated down the cloister walk, the gown billowing softly like an angel's dress. She was ready to face Edmund, feeling like a duchess or even a queen. Her mind went back to those long, lazy afternoons she had spent on the hillside with Jake listening to his dreams of adventure. Who could have expected that one day she would dine with knights and ladies wearing a silken gown?.

The banquet was held in the warming room, a chamber never used by the students. A fire burned in this room from All Saint's Day to Easter, and the nuns often gathered in its comfort to embroider.

Whatever confidence the gown had given Isabel vanished like a morning mist when she stood on the threshold. The vaulted chamber was filled with people dressed like peacocks, one brighter than the next. Sumptuous tapestries of blue, silver, and gold hung over the bare walls, three tables covered with shimmering white linen erected in the shape of a "U" were loaded with trays of food, the air was filled with the mouthwatering scent of hot buttered bread. The room was lit by huge torches set in iron holders mounted on the wall.

When everyone turned to face Isabel, she felt as if she had turned to stone, suddenly awkward and unable to move. There was a movement and a cloud of white broke from the swirl of colorful silks and satins and floated toward her. It was Clare, in a virginal-white habit.

Clare smiled encouragingly. She took Isabel's elbow and led her to the group she had been standing with. "I'd like to present our most brilliant student, Isabel Cole," she said to one lady who stood slightly apart from the others. "Isabel dear, this is Lady Hilda Decourcey."

Hilda was not-quite-pretty, with stern features and frizzy yellow hair. Isabel inclined her head, stunned as much by Hilda's costume as by her name. Hilda wore a hat the shape of a truncated cone with a lavender veil billowing behind, and a deep velvet gown set with pearls.

"She's very beautiful," Hilda said to Clare, after inspecting Isabel. "Will she remain in the convent, or will she marry?"

"Her future hasn't been decided," said Clare, as if Isabel were a royal princess, or at least a great lady with a respectable dowry instead of a common village girl.

Isabel looked around. The knights, in their slashed cloaks over brightly colored silk shirts, and doublets with embroidered cuffs were every bit as splendidly dressed as Hilda and her attendants. She wondered which one was Tristin. Clare's glowing face told her he must be in the room.

"Supper will be served soon," announced an attendant from the side doorway.

"Where is Edmund?" said a knight near Isabel. "He has a way of disappearing."

"He's in the village at the foot of the hill," someone answered. "What he's doing there, I will not venture to guess."

"Most likely," said another, "he has a girl."

"It wouldn't surprise me," said one of Hilda's attendants, giggling.

"If he's not here soon," said Hilda, "we will begin without him."

Isabel knew he had no girl in Brotton — at least, she didn't think so. She wondered if he was visiting Alis.

The guests settled themselves on the benches around the tables, like exotic birds alighting in rows on branches. Clare led Isabel to a delicately painted porcelain basin, and Isabel imitated the way she washed her fingers. Then Clare showed her where to sit, among Hilda's attendants at one of the side tables. Clare herself sat at the center table with Hilda.

"How can you endure living here?" one of the girls whispered to Isabel as a serving man carried in a tray loaded with meat.

Isabel swallowed, afraid to speak.

"We just returned from the king's court," said another. "After that, anything would seem dull, but this gray convent is miserable."

"I suppose," offered another, "for those who love books and prayers, this is a wonderful place."

"I prefer dancing," said the girl nearest Isabel. "Let others do the praying."

Food was heaped onto plates, and Isabel imitated those around her, dipping her fingers into the water bowls as they did. The wine goblets were surprisingly heavy. A few sips of the thick wine went instantly to her head, giving her a light dizzy feeling. She set the goblet aside. The evening was going to be difficult enough without fogging her mind with rich wine. Instead she sipped water from the enormous goblet which was passed around the table. Several hounds sniffed through the rushes for crumbs, breathing hotly on Isabel's ankles.

As they ate, a young man played the flute in the center of the room. His music was soft, exquisite, and playful.

Isabel guessed that the empty seat beside Hilda was intended for Edmund. Would he turn up? Here she was, dressed like a lady, ready to face him again, this time with her pride intact, and he was nowhere around.

Hilda signaled to a youth who stood the side of the room near the back entrance. His costume was comic, alternating patches of red and white, shoes bent into huge curled toes topped with bells. The flute-player backed away as the strangely dressed youth took his place.

He bowed to Hilda, and announced himself in a soft, musical voice: "I am John, the minstrel, here to tell the tale of the three Mesopotamian monks who journeyed to find the terrestrial paradise where heaven and earth meet."

A memory stirred as Jake's words came back to her. He had spoken of that very place.

The minstrel strummed a small stringed instrument as he quietly sang his story: "The place lies far to the east, where no traveler has ever reached. Many have tried. I will tell you the adventures of the three monks who burned with desire to see the place nobody had ever seen.

"Paying no heed to the many warnings they received, they set off one gray winter afternoon. They traveled simply, and in the beginning, they passed through deserts and barren lands, and endured many hardships. After passing through Persia, they found themselves in lands unmarked on any map. Here lived huge lizards called dragons. As if sensing that they were monks on a holy missions, the dragons left them alone, watching curiously from their caves.

"Beyond a fruitful region, the monks came to a country of rock dwellers who spoke a strange and ancient language. Another hundred days travel brought them to the land of Pichichi, a tribe of people less than two feet high who ran from the monks in panic.

"Amid still higher mountains, the monks found elephants and tigers. Still further was a region of continual darkness. Another forty days brought them to a place of terrible torments. Shrieks and mourns came from sinners who never repented their sins. The sinners were chained knee-deep in a noxious lake filled with snakes. One sinner, a woman who had once been beautiful, was pinned to a rock by coiled snakes which bit her tongue whenever she tried to speak.

"The monks crossed a river to a huge cave where a silver-haired man wearing a jeweled crown identified himself as St. Macarious. He told the monks that he, too, has sought the end of the earth, but was warned in a vision not to complete the journey. He warned the monks to turn back. Although they were only ten days from their destination, they heeded the warning and turned back."

He strummed a few concluding notes, then bowed.

"They never reached the place?" asked a lady near Hilda.

"They never did," said the minstrel.

Hilda stood up. "That's absurd. They never should have set out on such an adventure to begin with. Who told you to tell such a dreadful story?"

"I did," came a voice from the doorway. Everyone turned toward the voice. Isabel caught her breath at the sight of Edmund, leaning easily against the door post.

"The story fascinates me," he said. "You didn't like it, Hilda?"

"There is no such place, and if there is, the monks had no business trying to find it," she said, but in the face of Edmund's utter assurance, her voice had lost some of its force.

"There certainly is such a place," he said, tossing a gold coin to the minstrel, who caught it, grinning. "But you made a mistake," Edmund told him. "The place is not to the east, it is far to the north."

"My apologies, your lordship," he said bowing low.

"But then some say it is in the west."

"My apologies again, your lordship."

"Enough of this ridiculous talk," Hilda said. "You have missed dinner, Edmund. Where have you been?"

"Visiting a friend." He turned to a serving man who was gathering goblets and said, "Bring me a bit of meat."

The servant brought his meat, and Edmund ate quickly. The trays, now only half-filled with food, were carried from the room.

"Come," Hilda said, "let us walk in the garden."

At her words, the diners rose, formed groups, and idly drifted toward the door. A cluster of ladies surrounded Edmond.

"Really Edmund," said one, smiling coyly and tapping him lightly on the arm, "who were you visiting? A village girl?"

"Sort of," he said lightly.

The ladies laughed as if this were terribly clever. "She was sort of a girl?" one asked.

"We hated to begin supper without you," said another, in a sticky-sweet voice.

It was then that Edmund noticed Isabel. First he simply stared, then grinned broadly, as if they were fellow conspirators. The chatter around her died as others became aware of his gaze. Isabel reached for the edge of the table to steady herself.

Hilda stepped forward and took Edmund's arm. "Isabel is a very pretty girl," she said.

"I would like to be introduced, please," he said.

"Certainly," Hilda said coldly. "Edmund, allow me to present Isabel — what did you say your last name was, dear?"

The seconds ticked by as Isabel swallowed and fought for breath. "Cole," she said after what seemed like an eternity.

"Isabel Cole," Hilda repeated. "This is my brother, Sir Edmund Decourcey."

Isabel bobbed a curtsey.

"Shall you become a nun?" he asked gravely. He knew well enough that only wealthy girls with large dowries could remain permanently in the convent as nuns.

Isabel didn't answer.

"I understand Isabel is an excellent student," Hilda said, as if that answered the question. "Now come Edmund, I must speak to you." She took his arm and led him out to the cloister walk.

"Well, well," one of the attendants whispered to Isabel. "That was some inspection."

"Indeed," said another. "How fitting that the baron's brother soon to be a priest should take an interest in a nunnery student."

Isabel turned away as a hot flush crept up her neck and throat. Where was Clare? She felt thoroughly flustered. Just then, as if by magic, Clare appeared behind her.

Clare lightly touched her elbow and whispered, "I want you to do something for me."

"Of course."

She slipped the cold metal of a key into Isabel's hand. "Go to my chamber and lock it. Anyone who checks must think I am inside sleeping."

"When will you be back?" said Isabel.

"Before Lauds," she whispered, "don't worry."

"I don't know which are your chambers," Isabel said. She knew the building, but had never been inside.

"The center door at the top of the stairs. Be careful not to let anyone see you. Everybody should be sleeping, so be very quiet. Go now." Clare had evidently not witnessed Isabel's exchange with Edmund, or, if she had, she had more pressing matters on her mind.

Isabel dropped the key into her waistband and slipped into the cloister walk. The night was cool, the air surprisingly crisp and clear. The round white moon bathed the cloister walk with luminous silver light.

Dim laughter came from the nearby gardens where the company had retreated. The sound of laughter was strangely out of place in the convent. The bright colors, music, and luscious food in the transformed warming room had made her feel that she had stepped into another world. How odd it was to glide through the cloister walk wearing a shimmering silk gown, listening to distant laughter.

Suddenly she heard the tap-tap of footsteps behind her. She whirled, thinking it was Clare. Instead, she found herself staring at the broad shoulders of Edmund as he advanced toward her.

"Wait," he said.

He stopped a few feet in front of her, and for a moment looked as if he forgot his purpose. "You have bewitched me. Perhaps you borrowed one of Alis's potions."

She knew from the glitter in his eyes that he was teasing. Yet the accusation of witchcraft was not one to be taken lightly.

"I've done no such thing," she said, unconsciously repeating the tone Alis had used during her trial.

"But you have. Thoughts of you haunt me constantly."

He moved closer to her. She shrank away.

"Come," he said, grasping her arm and pulling her toward the shadows. "No one will see us here."

Inwardly she braced herself against him, but curious and held spellbound by the moment, she allowed him to lead her away from the moonlit walk. The nearby rosebushes filled the air with a sweet musky smell. She knew she must run from him, and soon — very soon — she would.

She lifted her chin and said, "You aren't acting like a priest is supposed to."

"I've not taken final vows," he said.

"Not yet, but you will." She tried to shake herself free. "I won't be another girl you forget the moment you take your vows."

"I doubt you'd be so easy to forget, Isabel. Besides, you overestimate clerical vows. How many priests do you think give up women?"

"You all but admit—"

"I admit nothing." His face was hidden now in the darkness, but she felt the nearness of him.

"You not only want to be a priest, you want to be a dishonest one!"

"Who told you I want to be a priest?"

"You're going to be one," she said, faltering. "Aren't you?"

"Does it matter to you?"

"No." A baron's son, priest or not, could only mean trouble for her. All she needed was to be expelled from the convent and her life in Brotton — if she even dared return — would be sheer hell.

"I just want to kiss you." His whisper was hoarse, yet surprisingly humble. Intrigued, she held still. He bent forward and pressed his lips to her hair. He tilted back her face, slowly and very gently, and kissed her cheeks and eyes. She leaned into him and his arms tightened around her.

"No," she said, turning her face away. "I shouldn't be here." Her voice sounded distant and timid, even to her own ears.

"But you are. I shouldn't want you, but I do." His voice held a note of triumph, as if the matter were therefore settled.

He pressed her tightly to him, and her head spun as he kissed her again, this time deeply, dizzily.

A sudden rustling of the wind in the trees made her jump for fear someone was coming. Then she remembered the key tucked into her waistband. If she didn't lock Clare's door and Clare got caught — Isabel shuddered to think of what would happen.

"I've got to go," she said, fiercely shaking herself free. "If I'm missed, there will be trouble. I must leave."

"Will you meet me again?"

"I'd be a fool if I did."

"I'll find us a messenger," he said.

"But I just said —"

"I believe you will change your mind."

She scooped up her skirts and turned to run toward Clare's room.

CHAPTER 2

Edmund took aim and sent his arrow flying, watching it sail toward the target strapped to a tree at the far end of the meadow. The arrow struck just off center. Although it missed the bull's eye, his younger brother Albert drew in his breath, as if inspired by the sight of Edmund's superior marksmanship. Albert stepped forward and lifted his bow.

"No," Edmund snapped. "Loosen your arm. Let the arrow rest on your fingers, like this."

Albert tried to obey, but when his arrow flew, it curved to the left, missing the target by several yards.

"I just can't do it," Albert whined. He had very pale skin, brown hair, and the large soft brown eyes of a puppy.

"You're the Baron Decourcey now," said Edmund. "It's time you learned."

They were in the grassy meadow in front of the outer castle walls. It was late September, the grass and leaves overhead was tinged with the transparent yellow that meant the trees would soon turn. The day was windless but cool with lightest chill of autumn in the air.

Edmund let another arrow fly. This one, too, struck close but missed the center.

"Your aim is off today," Albert observed. There was no maliciousness in his voice. He fully accepted that Edmund

182

consistently hit the bull's eye whereas he had trouble hitting the target at all. "You must be thinking about Sunday."

On Sunday Edmund was supposed to take his final orders. Not knowing what else to do, he'd been biding his time, postponing his vows for months with one excuse after another, watching for his avenue of escape, knowing it must come. But the day he was to take his final vows was almost here and he still didn't know how he could delay them further without outright refusing to take them.

"I'm not thinking about Sunday at all," Edmund said. "I'm thinking about a beautiful girl I saw at the convent."

Albert slumped his shoulders. "Edmund!"

Edmund smiled. He always enjoyed shocking his brother. "I really must find a way to see her again. Perhaps I can sneak into the girl's dormitory."

"Edmund!"

The smile stayed on Edmund's face as he lifted his bow again and aimed. He thought about Isabel. God she was beautiful. He had forgotten how beautiful she was until he saw her again outside the convent gates. She was an interesting mixture of shy and bold. For all the demureness of her modest white convent shift, there was a tantalizing wildness in her eyes.

The sky had cleared and the early morning sun reflected off the red sandstone walls, making Edmund squint against the glare. He took aim and let his arrow fly. This time his arrow hit the mark.

"You must have put the girl out of your mind," said Albert.

"Not for a moment," Edmund said, grinning at Albert's perplexed expression. "I'll find a way to get to her."

"Edmund, really. You just try to be difficult. Why do you do it?"

"I can't help myself."

"Why? Everything's arranged for you. You have nothing to worry about. Why do you make trouble?"

"It's nothing I can explain."

"You're just nervous about Sunday."

"Think that if you want to," Edmund said, dropping his bow to the ground. Suddenly needing to be alone, he strode away, leaving Albert to practice by himself.

He wandered around to the east side of the outer wall where the precipice of the hill overlooked the valley which cradled the village of Brotton. Edmund found a grassy spot where he could lean against the sandstone wall. He closed his eyes and tipped his face into the sun. He sat still for a long time, thinking. By the time the evening bells rang, his mind was made up.

Next morning, Edmund was awake and dressed before the morning bells rang.

He strode past the grooms who slept in the anteroom of Albert's chamber. They awakened as he passed through, but they didn't bother trying to stop him. The night candle on the mantle in his brother's chamber had almost burned down, and the shutters were tightly closed. In the dim room, Edmund's shadow fell across the floor and loomed halfway up the wall.

He stood several feet from the bed and said, "Albert, wake up."

Albert groaned and rolled over.

"Wake up, Albert."

With another moan, Albert stretched himself to a sitting position and squinted at his brother.

"What are you doing here? It's the middle of the night." No sooner had he finished speaking when, from the courtyard, came the crowing of the roosters.

"I've come to tell you that I've decided not to take vows. I thought you might like to know."

"You've gone mad."

"I've made up my mind," said Edmund. "A church career is not right for me."

"You can't refuse."

"But I do."

Albert slid back down, dropping his head onto the pillow and staring blankly at the ceiling. "You can't refuse," he repeated, evidently not knowing what else to say. But there was no conviction or authority in his voice.

"After church, I will inform the chaplain of my decision, but I thought I should tell you first. After my announcement we can discuss my plans further, if you wish."

Edmund turned and left the room.

Within minutes the bells summoned the household to Mass. Edmund was the first to arrive in the small, vaulted chapel and take his place in the first row of polished curved benches. Soon the baron's retainers and high-ranking household servants entered and took their places in the back of the chapel.

Albert entered and, before taking the seat their father occupied when he was alive, he sent Edmund a pleading, desperate look. Edmund returned a confident smile. It was devilish of him to enjoy tormenting his brother so, but sometimes Albert was such a pitiful figure, looking so uncomfortable in their father's seat, it was hard to resist. Albert pulled at his tunic collar which seemed too tight.

Albert's mother — Edmund's stepmother, the dowager baroness — sat to Albert's right. She meddled very little in affairs of the barony, leaving all business matters to her son and his advisors. Edmund didn't care much for her, but he had no particular reason for disliking her. She regarded him as insignificant, the illegitimate older son who in no way threatened her son's inheritance, so she left him alone.

Edmund and his half-sister Hilda sat on the bench immediately to Albert's left. This morning Hilda wore a bright orange gown fringed with silver and a matching cap. Her wild and extravagant clothes amused Edmund and annoyed Albert.

The chaplain, an elderly dimply man with an open, easily approachable manner, entered last. Although he presided over the Mass, he seemed more like a secular servant because he kept the baron's seal. Part of his office was to write the baron's business and personal correspondence.

The chaplain began speaking in a dull monotone which Edmund easily ignored. His richly embroidered vestments of silver and gold outshone all other garments in the place, even Hilda's, and she loved to dress like a peacock. In Rome, Edmund had heard, the cardinals were even more richly attired than the secular princes.

After the service, when the others left the chapel, Edmund went to speak to the chaplain. "I have something of the utmost importance to speak with you about."

The chaplain closed the book in his hand. "What is it, Edmund?"

"I cannot become a priest. I will not take the vows."

For a moment, the chaplain simply stared. He hemmed a few times, but still said nothing.

"Why are you surprised?" asked Edmund. "You know I've never been happy about my future."

"If you refuse," his words were slow and deliberate, "you will find yourself in prison."

"I shall convince the king that I pose no threat, and that I have harmless reasons for wishing him to reverse his command."

"And what reason can that be?"

"There is a girl I wish to marry."

"Don't be ridiculous. If you want a girl, fine. You can't marry her of course, but have what you want."

Edmund wasn't prepared for this. He wasn't even sure he wanted to marry. While he'd thought of Isabel constantly, marriage had never entered his mind. He was looking for a convincing excuse, and he'd assumed the wish to marry was convincing.

"I want to marry her. And I don't want to become a priest."

"Don't be a fool. With your brother as a baron your career in the church is assured. With luck, you may even see Rome someday."

"My decision is made."

"Fine. When the king imprisons you for disobedience, you'll have plenty of time to contemplate your folly."

The chaplain turned and walked from the chapel, no doubt to find Albert and his advisors, who were probably already discussing the matter. Edmund was glad to have a few minutes alone. He was apprehensive, for he was no fool, but at the same time he felt wildly exhilarated and free.

Just then the door swung open and Hilda strode into the chapel, her face tense and angry, even the thick straw-colored hair that escaped from her cap frizzed wildly, as if to punctuate her fury.

"What is the matter, Hilda."

"You are taking advantage of Albert," she said, "because he doesn't know what to do."

"I'm not taking advantage of anyone. I'm doing what's right for me."

"Do you know what's right for you? Do you have a plan? Any idea what you'll do now?"

"First I plan to convince Albert to work with me, to mitigate the king's anger."

"Then what?"

"I will present my case at court. I'll convince the king that I pose no threat, and should be released from his command to enter the church. If necessary to show my good intentions, I will ask for a post serving him."

"How will you plead your case? He'll think you've been seized with a sudden madness, and he'll be right. How will you convince him otherwise?"

"I'll tell him the truth, that I have fallen in love, and simply wish to marry. How can he refuse so humble a request?"

"Marry?" Hilda blinked. "You're jesting."

"I'm perfectly serious."

"Who is she?"

"I prefer not to disclose her name until I have obtained her consent."

Hilda shook her head, aghast. "You're refusing vows and planning to present this case at court, and you don't even have the girl's father's consent? You're too much. You have no living; you have nothing. I do hope she has an enormous dowry, for your sake."

"I don't believe she has any dowry at all."

"Edmund," Hilda said, with a groan in her voice. "She has *nothing*?"

"Possibly a few chickens, but I can't be sure."

"That girl in the convent," she stated rather than asked. Her first response was to raise her hands to her temples in dramatic and exasperated gesture. "You don't fool me, Edmund Decourcey. I know you are looking for a good excuse. You may be rash and impulsive, but you're not stupid. I know very well that you haven't given a serious thought to marrying that girl. You haven't any idea what you want."

"I want to make my own choices."

CHAPTER 3

✦✦✦

Isabel locked Clare's door as she had been instructed and returned to the dormitory, too excited to sleep. *I'll find us a messenger,* Edmund had said. She wondered if he would.

A stern voice in her head warned her to take care. *I've heard stories about what knights do,* Jake had said. *They come around with presents and gold, and then leave you with a big belly.*

Next morning, as they dressed, the girls demanded a full report of her evening, drawing close to listen. Isabel described the sumptuous clothes and food, the flute-player and the minstrel.

"They say Edmund Decourcey is very handsome," said one of the girls.

Isabel tossed her rope of freshly braided hair over her shoulder, shrugged and said as lightly as she could manage, "I suppose."

The baron's entourage had left early that morning before breakfast, and with them gone, the place seemed bleaker. There were eight days left until her next free afternoon and they seemed interminably long.

Later, in the refectory, Clare stood alone, solemnly eating her bread as if nothing unusual had happened the night before. Isabel and Clare looked at each other, but weren't able to speak. Three days passed before they were able to steal a few moments in a corner of the cloister walk, hidden by an ivy-covered trellis.

"A thousand curses on my father for shutting me up here," Clare said.

"You will run away," said Isabel.

"Yes," Clare said, "as soon as we can. We will go to France, as Tristin promised."

Isabel tried to imagine what the convent would be like without Clare. How would she bear it?

Meanwhile, Edmund was in his room, waiting to see how his brother and the others would respond to his announcement that he would not take vows when a page entered his chamber with a sealed envelope. Edmund reached for the envelope, assuming it was a summons from his brother's advisors, but glance at the seal told him it was from Tristin. He broke the seal and scanned the lines, the contents coming as no surprise. "My visits done, and all's arranged," wrote Tristin. "I've found a cousin who's willing to help. May I stay at the Decourcey castle for a few days?"

Edmund understood the full meaning between the cryptic lines. Tristin had been visiting his mother's family in France, trying to arrange a place for him and Clare to go when they ran away.

"Prepare a room for Tristin of Northumberland," Edmund told the page. "Inform the steward and my brother that we will have an overnight visitor."

The page bowed and left.

Edmund felt envious of Tristin. He had known Tristin for years, since they were both young boys, for Tristin's mother and Edmund's stepmother had been friends. Edmund's stepmother had hoped Tristin would fall in love with Hilda, but there was no chance of that. Tristin's heart was set on the beautiful and seemingly unattainable Clare.

After Clare had been betrothed to the son of the duke of Northumberland, she and Tristin met in secret for months before they were caught. When their love and secret meetings were discovered, the duke of Northumberland refused to let his son marry her, and the wedding was cancelled. Her father then placed her in the convent.

It wasn't long before Albert's advisors summoned Edmund to them. Edmund arrived to find that his brother's advisors had already drafted a letter to the royal court requesting a personal audience for Edmund.

"Edmund, what is this nonsense I hear about a marriage?" Albert said in an irritatingly patronizing tone.

"What could be a more harmless reason for not wishing to take vows?"

"If you are released from your vows, we'll find you a suitable girl, one with a respectable dowry."

"I believe that might be nearly as dismal as a life in the church. I will choose my own bride, thank you."

"Edmund," the chaplain's voice was low and threatening, "if you wish to avoid prison, you must stop rebelling."

"He won't listen," snapped Albert's chief advisor. "If the king grants you an audience," he said, turning to Edmund, "you'd better be convincing. Any of your sarcasm, and you may find yourself in prison for flouting royal authority."

"I can be very convincing," said Edmund.

"I do hope so," said one of Albert's advisors. "Not that I really care. You're the one who will languish in prison, not any of us."

"Your concern for my welfare is touching."

"My concern is for the safety and well-being of the baron your brother, who has always shown himself to be the king's loyal subject."

Edmund inclined his head in something like a bow and clicked his heels together to indicate that he was leaving.

He found Hilda waiting for him in the anteroom. She looked up anxiously when he entered.

"What happened?"

"They're writing to the king to request an audience for me." Edmund studied her as he spoke, surprised that she was so concerned. Her next words made him know what was really on her mind.

"It is true that Tristin will be here tonight?"

She tried to sound casual, but the unnatural strain in her voice gave her away. So she still hoped, as her mother did, that Tristin would offer her marriage.

"He'll be here for just a short time," Edmund said. "I doubt any of us will have much chance to see much of him."

From the way Hilda's head dropped slightly, he knew she understood his meaning. He was thus surprised when she persisted. "He's not still thinking about Clare, is he?"

"Maybe he is."

She sniffed to show her disapproval. "He'll get over her sometime," said Hilda. "He'll have to, now that she's in a nunnery."

"Yes," Edmund lied.

Tristin arrived early that afternoon. Edmund met him at the gatehouse. The two squires and three servants who rode with Tristin were dusty and exhausted from the long journey, but Tristin seemed relaxed and exhilarated. His face was tanned to a deep bronze, his hair tossed carelessly back from his forehead, his smile easy and warm.

"We rode sixty miles today," he told Edmund as the Decourcey stable hands came forward to take the horses. He lowered his voice so only Edmund would hear and said, "Tonight when we leave, I'll need fresh horses, and an extra horse."

Edmund nodded, knowing the extra horse was for Clare. "You have your pick of the stables."

"At the port, I have a ship waiting to convey us to the continent. But now I need rest."

It was clear Tristin had no idea Edmund had announced his refusal to take vows.

"I've had rooms prepared," said Edmund. Then, after a pause, he asked, "Have you devised a way into the convent?"

Tristin smiled. "I have. My plan can't fail."

At the idea of Tristin sneaking into the convent, Edmund thought about Isabel, and felt a small thrill. After all, he had implied he wanted to marry her. The least he deserved was another look at her.

"Will you deliver a note to a girl named Isabel?"

"Of course. Isabel," he mused over the name, as if trying to remember if he knew her. "What's her family name?"

Edmund chuckled. "To tell the truth, I have no idea."

"I'm sure Clare knows her and will help."

Edmund's note was short and to the point: "Please meet me at the west gate after Matins. I just want to talk to you. Yours, Edmund Decourcey."

Much later, several hours after Vespers, Tristin came to Edmund's chamber door. "She received your note," he said, "and I think she'll be there."

"Did you see Clare?"

"Just for a moment. She thinks my plan will work; we'll leave tomorrow."

CHAPTER 4

✦✦✦

Edmund spent the afternoon waiting impatiently for nightfall. Thinking about Tristin's intended flight to France increased his restlessness. He was anxious, too, about how his request for an audience would be received by the king. He paced about, trying to decide how to pass the afternoon, when he struck upon the idea of visiting Alis.

The afternoon sun slanting low through the trees and the yellow-tinged leaves gave the forest a warm golden glow. Edmund walked down the rear of the castle hill where no trail cut through the dense woods and there was also no chance of him being seen.

Alis was sitting on a mat on the stoop of her hut, whittling. Honeysuckle and ivy climbed up the hut's and framed the doorway. A few chickens clucked about behind a tiny lean-to shed at the rear of the hovel.

As he approached, she smiled. In the short time since he had seen her, she seemed to have aged considerably.

"How are you feeling?" he asked. He sat in a grassy spot a few feet from her.

"I feel fine."

But she wasn't fine, he could see that. She seemed shriveled, her elbows protruding through her loosened skin. The hand that grasped the whittling knife seemed bony and awkwardly bent.

A hen cackled and poked around, brushing against her leg. She pushed it aside absent-mindedly. A brisk breeze sent a chill through Edmund, making him shiver. The sun in trees in the glad had deepened to a rich gold, the color of light through amber-stained glass.

"What is on your mind?" she asked.

"I've refused to take vows," he said.

"Good for you. What will you do now?"

"I will journey to the king's court and convince him that I pose no threat." After a pause, he said, "That girl is living in the convent now."

She seemed undisturbed by his abrupt chance of subject. The hint of a smile came to her face.

"Back when she was younger, you sent me into the exorcism ritual because you wanted me to see that girl," he said.

"That was part of my reason."

"I thought it was because you wanted me to stop the nonsense."

"I did want you to stop the nonsense, and I wanted you to see Isabel. I knew she would make an impression on you. How could she not?"

"You have put a spell on me concerning that girl."

"I did nothing of the kind."

It was her usual protest. She liked to pretend she had no magic, and that she couldn't read the thoughts of everyone around her. She had a piercing intelligence and acute perception, what the superstitious called the ancient Sight.

"Exactly who is she?" he asked. "What is your interest in her?"

"Isabel is no ordinary girl. Her grandmother was a tribal princess, so she was born royal. Now she has the education of an English lady. She is fit for a prince."

"You wanted her there? I didn't think you cared much for the church."

"The convent was a good place for her to spend these past few years. She got out of the village. She's learned to read and she's become familiar with the church's magic. The goddess's magic is more powerful of course, but she wasn't ready to know about the goddess."

"I may be seeing her tonight," Edmund said.

"You will take good care of her for me," Alis said.

The moon was full, just over the horizon when Isabel ran softly to the gate, which was locked with an enormous metal bolt. She would have been able to steal the key as she had done the first night she had visited Alis, but she was too cautious — and too wise.

Edmund stood watching her approach, his horse tied to a nearby low-hanging branch. He turned at the sound of her slippers tapping over the paved walk and smiled at the sight of her. Her hair, loose over her shoulders, caught the moonlight, shimmering like a flame.

She stopped a few paces from the gate and waited for him to speak. He grasped the metal bars with gloved hands.

"Thank you for coming," he said. "I had to see you again."

"Why?" Knowing she was safe because of the locked gate between them, she leaned forward against the bars.

"I had to see if you're for real," he said. "I thought maybe you were a vision the witch concocted to tease and torment me. If I touch you, will you vanish?"

"Why would she want to torment you?"

"To make me see the error and futility of entering the priesthood."

"I cannot imagine you as a priest."

"Neither can I."

He could smell the nearness of her. He wanted to reach forward and touch her hair. It struck him that although she was remarkably different from Alis, she had a similar aura of mystery. Alis was quiet and serene, Isabel had a wild air about her. He realized that he had never learned their connection.

"How do you know Alis?" he asked.

"She is my aunt. Well, I guess my great-aunt. My grandmother was her sister."

"I thought she had no kin in the village."

"None but me. My mother was born in York. Alis brought her, as a babe, to the village and left her on the church steps. My mother was believed to be a foundling from Threshfield. Nobody in the village knew of her relationship to Alis, and nobody knows of mine."

"Very smart, to keep it hidden."

"I was always in enough trouble, as it was. I used to be afraid to visit her. Now I am eager to go again. She's the kindest person with the most loving heart I've ever known."

Edmund pulled his gloves off, tucked them under his arm, and put his hands over hers. Her hands felt cool beneath his. As he rubbed her hands to warm her, she turned her face down. He would have lifted her chin, but he didn't want to let go of her hands.

She shivered again, then turned her magnificent eyes toward him.

"You are very lovely," he whispered, sliding his hands beneath her sleeves to caress her bare arms. He pulled her as close as he could, with just the metal bars between them. She was so close he could feel her breath and the beating of her heart. Then he touched her hair, which felt just as he had imagined it would, like heavy strands of silk.

"If you're a witch like Alis," he said, "please make this gate disappear."

He glanced into her face, expecting to see a smile, but instead he saw a bright glow in her cheeks and a shimmering luster in her eyes. How beautiful she was, full of joy, life and spirit, too full of intense, ungovernable emotions for the confines of these walls. She didn't belong in the convent. He wanted her out, with him.

"Who would ever have expected the little girl I saw that day in the village church to come to be a student here?"

"Lots of people have wondered the same thing, I'm sure," she said.

The skin of her arms felt like satin beneath his fingers. He wished he could kiss her. "Can you come outside?"

"First I'd have to steal the key."

"Will you?"

She tossed her hair back over her shoulder and smiled. "If I want to."

"Please, Isabel, steal the key soon. I may die if you don't."

"I must go back now," she said.

He nodded, but neither of them moved. He remembered the game she had invented under the waterfall as a young girl and he felt himself growing warm.

"Tomorrow night," he said, "at the same time, please come — and bring the key."

Next morning, Edmund was awakened by a knock at the door. Hurriedly Edmund rose and wrapped a robe about him. "Enter," he called.

It was Hilda, who seemed slumped and tired. "Tristin left already. I thought you might want to know."

His surprise was genuine. "Already? I knew his stay would be short, but I had no idea it would be this short."

"Will he be back?"

"Maybe not for a long time, Hilda."

She looked away.

"Forget about him. He's not right for you. He can't be."

She slumped even further and turned and left.

Minutes later, his most trusted page entered with a sealed note from Tristin. "We're on our way," Tristin wrote. "I dare not say more for fear of this letter falling into the wrong hands. I will write when I can."

Edmund imagined Tristin and Clare galloping away, as they must have done sometime in the night. This time the thought brought no envy. He was filled instead with a wild exhilaration. Good for you, he thought. Good for both of you.

That night, Edmund waited in the darkness of his room until he heard the Matins bells, then stealthily he made his way from the castle grounds to the meadow beyond. His horse was awaiting him where he had tied it earlier that evening. As he neared the monastery walls, he dismounted and led his horse behind him, afraid he might attract attention if he rode.

The gate was locked. He peered through the bars to see if Isabel was coming, but the grounds were deserted. He thought that perhaps she hadn't been able to get away, and felt acute disappointment.

At last she appeared at the far end of the cloister walk. Her hair was pulled into a heavy braid which hung forward over her shoulder, dangling past her waist. The simple white cotton bodice laced over her breasts and the white ribbon woven through her braid and tied at the end gave her the simple, but enchanting look of a woodland nymph.

She stopped in front of the gate and put her hands on the bars, near his. "Could you get the key?" he asked.

"The gateman was there every time I went by. I had no chance to take one."

He touched her hands, then slipped his arms through the bars. Smiling, she stepped close so that he could put his hands behind her back, where he could touch her neck and back and hair. He pulled her as close as he could, her breasts pressed against the gate. The smell of her was dizzying.

"Clare ran away this morning," she said.

"When did they find out?"

"No one knows yet. Tristin and his riding party disguised themselves as emissaries from her father's castle and said she was needed at home for a few days. The abbess will guess the truth as soon as she learns that Clare never went home."

"What did Clare tell you about her plans?"

"Not much. She said it's better if I didn't know too much, for my sake."

"She's wise. Listen to me, Isabel. If there is trouble of any kind, and if you are interrogated, you must not lie, about anything."

"Even my mother's origins?"

"Nobody is going to ask you about that because such a question wouldn't occur to them. They will ask about Clare, and maybe me. It's important not to lie. Clare was wise not to give you any details."

"Why would they care that much about Clare running away?"

"Clare has a powerful father who might make everyone squirm when the truth is discovered. Just take care. Tristin didn't even tell me where they were going."

"I don't know anything. Just that she ran away. We also heard what you did, refusing to take vows."

"So far I've offended no one except the king, and I hope to make amends as soon as I can. When I'm out of trouble, Isabel, I'll come back for you. Would you leave this cloister to be with me?"

She looked at him as if she couldn't believe his words. Then she said, "Yes, I would," she said. "If you mean it."

"Of course I mean it."

He turned her face up to his, cupping the back of her head in his hands. Through the bars, he kissed her, his cheeks pressed against the cold metal. She warmed under his hands. He touched her cheek and it was burning. Drawing back to look at her, he saw that she was flushed.

She started to speak, but stopped.

"What is it, Isabel?"

Her cheeks flushed deeper as she reached into her waistband and pulled out a key. She took another step back as she held it up for him to see.

"You have it," he said. "Why didn't you say so?"

Her eyes grew wider and he was astonished to see that she was frightened, for he had thought her impervious to fear. Something about the way she held herself, tense yet alert, almost eager, made him ache to hold her.

He reached his hand through the bars. "Give me the key," he said quietly, his voice gentle yet strained with emotion.

She dropped it in his hand. He unlocked the gate, creaked it open, and reached for her wrist. She came to him. He led her away from the gate, to the shadows of a nearby hedge of hawthorn. He put his cape on the ground, and drew her down with him. He kissed her and touched her, his touches gradually becoming more insistent and probing. She lost herself in the feel of his hands on her body until she felt a rush through her like an exquisite burst of energy. She was so stunned, she laughed out loud.

"What?" he asked.

"The game under the waterfall!"

He laughed with her, his arms around her, his hands stroking her as if she were something precious and delicate. They remained as long as they dared, until the position of the stars told his trained eye that it was nearly time for the Lauds bells.

"Can you steal the key again tomorrow night?" he asked.

"I'll try."

"I'll be here every night until I find a way to take you out of here."

"If the king forces you to take vows —?"

"I will never take vows. I don't want that kind of life."

"What do you want?"

"I want you, my beautiful Isabel. Nothing else."

CHAPTER 5

After Edmund galloped away, Isabel turned back toward the dormitory. With Clare gone and no free afternoon coming up to visit Alis, there was nobody to whom she could tell the delicious secret of his love. During the days, she had to carry it with her, trying not to blush and smile at odd times while she remembered his embraces, fighting to keep her mind on whatever task was at hand. But now, alone in the dark cloister walk with no one to see her, she could throw her arms wide and giggle silently. The laughter bubbled inside her, and she thought she would burst with happiness.

She entered the convent and locked the gate behind her. At the sound of approaching footsteps, she whirled around to face two monks walking toward her with long, purposeful strides. A third one, with walnut-colored hair striped with gray and clipped into a perfect bowl around his head, came from the direction of the watch tower.

When she realized what was happening, her heart beat erratically. The furthest thing from her mind just then had been getting caught. She had stopped worrying about it completely. With Edmund who seemed to fear nothing, and the example set by Clare, who entirely ignored the strict rules, Isabel herself had forgotten the dangers of getting caught.

The monk with walnut-colored hair stopped in front of her and said, "Give me the key."

She took the key from her waistband and dropped it into his waiting palm. Then he turned, saying, "Come along."

Two monks walked on either side of her, and the third came behind, as if she were a dangerous criminal. They were so solemn it was absurd.

"Where are we going?" she asked.

When nobody answered, she repeated the question. Again they all remained silent. She was filled with a sudden confusion when she realized they were taking her toward the monastery. Women seldom entered that part of the complex.

"Please tell me where we're going," she asked, but they continued to act as if she hadn't spoken. As they passed through the main gate into the monastery grounds, her pace slowed. They led her through a doorway into a narrow corridor lit by torches lining the wall. At the bottom of a stairs was a windowless cell containing only a thick sleeping pallet and blanket and a writing desk. After she entered, they locked the door from the outside, leaving her alone in the dim room.

The only light came in through a tiny slit of a window cut in the door, throwing strange shadows across the room. She peeked through the slit, then called, "Hullo? Is anyone there?"

The way her voice echoed down the hall made her feel she was alone in the world. No answer came. Of course there was a rule of silence and anyone around would ignore her call. She had heard that low-ranking monks lived in cells such as these, but it seemed more like a prison. The smell of the interior told her the walls had been freshly plastered and the floor rushes clean, but the low ceiling and sparse furnishing gave the room a gloomy air.

Without a doubt she would be expelled, shamed and humiliated. She paced back and forth, unaware that she was tugging at her hem until she heard the rip of cloth. She hoped Edmund would find out quickly that she'd been caught.

Exhausted, she lay on the pallet, putting her head on the folded blanket. She must have slept, but she remembered nothing until the pre-dawn Lauds bells. She waited, but nobody came for her. For the first time since her arrival at the convent, she was not present for the singing of Lauds.

After that she slept again, but this time she tossed restlessly, her thoughts wandering through strange and disturbing dreams, the details of which she forgot the moment she opened her eyes. She was left with a queasy, uneasy feeling heightened by the fact that she had no idea what the hour was.

Some time later she heard the sound of a key turning in the lock. The door swung open, and a servant brought in a small loaf of black bread and a cup of ale. After he set it down on the table he turned to stare at her. He was about twenty and very thin, with hardened, narrowed eyes.

"You're in serious trouble," he said.

"Oh, really," she said. "What sort of trouble?"

"You were caught last night with the gardener and you helped one of the nuns run away."

"You're wrong about both."

"That isn't much bread, you know. I can help you get more."

"I don't want more. I want you to leave."

He stepped toward her, and like a caged animal she backed toward the writing desk.

"I wouldn't think you'd be so coy," he said. "From what I've heard about you."

He took another step forward. She grabbed the cup and flung the contents in his face. Sputtering, wiping the ale from his face with his sleeve and shaking it from his hair, he hissed, "Fool."

"Get out or I'll scream."

"You're a fool," he said. "I'll have to report to the abbot that you attacked me like a wolf."

"Tell him what you want, just get out."

After he slammed the door behind him, his footsteps fading away, she tore off a chunk of bread with trembling hands and took a bite, but it felt like sawdust in her mouth and she had trouble swallowing it. She flung the loaf back onto the desk, and resumed her pacing. The prime bells rang, and what seemed like days later, the mid-morning Terce bells.

She nibbled again at the bread. The smell of the spilled ale made her thirsty.

Another servant entered shortly after the Sext bells with more bread, ale, and a piece of chicken.

He looked at the spilled ale and laughed. "Rob told me what happened. You're a fiery one, eh?"

She didn't answer. He tossed her a rag to clean the mess.

The hours dragged by. Every four hours the bells tolled but she lost track of which bells they were. Without an outside window she became so disoriented that she had no idea whether it was day or night. She began to feel she had always been in the cell and always would be.

Listlessly she counted her paces, reciting verses to the rhythm of her tapping feet. She felt herself growing agitated, wanting to scream or pound the walls with her fist like a mad woman. But she knew that if she exhibited any such behavior, someone would say she was possessed by the devil.

Meanwhile, an hour or so after sunup, a troop of riders thundered up the road to the castle. When Edmund first caught sight of them, from the high window of a stair tower, they were far off in the distance and could have been any small retinue. But as they approached, he knew from the quality of their mounts, the finest of steeds, and the way they glittered all silver and gold, boldly displaying the royal insignia that they were from the king's court.

Edmund was surprised to see them so soon, and he was astonished to see so impressive a riding party. He had expected perhaps a single messenger. They paused to speak to the porter, then continued past the outer gate and entered the keep, with none of the usual timidity usually exhibited by visitors.

Albert was already busy with his round of conferences. Edmund knew the visitors would be taken immediately to his brother and soon after he would be summoned to hear the king's response.

He went to his brother's antechamber to wait but felt too restless to sit. For the first time he thought perhaps his mission wouldn't be as easy as he had imagined. His father, after all, had been a rebel and his mother a foreigner executed as a witch.

He stood at the window overlooking the valley. The yellow meadows and green hills stretched out to the horizon with roads winding along the ridges and plowmen in the fields.

At last the door to the anteroom door opened. "You may enter, sir," a page told him.

Edmund stepped inside. Albert, who sat in their father's chair, said, "Come forward."

It was always a bit ridiculous to hear his brother give commands, which he did only when officials were around. Surely everyone could hear how stiff and awkward he was.

Edmund crossed the room and bowed low to the royal messenger.

"The king has granted you an audience. He understands your request, and has several services for you to perform on his behalf. I have brought a retinue to escort you to the court. We shall leave before the midmorning bells."

"So soon?"

"We will live by midmorning."

Back in his room, he hurriedly wrote a letter to Isabel. He explained that he was on his way to the king's court. If everything went as he planned, he would return to make her his wife. He added several lines imploring her to be patient.

He started to seal it with his own seal, but paused. Better not to reveal himself as the sender. That way, it may prove easier to smuggle in to her. He sealed the letter with plain wax, and called for Robin.

"See that Isabel gets this letter," he said. "She's a student in the convent."

Robin bowed and promised he would. That done, Edmund packed his personal belongings: his best cloak and gloves, an extra doublet, and several pairs of finely woven hose. As his servants packed and prepared for the ride, he slipped down the back of the castle hill to the forest glade.

As he entered the glade, Alis emerged from the hovel, leaning on a walking stick, her hair clasped behind her neck, her face whiter than he had ever seen it.

"Let me help you," he said, taking her arm. She leaned against him as he ducked into the doorway and led her inside to sit by the low fire.

"You can't live out here anymore," he said. "I'll find you a room in the castle."

"I don't think you're in a position to offer any such thing," she said, "given the trouble you're in."

"I can find you a better place to live."

"No. Now, tell me what you plan to do."

"I will go to court," he said, "to plead my case in person.

"What is your case?"

"I cannot take vows because I wish to marry."

"Yes," she said calmly. "See how wise Maya was when she told me to make the villagers believe Nan was a foundling? Now nobody can trace Isabel's roots to the Holy Isle."

"I don't understand why I cannot find you a better place to live."

"There is no better place to live then here, in the ancient ring of stones. I will live my last days on earth content to know Isabel will be well cared for. She's right for you, Edmund. It's hard to imagine another girl who could match your courage and spirits, but Isabel can. You're both so young and so right for each other, it's frightening."

Her voice was packed with such emotion, and she looked off into the distance as if it were someone else she was thinking of. He suspected she was thinking of his father.

"He loved you," Edmund said. "I know he did, I could tell from the way he looked when he said your name. But it wasn't his way to talk about such things."

The calm settled back over Alis's face. "By the time your father and I found each other, it was too late. He thought he loved me the way he had your mother, but his love for me was too full of need, and his actions constrained by fear. He'd had the courage once to rebel against everyone: king, army, and country, but he couldn't risk everything again. That's why he wanted you to be cautious."

"I have no idea how long I will be at the court. If I succeed in being released from my vows, I still have much to negotiate. I need to find some means for Isabel and I to live, so that I can marry her. Perhaps if I am granted some minor post away from the court, but such posts are difficult to obtain."

"Would money help?"

"Money always helps," he said, "particularly at court. There are doormen to bribe, and countless other expenses."

She rose, and took a few steps to a corner of the hovel where she removed a mat, reached beneath it, and drew out a burlap sack which was tied with a heavy rope. Returning, she spilled it in front of Edmund. It was filled with gold and silver coins, and several heavy silver amulets."

"Where did you get this?"

"The amulets were my sister's," she said. "The silver my sister and I earned in York, many years ago. The gold," she hesitated, "the gold, your father — I planned to use it for Isabel somehow, so I give it to you, if you think it will help."

"It will help."

"Then you must take it and spend it as you wish. Except the amulets. Those are too precious to part with."

"Then you must let me do something for you. There must be something you need, if you insist on living in the forest."

"I need nothing. Every day I age a few more years, and there's nothing you can do about that. You would be shocked to know how old I am, my dear Edmund. I've not much longer in this world. With your father gone, I've outlived everyone who was here before me. There's no one left who remembers my arrival or my marriage. This generation knows only the stories, and the rumors, and I have no defense against those."

"I have a page who I would trust with my life," Edmund said. "I will have him check on you every day."

"When I die," she said, "I want to be buried here."

"Don't talk about dying."

"At my age, after the things I've done and seen, death holds no terror for me. I only want to know that Isabel will be cared for."

"I give you my word on that."

"And I accept it. You've grown into a remarkable young man. Your father would be proud, because, you see, once, before either of us knew him, he was very much like you. Farewell, Edmund. May the gods go with you and protect you."

CHAPTER 6

Isabel didn't know how much time passed before the sound of approaching footsteps told her that several people were coming. Rising, she turned to face the door as it opened. In the doorway stood the same monk with the striped hair who had led her to the cell, trailed by two others who she didn't recognize.

"Come along," he said, keeping his eyes averted so as not to look at her, as if the sight of her were offensive.

She knew from the position of the sun that it was early morning. As they led her across the open garth, Isabel's eyes drank in everything around her. The pure exquisite light of the sun, the deep green leaves now touched with the reds and yellows of autumns. How lovely the fresh air was, filling her chest with a brisk, clean feeling. She had a hard enough time suffering the confines of the daily convent routine, but the cell was unbearable.

They approached a stone building with a magnificent marble staircase leading to the door. The interior was more luxurious than anything she had seen in the convent: polished wood walls, delicate rose petals strewn thickly among the rushes, pewter statues of the Virgin Mother. Through a large double door, the abbot sat on a carved chair resembling a throne, surrounded by four elderly, bespectacled monks. His manner was grim, his steely gray hair gave him an air of authority.

After Isabel entered, one of the monks locked the door behind her. The locked door seemed as ridiculous as their overly solemn manner. She couldn't run away even if she wanted to. How would she get out of the monastery?

The monks went forward to speak to the abbot but they were too far away for her to make out their whispered words. To stop her limbs from trembling, she tensed them, clenching her fists by her side. Everything will be all right, she told herself. With Edmund's love, she was safe. As long as she wasn't accused of witchcraft or heresy, she would live to see the outside of these walls.

At last the monks turned to her and indicated that she should approach.

"I understand," the abbot said gravely as she stepped forward, "that you were in the woods with one of the gardeners."

His words so took her so by surprise. "No, sir, I wasn't," she said. "I was with Edmund Decourcey."

"The baron's brother? You cannot expect me to believe that. What would a baron's son want with a common villager?"

Wildly Isabel's eyes sought the monk with the striped hair who had been in the watch tower. Surely he had seen Edmund gallop away.

"He rode away, toward the castle," she said. "Please tell him."

"A gardener," the monk said. "I saw him myself."

At that, Isabel became too confused to sort out what was happening. Had the monks lied to the abbot? Or were they all simply trying to torment her?

"It's true," she insisted.

"Even if it is," said the abbot, "and I'm sure it isn't, you shouldn't be proud of being his whore." He paused for a moment, as if to let the force of that word hang in the air.

"Who you were with in the woods does not concern me. We have the more pressing matter of the runaway nun. What was her name?" he asked one of the monks.

"Clare of the Weston estates," he answered. "Eldest daughter of the Earl of Weston."

"Yes, yes," the abbot said with a slight wave of his hand, as if her name were too inconsequential for him to remember. When he turned back to Isabel, his manner became stern and forbidding. "Where in France has she gone?"

"I have no idea."

Surely they would be able to see that she spoke the truth, but the abbot glared at her and said, "If we suspect you of lying, we can send you to prison."

"That's all I know."

The abbot rose to his feet. Although he stood several paces away, his enormous body seemed to tower over her. He moved slowly, but he seemed tensed with an animalistic force.

"You are lying," he said.

She felt herself ready to crumple. From somewhere she found the strength to lift her chin and stare into his face. For several eternal minutes he stood like a statue, then he turned to the nearby monk.

"How did such a whore get into this school?"

The monk merely shook his head, as if in sad realization that a terrible mistake had been made, but he said nothing, for the abbot didn't seem to expect an answer.

"Take her back to the cell until we decide what to do with her."

They led her back across the garth. She was seized with a wild impulse to run. How could she endure another hour in that cell without completely losing her mind?

Several more days passed with no visitors except servants bringing food and fresh linen shifts for her to wear. Then sometime later, a key turned in the lock, so quietly and gently that she knew it couldn't be a servant bringing food. To her surprise Sister Agathe entered the cell, alone.

She was a large, stout woman with friendly, florid features and watery blue earnest eyes. She sighed, standing erect, her back inches from the wall, and said, "Are you prepared to tell us where Clare is?"

"She's in France with Tristin. That's all I know."

"Where in France?"

"I don't know."

"You must think very hard, Isabel. Try to remember if she gave any clue about where she might go. Think back over each conversation you had with her before she left."

Sister Agathe's manner, so friendly and coaxing, was entirely different from the abbot's. Edmund had told her not to lie, and so far she hadn't, but she kept her mind blank. If there was a hidden clue that would help them find her, she didn't want to remember it.

"All I know is that she may have gone to France.".

"I understand, Isabel, that you were caught with a gardener."

"I was with Edmund Decourcey."

Sister Agathe shook her head sadly, as if Isabel had been seeing visions.

"It's true," Isabel insisted. "You will learn it's true because he's in love with me and is going to find a way to take me out of here."

"I have something to show you," Sister Agathe said. Isabel noticed that she carried a piece of rolled parchment tied with a string. Slowly and deliberately, she unrolled it and handed it to her.

At the top and bottom was the baron's seal. In beautiful Roman style script was written: "The Baron Decourcey is proud to announce the entrance of Edmund Decourcey into the church. His final orders were taken this morning, the nineteenth day of September, the year of grace 1148. He will enter order of — "

Isabel dropped the parchment, unable to read further. "It's not true."

"I'm afraid it is," said Sister Agathe. "I'm sorry to have to tell you this, but the instructions to say you were with a gardener came from the castle. It was to protect Edmund."

"Then everyone knows the truth!"

"Under orders from the castle, to protect Edmund. Edmund himself wanted it that way." She produced several letters containing orders, threats to the convent, that they must hush up the story. Edmund had left, and he wouldn't return until he had completed his vows.

"It's not true," Isabel repeated.

"Then where is he, this lover of yours? He's not at the castle, that much I can promise you."

"How can I know where he is? I've been locked up here, and haven't been able to see him."

"Here's someone who can tell us where he's been." She gestured toward the door.

To Isabel's surprise, Hilda moved into the doorway. She stood just inside, erect and proud.

"I'm sorry to tell you the truth," she said coldly. "Edmund was only looking for an excuse. He thought if he claimed to want to marry a village girl, his reasons would not be seen as political. I'm sorry if my brother has led you to hope for the impossible."

"That's a lie!" Isabel said. Then: "What's going to happen to me? Why am I being left in here?"

"We are awaiting further orders," said Sister Agathe. She and Hilda swept from the room. The key turned in the lock, and Isabel was again left in silence.

Sister Agathe's final words puzzled her as much as everything else. Further orders from whom? Had the abbot appealed to a higher authority? It was hard to believe that either Clare running away or her being caught with Edmund was as important as that.

Isabel didn't know how many more days had passed before she was brought copying work to do. "No sense leaving her idle," Sister Agathe had remarked to her companion when they brought her a stack of blank parchment, a writing quill, candles she could work by, and a text to be copied. Sister Agathe's manner this time was more in keeping with her character, for her words were clipped and haughty.

Isabel was afraid to let her relief show for fear they would take the text away. As soon as she was alone again, she sat at the desk and began work. With something to concentrate on, the time flew by, with the hours between the tolling bells seemed shorter.

She now measured the passing days by how much copying she did. She wondered if the other girls wondered what had happened to her. Surely they must have heard something of the trouble she was in. Most likely they'd heard the gardener story. She knew well that rumor of anything interesting spread quickly through the convent.

As she worked, Hilda's words tugged at her. Could any of what she said be true?

CHAPTER 7

Isabel had just finished a meal of cooked oats and apples when the key turned in the lock and Sister Anne entered.

"You are to return to the dormitory, gather together your personal possessions, and straighten your chest, leaving it exactly as you found it. The abbess will be waiting for you in the warming room to give you further instructions."

Without waiting for a reply, Sister Anne turned and left, leaving the door slightly opened.

Dazed, Isabel looked one last time around the tiny cell which she felt she had occupied for years. Then she hesitantly walked into the narrow corridor and up the stairs.

How strangely bright and foreign the sunlight seemed, pouring in through the open door. During the time she had been in the cell, the trees had deepened to shades of red and yellow. The air was brisk, cold, and invigorating. The gate separating the monastery from the convent was closed but unlocked. Nobody was around as she opened the gate and stepped into the convent.

Once inside the nunnery, she paused to reorient herself, then walked toward the dormitory.

The girls were dressing, moving silently about the room. Isabel stood on the threshold watching them until one by one, they turned to stare. Sister Anne must have forgotten that the girls would still be in the room, or surely she would have waited to send Isabel when the room would be empty.

Ignoring their curious stares, Isabel crossed the room and bent over her trunk to straighten it, as Sister Anne had instructed. Behind her, she was aware of the girls filing out of the room. When she thought the last of them had gone, she glanced back.

To her surprise, Elizabeth stood a few paces behind her, waiting, her expression gentle and inquiring. Her words came out in a rush. "I've wanted to tell you that I'm sorry for the way I treated you when you first came here."

"I know," Isabel said. "It's all right. That was a long time ago."

"Clare was your friend. She would have tried to protect you from this, if she could have. If she were still here, this wouldn't have happened."

Isabel smiled at how simple Elizabeth thought things were. She imagined Clare as an all powerful saint who would always have her way. She didn't realize that if caught, Clare would be in far more trouble than Isabel.

"Thank you," Isabel said.

"And," Elizabeth went on, her voice hardening, "if you say Edmund Decourcey is in love with you, I believe you."

"Everyone must have heard the whole story," Isabel murmured, more to herself than Elizabeth.

"We heard that you were caught with the gardener but you insist it was Edmund Decourcey. The abbess says if Clare had not become friends with someone like you, she never would have done something so dreadful as run away."

"How little she knows." Or, Isabel silently corrected herself, how little she chooses to know

"Did you know a letter arrived for you?" Elizabeth asked

"A letter? From who?"

"I don't know. The abbess burned it."

When footsteps came down the hall, Elizabeth said, "Farewell, Isabel, and good luck."

A voice boomed from the doorway. "Elizabeth, for shame," Sister Agathe said. "Were you speaking to that village whore after you were strictly forbidden not to do so."

"No, Madam," she said. "I'd forgotten something, that's all."

"Well, be off."

Isabel hid the amulet Alis had given her in her stocking. The amulet and a shawl she had woven and dyed herself were her only personal possessions. She wrapped the shawl around the plain linen shift she wore.

Sister Anne appeared in the doorway. "The abbess is waiting."

Isabel nodded and followed her to the abbess's office. The abbess was bent over a writing desk when Isabel entered the room. She looked up at Isabel, but then continued her work for several minutes before turning and saying, "You are expelled from this school. I'm sorry you were ever admitted in the first place. That is all." Turning to Sister Anne, she said, "Escort her out."

I certainly won't miss this place, Isabel thought as they passed through the convent grounds.

The question was: Where would she go now? Not knowing what else to do, she set off in the direction of Brotton. When she saw the castle, perched on its distant hilltop, she stopped. If she walked the perimeter of the valley, she could bypass the village, climb the hill to the castle, and see if she could learn anything about Edmund.

As she walked toward the castle, the sunshine and brisk air revived her spirits, making her feel alive again. The days and weeks in the cell seem like a vivid, but unreal nightmare.

She approached the gatehouse. The guard turned idly, watching her without interest.

"Excuse me sir," she said, "could you tell me please if Edmund Decourcey is here?"

"What's it to you?"

"I'm a friend of his."

"He's not here. He's been gone for weeks."

"Can you tell me please where he is?"

"If you were a friend of his, you would know he's at the king's court, where he's likely to stay. Now be off before I call someone to get rid of you."

"When will he be back?" she persisted.

"That's none of your concern. Get away from this gate."

She backed away. Alis would know when he was coming back and why he was taking so long. Edmund had told her that there was a back way down the hill to the glade. Better to try to find her way through the woods than to risk someone seeing her enter the black forest.

That part of the forest was darker than she had anticipated. She wandered about for a long time, believing herself lost, trying to point herself in the right direction, using the position of the sun when it peeped through the branches as her guide. At last she burst into the open sunlight of the glade, the blinding light gleaming from the white stones.

The unearthly stillness told her instantly that the glade was deserted. The door to the hut was ajar, pulled slightly from its place, as if the wind had blown it but nobody had bothered to set it back properly.

"Alis," she called, timidly approaching the hovel. There was no response.

Inside, the mats were placed neatly on the floor, the pallet rolled out for sleeping, the sheepskin blanket folded neatly in the corner. The lids of the pot-bellied jars were all in place, as were the fire irons and cooking kettle near the hand-carved clay mantle. The thin layer of dust that covered the stool and tiny rickety table told Isabel that Alis had been gone for days, possibly a week or longer.

"Alis," she whispered, her chest constricting with fear. Where on earth could she be? Feeling that the musty air of the hovel would suffocate her, she stumbled out to the stone ring and found a place to sit, leaning against one of the cold stones, hugging her knees to her chest for warmth.

If she waited, she told herself, Alls would return. Perhaps she had gone to pick berries or fetch water.

When Isabel realized that she was shivering from the cold, she went to fetch the blanket from the hovel. Even wrapped in the blanket, she continued to shiver. When she grew hungry she picked a few turnips from Alis's garden and raided her jars for nuts.

In a short time she felt as agitated and listless here as she had in the cell. She paced about to shake her anxiety and keep warm. How could Alis bear to live here, all alone? Once, when she stopped and absorbed the magical beauty of the light through the trees, she sensed the comfort and solace Alis derived from this place. Nonetheless, the thought of living here like Alis seemed to Isabel like a lonely prison sentence.

At last, when the deep slant of the sun told her the afternoon was growing to a close, she knew Alis would not return. She folded the blanket, replacing it where she had found it, and took the trail which led directly to the whortleberry thicket, too dazed to care if anyone saw her emerging from this part of the forest.

It was not until she was on the main road that led past the church that anyone noticed her. She passed John Durbey, Jake's cousin who had seen them together that long ago day on the hillside. He chuckled and said, "We heard you'd be returning soon."

Without a word, Isabel continued past him.

One of Meg's sisters was at the well with the wheelwright's wife. Isabel knew from the way they stared, smiling in a superior and irritating way, that they, too, had heard the story. A group of boys played in the road, batting a lambskin ball around with a stick. The group of them fell silent as she passed.

When she found her father's cottage empty, she guessed that he and her brothers were still in the fields. She climbed the ladder to the loft, and discovered her sleeping space gone. They had moved the hanging blankets which divided the space and expanded their own sleeping quarters, absorbing hers, as if she would never return. Her crate was now filled with someone else's clothes, and her blanket was folded on one of her brother's pallets.

She climbed back down from the loft just as the door opened and her brother Marc entered. She started to say something, and then stopped when her father came up behind him.

"You thought you were so smart," her father said, "going to that school, like you were better than the rest of us, didn't you?"

"My things are gone," she said. "Where am I going to sleep?"

"Find yourself a place."

"My pallet's gone."

"Then you'll have to make another one, won't you." He kicked off his heavy boots and said, "Acts like she's a princess."

"We weren't surprised to hear about you and that gardener," Mark said. "We were just surprised it took you so long to get expelled."

I wasn't with the gardener, she started to say, but stopped. Their laughter would be worse to bear than their scorn.

"What we're going to do with her now, I don't know," her father muttered as he pulled the cooking pot down from the peg. "She's going to be the ruin of this family. There's hardly money to feed her, much less dower her. And with the scandals she's caused, not a respectable village boy would marry her."

And there's not one of them I'd even want to marry, Isabel thought. How surprised they would all be when Edmund returned for her. She just hoped he would come back soon.

Then came the nagging doubt. What if he never came back? Clare had told her his reputation with ladies. Suppose, just suppose, she had been a fool, and he was gone forever.

CHAPTER 8

Everything to do with village life was more difficult now than before she had gone to live at the convent. The exhausting work wore her out as never before. Knowing Latin and being able to quote church scholars was very little use in the fields. She hated attending church, with everyone gazing at her as if to say: "You thought you were so smart, so special, but here you are, in trouble again." She dreaded fetching water each morning from the well when she often saw Meg and her sisters. They ignored her as if she had never been away, as if she had not learned to read and write in the nunnery like a lady.

The situation worsened when one of the villagers claimed to have seen her emerging from the dark forest. "It was dark," he had reported, "and difficult to see her face, but it certainly looked like her. And who else could it have been?"

Nonetheless she returned often to the glade, hiding her visits the best could, but Alis had not reappeared. The layer of dust accumulated on the furniture and jar lids until Isabel found a cloth to clean it off. She pulled the stray weeds from the garden and fixed the door hinge.

She climbed the hill to the castle to try to find out something about Edmund. On her second trip, she found a new guard at the post, a much younger man with an open, friendly face.

"Can you tell me please," she asked, "when Edmund will be back?"

"He's gone to the king's court," he said, as if that answered her question.

"I know that, sir, but do you know when he'll be back?"

"Impossible to say. He may stay there."

"Do you know anything about Alis, the village witch?"

At her question, he turned to gaze curiously at her. Her chest tightened when she realized what she was risking by asking such a question. To her relief, he showed no fear at her question, merely a deep curiosity.

"Edmund's left orders that she's to be cared for."

Thank goodness for that, Isabel thought. "Where is she?"

"I'm not sure, really. She was sick, and a few of Edmund's men had to obey his orders and see that she's tended to, but I don't know where she is."

"Maybe she's in the castle," Isabel said.

"Maybe," he said. "Probably not." His stare became intense, making her acutely uncomfortable. "What's your name?"

"Never mind," she said, backing away. "Thanks for your help." She turned and walked down the road.

As time passed, and she readjusted to life in Brotton, she began to think Edmund would never return. At times she felt that she had dreamed their hours together.

One day she returned to the glade, and discovered a mound of dirt between the gardens and the lush hawthorn bushes which marked the trail leading back to the village. The ground was freshly dug.

Isabel stared for a dazed moment before she absorbed the fact that it was Alis's grave. Her thoughts suddenly jumbled, and she felt she must be dreaming. When and where had Alis died? Surely Edmund's men had brought her back to bury her here? If only she could speak to his men. If only he would return.

A strange emptiness, like a numbness crept over her. Wandering over to the stones, she settled herself in the spot where Alis had liked to sit.

It didn't seem possible that Alis was dead. It seemed that she would appear at any moment, from one of the trails leading through the woods, or from the hovel. She would smile the way she always did, with her air of quiet dignity. They would talk; Alis would straighten up the whole confusion of what had happened to Edmund.

"Where is Edmund? Is he coming back?" Isabel whispered. Had Alis been here still, she would have responded.

"Of course," Alis would surely have said.

One evening, several months after her expulsion from the convent, a thick-set, red-faced man with a shock of orangish hair came to the door of their cottage. He had come before, gazing at Isabel with a mixture of curiosity and contempt, but she had paid little attention to him. She should have taken more notice, for they rarely had visitors. He was a stranger, probably from a nearby village with kin in Brotton. He wore a tattered tunic and mud-splattered boots.

Isabel hid in the back entryway. She watched curiously through the darkened kitchen as her father and the man greeted each other. She was tense and still, her eyes fixed forward like an animal on the verge of flight.

"Six shillings," the red-faced man said.

"She's worth more than six," her father said. "She spins and cooks. Twelve."

For the space of a heartbeat, Isabel stood motionless, shrinking inwardly as the meaning of their exchange crept up on her.

"Eight," said the man, "and no more. You'd be well rid of her. She was thrown out of the convent and keeps company with witches. Who else'll want her?"

Her father chuckled. "Plenty want her, and you know it. Twelve shillings."

Isabel backed further into the shadows, inching her way to the back kitchen door as quietly as possible.

"Twelve," agreed the man, "but I don't promise to marry her."

No, she thought. He wouldn't dare! But she knew he would. Her fists clenched of themselves as she told herself that she refused to be sold like crude wools in the harbor at Grimsby.

She lifted the heavy wooden latch and creaked open the kitchen door. Glancing one last time at the soot-blackened kitchen walls and sparse oaken furniture she stealthily backed into the darkness of the garden. For months, since her expulsion from the convent, she had wanted to go. Now she had no choice. She had about her shoulders her heaviest shawl with the amulet tucked in the hem. She couldn't be better prepared had she known this would happen.

She picked up her skirt and tried to step gently, but twigs and dead leaves crunched and snapped. She stepped through the garden she had carefully tended, but the night was too dark to see the neat rows of herbs and vegetables. The moon was a transparent sliver, veiled with soft white clouds. Droplets of water collected around her hairline from the heavy mist and the softened leather of her boots grew damp. The grass, sown thickly with buttercups, was soft and springy.

She came down into the gully, divided by a narrow spring, and stepped carefully over a bridge of loose stones. At the slightest noise she froze to hide herself, not knowing if she hid from a man or an animal. Soon she would be at the river where the ground was damp and the leaves quieter. There she would be safe.

She would go to York, maybe even all the way to London. In the city she would find a way to live.

The whisper of water came from the distance. The ground softened as she neared the river, and there came the scent of the damp, mucky riverbed. The whispering trees arched over her. All around her she sensed hundreds of breaths, some of animals, and some of spirits. When she listened carefully, she could hear the song of the spirits in the wind. They sang a low, hollow note that was both mourning and comforting. Was Alis among them?

"I've run away, Alis," she said softly, but there was no need to look for token of her response. She knew that Alis would approve.

After reaching the river, she walked until the moon was ready to set, then she made a bed out of dried leaves. Fitfully she dozed in and out of sleep. When at last the eastern sky grew light she felt that she hadn't slept more than a few hours.

She walked steadily, stopping every few hours to gather berries or whatever she could find to eat. When she found a tree bearing ripe apples, she ate until she couldn't eat another bite. After gathering as many as she could carry in her bundle, she walked on.

On the third day she came to a fishing village. The cottages ranged up a hillside overlooking the river, with the church perched high on the hill, its white-washed bell tower peeping through the red and yellow foliage.

She stayed amid the brush that lined the riverbed, hoping to keep out of sight of both the fishermen and the cottagers. Her braid had loosened, and she had no comb, so she pulled her hair into a long tail that hung, tangled, down her back. Her shift was dusty, the tattered hem hitched up so that she could step more easily.

Several hundred yards past the village was an inn with a orange sign on which was painted a boar's head. To the side of the inn was a well. The thought of cool fresh water lured her. Creeping from the hedges, she moved stealthily like a cat toward the well. Quickly she dipped the bucket and gulped thirstily. As she turned away, satisfied, she saw an open door leading to a buttery. Inside hung chunks of cheese along the walls.

Instantly Isabel retreated back into the brush, but she couldn't put the cheese from her mind. All she had of value was the amulet, which she hoped to sell in the city. She couldn't trade something so valuable for a chunk of cheese. No, she would just have to steal some. After a diet of nothing but berries and apples, a good, solid bite of cheese was worth the risk. She had no idea what would happen if she were caught, but she was so hungry that she knew she must take the chance. One of those large chunks of cheese would last weeks, until she reached York. There she could sell the amulet and find a way to earn her living.

She found a hidden place to sit near the water where she could wait for nightfall. She worried only that the buttery would then be locked. If so, she would try to unlatch the window and climb in.

At last the sun set. After she was sure the darkness would hide her, she walked stealthily back to the inn. All the windows were lit, and the sound of voices and laughter came from inside. She peeked into a low window. A row of sleeping pallets were lined up near the wall, and about a dozen men sat at a table in the center of the room, laughing and drinking. Certain that nobody was paying attention, she hurried to the buttery, tried the door, and found it locked.

Reaching up, she jiggled the window shutter and discovered that it was unlatched. Not caring that she scratched her hands, she grabbed hold of the ledge and pulled herself up so that she could wriggle in, head first. She jumped quietly to the floor, pulled down the first chunk of cheese she laid her hands on, and dropped it back out the window to the ground. Just as she was squirming back out the window, a voice cut through the darkness,

"Hey, what's happening here?"

She sprang to the ground, scooped up the cheese and turned to flee.

The man called across the darkness, "A boy's stealing from the buttery!"

Her foot caught on a sprawling root, and as her ankle twisted under her, she fell across the grass, dropping the cheese.

"Stop that thief!" came a second voice from further away.

She should have left the cheese on the ground and fled but instinctively she groped for it, too tenacious to leave without it. As she did, a hand gripped her arm like a vise. She tried to jerk away, but she was held fast. In her peripheral vision, she saw the inn door open and the men stream out, a few carrying bright torches.

They were all around her, their voices blurring into a din. Someone held a torch near her face. She backed into the stomach of the man who was holding her, squirming as he pinned her arms behind her.

"Look at her," someone said, chuckling. "You said she was a boy, Micah. I think you're becoming senile."

A man pinched her thigh. "Under all that dirt, she's a beauty. What might she do for a piece of cheese?"

She tried to writhe away but she couldn't move.

"Wait," someone said, "I know that girl. Isabel?"

She blinked, trying to make out the speaker. The voice was oddly familiar, but her heart beat so wildly and her head pounded so that she couldn't place it. The speaker stepped forward, but in the darkness his face was contorted.

"Isabel," he said again, then turned to the man who held her, "let go of her."

Released, Isabel peered into his torchlit face.

"Jake?" she asked, unsure. She recognized his boyish features, slightly rumpled smile, and tuft of red hair that stuck up in front, but he seemed much larger, more filled out, with broader shoulders and heavier brows. The different proportions made his boyishness almost grotesque.

"Isabel, what are you doing here?"

"I—," she hesitated, aware of all of the men staring, unable to finish her sentence. A flush crept up her neck, and hot tears spilled to her cheeks.

"It's all right," he said. "I was in Brotton twice looking for you. They said you'd gone to live at the convent. Imagine you turning up here!"

She swallowed and looked around at all the faces. Jake understood her glance and said, "Everyone, back inside. I want to talk to Isabel."

"She was stealing my cheese," one man said, crossing his arms over his chest.

"For heaven's sake, Hal, forget it. I'll pay you for it."

Reluctantly, the others shuffled back toward the inn. At last the door was closed behind them, and the laughter and talking of the men became a distant buzz.

"Let's sit over here," Jake said, leading her to a rock large enough to serve as a chair for both of them. After they settled against the rock, he moved closer and said, "Tell me what you're doing here."

He was so close she could feel his breath on her as he spoke. Instinctively she cringed, drawing away from him. She felt that she should thank him, but instead, in choppy sentences, she told him everything, omitting only Edmund's name.

When she finished speaking, he said, "You don't really think that man's coming back, do you?"

She recoiled as if she had been stung. Never had she known Jake, with his easy going manner, to be cruel. The coldness of his words dazed her.

He was waiting for her to speak, so she said, "For a long time I thought he would."

He sighed deeply and shook his head, as if at her simplicity. He seemed to forget that, although it hadn't mattered to her in the least, he, too, had once deserted her in a time of trouble.

His arm seemed to be around her, hovering over her shoulder. "I've never stopped thinking about you," he said. "Have you thought about me?"

"When I went to live at the convent, it was so luxurious, I wanted you to know where I was. I thought, if you never made it to the east and the riches you talked about, you would be envious."

"I never got further than Turkey," he said

"There's a place called *Turkey*?"

They both laughed. It was one of those moments when laughter seems so wrong, yet so perfectly melts the tension.

"So you did get onto a ship," she said. "I'm happy for you, really. But why did you come back?"

"Because life on a ship was sheer hell. I worked like a slave on the galley, and was treated worse after we landed in Turkey. There are riches in Turkey, but I was lucky to get enough to eat."

"You live here now?"

"I work on a fishing boat that goes to sea for a few months each year. It's not bad."

His tone gave lie to his words. She knew from the way he spoke that he found working on a fishing boat complete drudgery.

"Why didn't you go back to Brotton?" she asked.

"I did, looking for you. But anything, even this, is better than village life. At least on a ship I can go to different places. This year we'll go to London."

"I thought I might want to go to London."

"London? What would you do there?"

She shrugged. "Find a way to earn my living."

For a long moment he studied her, as if trying to decide whether she was serious.

"There's only one way for a girl like you to earn a living by herself in London."

"Well, I have to go to London, because the plan my father has in mind for me is worse than whatever may happen in London."

He took her hand. She wanted to pull away, but he was so earnest and leaned forward so eagerly that she didn't have the heart.

"Come with me. I have a room near the docks in Goole near the port of Grimsby. I never stopped thinking about you, Isabel."

"I can't live with you."

"Why not?"

Indeed, why not? She told him part of her reason: "I'm in love with someone else." The other part was she simply didn't want to live with him. "Besides, I want to see a city like London. I want to know what it's like."

"I'll tell you what's there. It's filthy and crowded and bad things happen to people, especially beautiful girls who go alone."

Again, it surprised her to hear such hard and bitter anger in his voice, so unlike the boy she had known.

"I'm not afraid," she said.

"Well, you should be." After a pause, he said, "You're angry because I ran away."

"I was the only one who understood why you did it. So you should understand why I want to go, too."

"How can any girl be so mule-headed? Why won't you learn from my mistakes and the things that happened to me? At least come stay at the inn tonight and have a good supper. I insist."

He stood up and tried to pull her to her feet, but she resisted.

"Jake, I can't love you. I'm in love with someone else."

"I know. You already said that. But you're so hungry you were stealing cheese, and where is this man, anyway? Come on and have supper."

She went in with him, still uncomfortable under the gaze of the men in the room. Having been caught stealing was surely among the more humiliating things that had happened to her, and she felt a hot flush just remembering it.

Jake brought her a plate of dried mutton and a glass of ale. The smell of the mutton made her mouth water. She tried to control herself so that she didn't eat like a hungry wolf. Gradually the men turned their attention away, talking and laughing again among themselves. After eating, she was overcome with exhaustion. Jake led her to a pallet near the warming stove. Using a sack of sheep wool for a pillow, she fell asleep amid the laughter, vaguely aware of Jake stretched out on a straw pallet near her feet.

CHAPTER 9

Jake and several other fishermen rented rooms on the outskirts of the fishing village of Goole on the Humber River. The large half-timbered, gabled house in which they lived was owned by an old widowed fishwife. Isabel stood on the threshold of Jake's room, which was no bigger than the monastery cell in which she had been confined, but it had two windows including one that overlooked the river, which brightened the room.

He dropped his bundle on the floor and turned to her. When he took a step toward her, she moved back.

"You've changed. You're jumpy and touchy and you were never like that before."

As before there was a bite in his voice. No, she wanted to say. You're the one who has changed. Instead, she said, "I don't want to live here."

"There's a room in the loft. You can have it if you want. I pay enough rent for us both."

He showed her the room, which was smaller than his and completely bare, with only a tiny slit for a window. The cob-web covered ceiling was so low that Jake couldn't stand up straight and the top of Isabel's head brushed against it.

She sighed. "This'll do." For now, she added silently.

"It's better than your idea of going to London alone. Of all the feather-brained notions."

"I'll need work," she said.

"There's plenty around here," he said. "You'll see."

She knew his unspoken plan, and hoped he wouldn't guess hers. She understood that he was bewildered by her aloofness, so unlike the girl he remembered, and he imagined it was just a matter of time before she warmed to him again and moved out of the musty loft into his room. He asked no more questions about the man she loved, and seemed to assume that she would grow tired of thinking about him and waiting for him. After all, how would anyone ever find her in Goole — or London, for that matter?

Her own plan, of which she tried to betray nothing in her manner, was to stay here for the fall and winter, collect the things she needed for a journey, and in the spring, leave for York. She wanted to go to London but didn't think she would be able to get that far. York, she knew, she could reach in a matter of weeks. It would be better to go in the spring when she was prepared.

The fishwife who owned the house spent her days with the other local women on the dock mending the nets and making new ones. As payment they received all the fish they could eat, and enough to trade for other goods in the nearby town. The work was easier than the plowing, threshing, and harvesting work in Brotton.

For the first few weeks, Isabel's hands were painfully sore from the twine cutting into her flesh. Her fingers grew weary from tying the knots, but soon her hands became calloused and accustomed to the work. Tying the knots was every bit as monotonous as embroidering in the convent, but the fishwives were a boisterous bunch, laughing all day, making lewd jokes which in the beginning made Isabel blush but in time she became accustomed to.

The women welcomed her to their group, assuming, as did the fishermen, that she and Jake were lovers. In the beginning she denied it, but they brushed aside her denial. Then, by tacit agreement, she and Jake permitted them all to go on believing it, for the landlady was more accepting of her presence, and the fishermen left her alone.

The winter passed comfortably enough. Jake disappeared for days at a time to fish and congregate with other fishermen at inns and taverns. She knew there were women there, but she didn't care. He always returned tired and a bit subdued.

Despite the hardness that had come over him and the edge that often crept into his voice, he hadn't completely lost his good humor and easy going manner. When she refused to permit him to touch her, he shrugged as if he needed only to wait patiently.

"Isabel, please marry me," he would say every few weeks.

"Maybe someday," she would answer. It was like a ritual.

She would never marry him, she knew. Nor would she ever let him touch her as Edmund had, because if she let Jake touch her that way, she would become part of his life and part of this village and she'd never leave, and then she'd have no hope of finding a better life than this one.

As the winter months dragged on, she came to forgive Edmund for deserting her. She believed the pressure had become unbearable and he had given in. How could he fight his brother the baron, the king, and the church? She was sure he had nothing to do with the gardener story. She knew from Clare that even those highly born were restricted and treated like chess pieces on a chess board.

Other times she imagined Alis telling her not to lose hope, and that one day Edmund would be back.

"But how will he find me," she demanded silently, imaging she was speaking to Alis's spirit. "How will he know where I am?" For that there was no answer, and Isabel's confidence waned.

She learned to accept what her father had done, telling herself that nothing better could be expected of him. Once she felt something like forgiveness, a weight, like a burden she carried, was lifted and she felt light and content. Not happy; she felt she could never be happy again, but ready to begin a new life somewhere else.

She built up her little stash of goods which she imagined she would need for her journey to York: sturdy walking shoes, skirts that reached mid-calf and were thus better for hiking through brush, a small waterproof oilskin bag, a warm but lightweight woven blanket. She put from her mind Jake's warning of the things that might happen to her in the city. She didn't know what the wider world might offer. She only knew there had to be better than this life.

It was late March and the first hint of spring was coming to the hillside. The trees were still bare and the wind cold, but there was an indescribable change in the air which meant that winter was almost over. The time would soon come to leave for York.

Early one morning after Isabel had finished dressing, she bent to peer out the tiny window of her loft-room. Tied to the wooden docks were rows of wooden fishing boats, their masts bare skeletons against the gray sky. A mist settled over the hill that rose from the shore, enveloping the church's slender white-washed bell tower.

Goole had very few fields suitable for plowing because of the rocky hillsides and desolate stretches of moor, but there were a few good acres near the river, and already the plowmen were at work with their oxen teams, overturning the ground which was still frozen. They reminded her of Brotton.

She watched the fishwives gather in their usual place near the dock. They settled with the nets spread over their laps, and Isabel knew she should join them. As it was they may wonder why she was late. She turned, surprised by the sight of Jake standing in the doorway. He was usually off on the boats long before sunrise

"I need to talk to you," he said quietly. There was something different in his voice.

"All right," she said. "Sit down."

He sat on her pallet which she hadn't rolled up yet, and she sat on the floor, hugging her knees, waiting for him to speak.

He took a deep breath and said, "You will never marry me, will you?"

A burst of tenderness rose in her. She felt sorry for him, she was fond of him, she was grateful for his kindness, but no, she couldn't love him.

"I don't think so," she whispered.

He nodded, as if he had asked the question out of some duty, already knowing the answer. "Then there's something I have to tell you. I want you to hear it from me."

The quiet tension in his voice made her heart suddenly beat wildly. She caught her breath, waiting.

"A man rode through Goole last night. I only heard about it this morning. That's why I stayed, to tell you."

"What man?"

"He didn't say his name, but they said he rode a beautiful black stallion with a silver bridle. He asked if anyone had seen a girl named Isabel from Brotton. He said he'd been combing Yorkshire for you."

Edmund. It had to be Edmund. She was so stunned that several moments passed before she could speak. "Did someone tell him I was here?"

"Micah told him you were married to me, which is what they all think, anyway. They didn't know why he'd be looking for you."

"And now he's gone?" Isabel asked, already knowing the answer.

Jake nodded.

Instantly Isabel was on her feet. Edmund had been looking for her. Now he thought she was married to someone else.

"I have to find him," she said.

"How do you expect to do that?"

She reached for the sturdy hiking boots she had expected to take her to York. In another few moments she would have her clothes wrapped in the blanket, tied in a neat bundle.

"I'm going back to Brotton."

"To your father's cottage? You can't do that, Isabel."

"I didn't say I'm going to my father's cottage."

"I'll go with you," he said.

She stopped for a moment and considered his suggestion, but quickly rejected it.

"No, I want to go alone."

"At least let's find some good dried meat and cheese for you to take. You'll be there in three days, but," he paused to flash a sad grin, "you might get hungry along the way and try to steal some cheese."

She smiled gently. "And you won't be there to protect me."

He packed a pound of dried meat and a pound of cheese into a bundle for her and walked with her to the edge of the village.

"I'll miss you," he said.

She kissed his cheek then hugged him warmly. "Thank you for everything, Jake." It wasn't enough, but she didn't know what else to say.

She reached Brotton in mid-afternoon. Skirting the perimeter of the village so as not to be seen by anyone, she walked along the road that led to the castle. By the stream, the women were busy with spring washing. They were taking the clothes from the buckets and beating them with paddles and spreading them in the sun to dry.

Isabel was far enough away not to see any of their faces.

As she came over a low slope she found herself face to face with a team of plowmen coming her direction. It was too late to avoid them.

"Is that Isabel?" someone asked.

The speaker was Wade, whose cottage stood near her father's. The first time she looked over their group, she didn't see her father, who walked slightly to the rear. At the mention of her name, he stepped forward.

The men were far enough away so that she could try to run, but she found herself unable to move. She couldn't see her father's expression but she could tell from the way he held himself, leaning forward slightly as if curious, that she had nothing to fear. He seemed surprised, but not angry.

"Isabel?" he called out. "Is that you?"

As he advanced toward her she stood riveted, watching him approach. He stopped several yards away from her. His eyes were wide, his usually blank expression animated with something close to awe.

"The baron's brother has been looking for you," he said as if he couldn't believe his own words even as he uttered them. "Every few weeks he comes around, asking if we've seen you."

Her father stood about five paces away. She stared at his face for a minute, as if at a hideous monster donning a smiling mask.

She nodded to indicate that she knew, then turned away.

"Isabel, don't you have anything to say?"

"About what?"

"You ran away."

He said it accusing, as if she had no right to do so. "Is it any surprise?" she said. "You're the one who should have something to say."

He frowned, puzzled. "Like what?"

It was unbelievable that he didn't understand. "Like maybe that you're ashamed of offering me for twelve shillings."

"Anyone would have done the same thing. I thought we were lucky to find someone who wanted you."

She turned away, but this time when he called to her she broke into a run not stopping until she was past the first hill leading to the castle. After the long journey and the uphill sprint, she had to stop and lean against a tree, fighting the sick tension that gripped her throat.

He's not evil, she thought, remembering her father's expression and tone. He's merely stupid. Incredibly stupid, like one of the oxen in his team. She had hated his cruelty, but now she pitied his utter lack of intelligence.

He doesn't matter anymore, she told herself. Nothing mattered except finding Edmund. She reached the castle just as the monastery bells chimed Nomes. How strange the bells sounded, so familiar, as if their sound were a part of her being, but so far away, as if from another lifetime.

The guard was one she didn't recognize.

"I'm looking for Edmund Decourcey," she said.

He inspected her curiously for a moment, then said, "Is your name Isabel?"

Her heart seemed to stop beating. "Yes."

"He's not here."

"What do you mean? How did you know my name?"

"He was here, but he left. A few hours ago. He went that direction." He pointed down the back of the hill toward Alis's glade.

"Before that," she said, feeling she had to know the truth before she saw him, "he was gone for almost a year."

"Yeah," he grunted, as if to say: what of it?

"Where was he?"

"At the king's court. Turns out he was asking permission to marry." His gaze swept disdainfully over her, pausing at her tattered hem and mud-splattered boots. "Rumor has it he wants to marry a common village girl."

A moment passed before she trusted herself to speak.

"Why did it take him so long to get back?"

"Roads are bad in winter, you know." Then: "I think he looks for you in the haunted forest. Are you some kind of a witch?"

Instead of answering, she smiled. Then she turned and walked briskly down the hill toward the glade.

The first buds were on the branches, which were now brushed with the lightest hint of green. Soon the hills would be in bloom with wildflowers: primroses, daffodils, bluebells, and daisies, and the forest, bright green with new leaves, would be dappled merrily with sunlight. She had looked forward to spring, knowing it would bring a new beginning. Never could she have known it would bring this.

She thought of Alis, and understood how much Alis had done to bring her to this moment. Alis had lifted her above her surroundings and touched her life with magic. It was Alis who had made possible her love for Edmund, and his for her.

Isabel's exhaustion from the long journey, the days of walking, fell away from her as she approached glade. A light, airy feeling came over her as she found the narrow trail leading to the glade. She knew with absolute certainty that she would find Edmund there in the glade. She was so sure he would be there, the knowledge was like a vision, causing her to wonder if perhaps, like her grandmother, she possessed the Sight.

She entered the glade and saw the ancient ring of stones. Overhead, sunlight passed through the arching trees like light in a cathedral.

The door to the hovel opened and Edmund came out. He smiled at her, and she smiled back

"I've been waiting for you," he said.

ABOUT ANNE KINSEY

To learn more about Anne and her forthcoming fiction, please visit Anne's website at www.AnneKinsey.com. If you have any comments or questions, she would love to hear from you